ROSEMARY'S BABY...
THE EXORCIST...THE OTHER
...NOW THE ULTIMATE
INTRUSION OF EVIL—

W9-BII-429

TINEL

When the first agonizing headaches struck, Allison could not realize what was happening to her.

When she met her new neighbors in the old brownstone building, she could not recognize who they really were.

When even the man she loved began to shed the outer skin of his identity, she could not accept the most intimate evidence of her senses.

And by the time Allison could no longer deny the horror possessing her body and mind and soul, only a miracle could save her . . .

THE SENTINEL

THE SENTINEL

A MICHAEL WINNER FILM

Starring
CHRIS SARANDON
CRISTINA RAINES

•

MARTIN BALSAM
JOHN CARRADINE
JOSE FERRER
AVA GARDNER
ARTHUR KENNEDY
BURGESS MEREDITH
SYLVIA MILES
DEBORAH RAFFIN
ELI WALLACH

Screenplay by MICHAEL WINNER
Based on the Novel by JEFFREY KONVITZ
Music by JOHN WILLIAMS

Directed by MICHAEL WINNER

Produced by MICHAEL WINNER AND JEFFREY KONVITZ

A UNIVERSAL PICTURE

TECHNICOLOR®

THE SENTINEL

Jeffrey Konvitz

BALLANTINE BOOKS • NEW YORK

Copyright © 1974 by Jeffrey Konvitz

All rights reserved. Published in the United States by Ballantine
Books, a division of Random House, Inc., New York, and simul-
taneously in Canada by Ballantine Books of Canada, Ltd.,
Toronto, Canada.

Library of Congress Catalog Card Number: 74-8984

ISBN 0-345-25641-7-195

This edition published by arrangement with
Simon & Schuster, Inc.

Manufactured in the United States of America

First Ballantine Books Edition: January 1976
Tenth Printing: February 1977

*To Peter Lampack
for his encouragement.
To my family
for their love.*

Prologue

A plain manila folder lay on a briarwood desktop. In the upper right-hand corner the name ALLISON PARKER was printed in bold-face lettering. A piece of paper which contained a detailed resumé of Allison Parker's life was held over the desk by a pair of well-groomed hands. The folder was opened and the paper inserted.

Another folder, labeled THERESE, was placed on top of the PARKER file and the desk light was flicked off.

1

The taxi fought its way up First Avenue, past the United Nations, the Fifty-ninth Street bridge and the singles bars that lined the avenue.

Her head lay against the window; her mind wandered. Had it really happened? Or would she wake up at the sound of the alarm, squint at the reflected rays of light on the smog-coated windows and realize, as she wiped the sweat from her forehead and threw off the blanket, that the last four months had been one incredible nightmare—the hospital, the funeral, the agony and despair (while waiting and eventually hoping for Father to die)—all of it—and that everything she had experienced and seen would dissipate like visions, as they had when she had left home seven years before, forever, or so she had thought. She laughed softly to herself. No, it had all happened, as hard as it was to believe. She closed her eyes, thinking of New York City. Not a bad place once you got used to it. She had been happy here. In fact, returning to Indiana was the last thought in her mind last July when she raced from the shower and, out of breath, lifted the phone to hear Mother's strained voice plead, "He's dying. Come home!" Could she have said no? Perhaps. Every impulse told her not to go back. But if she had left Mother alone, she could never have lived with herself. She'd had to return, no matter what she'd had to give up. Even Michael. And though she could have spent hours reliving the subsequent events, it would have been a waste of time. She had survived—physically and mentally—and the memories that had plagued her could not have altered that fact. It was over.

The taxi cornered onto Seventy-first Street and pulled to a stop in front of a modern thirty-story apartment house.

The door swung open and the doorman extended his hand into the cab. "Miss Parker!" he said happily.

"Hello, George," Allison said, smiling. She was attractive. Angular and tall. With skin like silk and long brown hair that fell over her shoulders halfway down her back. She looked younger than twenty-six, her face highlighted by a delicately sculpted nose and two enormous blue eyes.

"It's been a long time," George said.

"Yes," she replied cordially. George was always enthusiastically attentive and pleasant. She liked him. "Almost four months," she added. She stepped from the cab and walked under the green canopy that extended from the doorway to the sidewalk. She glanced at her watch; it was late. She looked up at the doorman. "How have you been?" she asked.

"Good," he answered, walking to the rear of the cab.

"And your family?"

"Fine, very fine." He began to collect her luggage. "I asked Mr. Farmer about you many times."

She stepped back toward the polished glass partition. "I hope he said good things."

"Only the best." George smiled, as his powerful muscles began to bulge from the strain of the heavy baggage.

She would remember to tip him handsomely—if just to signify her friendship. And she would remember to thank Michael for his unusual display of affection and discretion. "Is Mr. Farmer in?" she asked. Of course he would be in. Waiting. It was her homecoming.

"No, he left town yesterday."

"He did?" He didn't say anything on the phone about leaving town.

"He left a note for you. And gave me instructions to let you use his apartment."

They entered the building. He put down the pieces of luggage, returned to the cab, brought in the last two suitcases, laid them next to the car packs, turned and disappeared into a small room just inside the door. He reappeared moments later with an envelope in his hand.

"Mr. Farmer told me to give you this myself." He bowed, obviously pleased with his conscientiousness.

She smiled thankfully and snatched the envelope from his hand. Quickly she tore it open, removed a note and read:

Allison:

Sorry couldn't be there when you got back. Had to leave Friday night for Albany. Business. Be back Tuesday. See you then.

Michael.

P.S. Will call Sunday night.

She folded the paper and shoved it into her purse.

That was just like Michael to disappear when she wanted him so badly. And leave a note that could have just as well been a telegram. Short. Direct. And unemotional. A perfect mirror of his personality, but then again she could never hope to change him into something that he wasn't—nor did she really want to. If she had thought about it, she would have had to admit that it was just his curt and businesslike manner that she found so appealing—and the challenge of every so often coaxing him to let his hair down and betray some of the emotions that he so carefully kept hidden beneath his impassive exterior.

She thought for a moment, then turned to George. "Could you help me with the luggage?" she asked.

"Of course, ma'am," he answered. He lifted the bags under both his arms, an accomplishment that she had thought impossible, and walked around the bend toward the elevators. "Mr. Farmer told me you gave up your apartment."

"Yes. I was going home for an indefinite period. It was best to let it go." She paused, then added, "I'm going to start looking for a new one first thing tomorrow. Preferably a brownstone. A change of pace."

She pressed the call button, looked up and watched the light start ticking downward from number seven.

"Weather's been bad," said George. "Lots of rain and it's been colder than the North Pole."

"Yes, I know," replied Allison.

"You're lucky you were away."

"I suppose I was," she answered just to agree, since it had probably been colder and rainier back home.

The elevator arrived; the door slid open. She entered; he stepped in behind her. The door closed, the cabin ascended and opened smoothly on the tenth floor. They walked out, turned to the right and George opened apartment 10 E.

She flicked on the light switch.

"Just put everything on the floor. I'll do the rest."

He placed the luggage at her feet and accepted the five-dollar bill which was offered. "Thank you," he said. "If there's anything you need, just buzz down."

He stepped out; she closed the door. Breathing deeply. Tired. It had been a long day what with the goodbyes, the flight to Kennedy International and the discouraging drive into Manhattan. She propped herself against the largest valise and surveyed the apartment. Living room straight ahead. Dining alcove to her right. Furnished early bachelor, endearingly tacky. He still hadn't thrown out the faded couch, or the rug, or the ridiculous painting of Napoleon Bonaparte. She would be sure to speak to him about that.

She removed her jacket and shoes, carried the car packs into the dining alcove and hung them one at a time in the alcove closets. She was pleased to see that the clothes she had left several months before were still neatly folded in place and apparently had not been moved or exposed to anything that might have injured the fabrics. She turned, grabbed two of the valises and hauled them down the hall past the kitchen and into the bedroom, where she laid them on the black shag rug next to the night table. She turned on the table lamp and pulled the white fur bedspread off the bed. It fell to the floor and lay crumpled, contrasting brilliantly.

The bed looked empty without him. But it would have to do. The note said he wouldn't be home until Tuesday.

She removed her clothes, washed, then climbed under the bedsheets, blinking at the lights that shone through the window. She threw Michael from her thoughts, turned off the night-table lamp and clutched the crucifix that lay around her neck. She pressed the cross gently against her lips, remembering.

The return to the old house during Father's funeral. She had refused to go with the mourners to the cemetery. She had felt too sick. It had started in the hospital, about an hour before Father had died. The pain had been relentless, noticeably increasing in intensity, the headache becoming a pounding migraine and the dizziness spiraling into disorientation. They had missed her at the cemetery. Just as they had missed her earlier in the day when she had refused to enter the church for the services. But neither impropriety had mattered. They had all understood. The family history was public knowledge. The why of it patently obvious. She had needed rest. And the opportunity to retrieve the crucifix. The house would be empty. She could trespass on her past undisturbed, satisfying that

curious impulse of redemption that had haunted her
since her return, waiting for Father's death to seek
its fulfillment.

Before opening the front door she had stood silently
on the porch. Then she had entered the main hall
and, climbing the staircase, had walked into a dimly
lit corridor that ended in a solid gray wall. To the
right was a solitary door. It had once been her parents'
bedroom. For seven years it had remained untouched
and locked.

Inserting a rusted key, she had turned the round
crystalline handle, gently pushing open the door.
It was poorly hinged; the squeaking had vibrated
through the halls. Terrified she had stepped inside
and looked about.

The bedroom was simply furnished. An old wooden
bed occupied the center. Above it hung a crucifix.
On the left side of the room was an antique dresser.
On the right were the closets. The room was carpeted
with dust; cobwebs covered the furnishings.

She had stumbled. Dizzy with the memory of dead
voices. Remembering her escape through these halls
all over again.

The confusion.

The police. "Allison, tell us what happened."

Mother crying.

"What happened?" Mother asked over and over
until her words had become nonsense.

"I don't know."

"Tell me."

Tears.

"Please tell me."

Then the truth.

The doctors. "Why did you throw away the cross,
Allison?"

"Because."

"Because what?"

"It was dirty. Everything was dirty."

"That's not true, Allison."

Silence.

"You know that's not true. Let's talk about it again. Let's talk about everything again."

"No."

"Yes."

"I can't. I want to die."

She heard herself cry as the blade bit into her wrists. Then there was nothing. She had looked around. The room was quiet, the voices gone, the past, attempting resurrection, dead again.

She had walked to the dressing table. The top had been covered with pictures standing in frames. She picked up several, viewed them briefly and returned them to their places. Searching the rest of the table, she lifted a small box behind the picture of Bugle, their black Newfoundland who had died many years before. She removed the top. Inside, on a wad of cotton, lay a crucifix about the size of a silver dollar. Trembling, she had carefully removed it. Could it have been that long since she had last held it in her hand? It looked the same. The figure of Christ was still intact; the chain remained unbroken. Slightly more tarnished, perhaps, but one would have had to expect that after seven years.

Glancing about the empty room, she had placed the chain around her neck and started to close the circular catch; she paused.

Father is dead, she had told herself angrily.

Then she had snapped the latch and looked in the mirror. The crucifix lay just right. It felt comfortable.

And still did, but perhaps even more so, now that she was secure in the confines of Michael's bedroom.

She rolled on her side, burying her face in the soft beckoning pillows. The impulse of redemption was still strong. Inciting a return, part conscious, part subliminal. The most terrible stigma had been removed by death. The others remained. Confront them? The disavowals? The reality from which she had fled? The attempts at self-destruction? The death of Michael's wife Karen with all its unspeakable horrors?

Reconcile her past with her future? Yes. It would happen. Slowly. It was inevitable. Whether she knew it or not. Whether by choice or momentum. Now in the silence of the bedroom or soon, wherever, whenever.

She fell asleep, her hand caressing the figure of Christ.

2

The ad was located in the lower right-hand portion of a page marked "Commercial Lofts and Storage Facilities." It read:

> ATTRACTIVE BROWNSTONE APARTMENT,
> OLD, PARTIALLY RENOVATED BUILDING,
> FLOOR THRU. ONE WBFP, UPPER WEST
> SIDE, 3½ ROOMS, FURNISHED. CALL
> RENTING AGENT, YU 6-1452. ASK FOR
> MISS LOGAN FOR APARTMENT 3 A.

It was out of place. It should have been entered under "Residential Apartments." If it had, she might not have wasted the entire day chasing from building to building, agent to agent. Yet, as she removed a dime from her pocket, she warned herself not to be overly optimistic. The apartment might have already been rented. Or it might prove unacceptable, as had most of the other "favorable" leads.

The day had started inauspiciously; she had overslept. Yet, she hadn't had much sleep. She had woken twice during the night, one time to go to the bathroom, the other to find something to kill the dull pressure that had gnawed at her temples, reminding her that the tension that had caused the terrible migraines and dizziness was just beginning to subside and that she would probably feel some discomfort for some time to come. Strangely, the aspirin had little effect. The headache persisted through her sleep, intensified during the morning and first began to dissipate after she had left the apartment. It was gone by noon and was only a memory by the time she found a phone booth in a midtown drugstore, called the listed number and, after speaking to Miss Logan, walked uptown toward Seventy-seventh Street and located the dilapidated brownstone that housed the agent's office. She opened the front door, consulted the directory—Miss Logan was the solitary tenant—and climbed a lopsided staircase to the second floor. She peeked through the open doorway. A woman was seated at a desk examining a handful of documents.

"Miss Logan?" Allison questioned.

"Miss Parker," stated the woman in a modulated contralto. She was neatly dressed but years behind in style. Matronly and spinsterish. With a strict posture, an old-fashioned hairstyle and bland, reserved features. "Please take a seat," she suggested. She leaned forward, removed some papers from a nearby chair and placed them on the already overloaded desk.

"Thank you," replied Allison as she entered the room and sat down.

Miss Logan quickly collated the piles in front of her. "I was about to leave when you called. I don't like to stay too late on Sunday so I'm straightening up. I'm sure you don't mind."

"Of course not. I hope I didn't cause—"

"No, it's no trouble at all."

"Nevertheless, I appreciate your staying for me.

The apartment sounds perfect. I didn't want to wait till tomorrow and perhaps lose it."

"Yes, I see," observed the agent.

"You sounded unsure on the phone. It is available, isn't it?"

"I believe so," she said as she leaned over the desk and closed the Venetian blind on the only unboarded window.

"Believe?" asked Allison.

The agent smacked her lips. "The landlord said he was going to cease running the notice. He didn't like the prior applicants. We assured him we would find someone suitable, but he became disenchanted and decided to leave the apartment unoccupied."

"He obviously changed his mind again."

"Can I see the ad?"

Allison extended the paper and pointed to the bottom of the page.

The agent read the blurb and nodded.

"Then I can see the apartment?"

The agent eyed Allison intently. "Well, I don't see why not." She paused, then added, "The building is on West Eighty-ninth Street. It's old but still in good condition." She turned back to the desk, shuffled through the piles of papers, removed a document and smiled triumphantly. "Our questionnaire. Standard information for us about you, and I'd appreciate your indulgence. There's also a document that defines our commission which you must sign." She handed the paper to Allison with a slightly raised brow. "Thank you," she said prematurely. "As soon as you've finished, we'll catch a cab."

Allison removed a pencil from her purse and addressed her attention to the forms.

Miss Logan completed the arrangement of her desk. The room was silent for several minutes, then she swiveled around, sat back and stated, "You're from the Midwest."

"Yes," Allison answered, lifting her head.

"I can hear it in your voice."

"I didn't know the drawl was so prominent."

"It's not, but it's there for someone who can recognize it. I'm from Peoria, Illinois, myself, but I've lost the intonation. I've been here fifteen years."

Allison smiled and continued to write.

"You just get to New York?"

"No."

"I didn't think so." Miss Logan was craning her neck, curious as to the answers on the form. "You'll be living alone?" she asked.

"Yes," Allison answered, annoyed at the constant interruption. "With an occasional visitor."

"I live alone."

Allison raised her eyes. "How nice," she remarked.

"I prefer it that way. It gives me more freedom. I can do what I wish whenever I wish. And solitude is good after dealing with people six days a week, ten hours a day."

Allison nodded indifferently, then completed the questionnaire and scanned the commission notice. "Where do I sign?" she asked.

Miss Logan leaned over and pointed. Allison scribbled her signature and returned the forms. The woman quickly reviewed them.

"A model," she declared. "That's a very interesting profession. All that glamour and excitement. Twenty-six years old. Single. No relatives in the city, but good references." She smiled reassuringly. "It looks fine. I'm sure the landlord will approve." She looked at her watch. "Shall we go?"

Allison stood and followed the agent as she walked to the door and pulled a fashionless tweed coat from a rusted nail on the wall.

"Are you sure the staircase is secure?" Allison inquired, half jokingly.

"Perfectly," replied the agent. She threw on her coat. "Just a little harrowing. To make life interesting." She motioned Allison out, set the lock and slammed the door. "I've been in this building five years, and though it looks like it's falling apart, it's sturdy."

The landing squeaked under her feet as she grabbed the banister. "I've thought about renovating a portion of the second floor and even the staircase, but that wouldn't make any financial sense. I suppose I'll get out of here sooner or later, but, you know, once you get used to something, you don't like to leave it. The office is like a second home."

"I understand," Allison replied. "I'm a little like that myself."

"Midwesterners are. They have a more finely developed sense of home and sentiment than New Yorkers. I rarely find New Yorkers having a sense for anything but sex and money."

"I guess there's something to be said for that too," observed Allison.

"Each to his own," said Miss Logan obliquely as she opened the front door.

They stepped onto the street into a tide of shattered sunlight painted in striations by a descending sun through barren trees; they hailed a taxi.

It was a standard New York brownstone. Five floors. Extremely old. Engagingly battered.

Allison paid the driver; they stepped from the cab.

"One of the nicer tree-lined blocks in New York," declared the agent as she started her sales pitch.

Allison pivoted and glanced up and down the narrow street lined with brownstones.

"And it's convenient," Miss Logan added. "There's a subway on Ninety-sixth and Central Park West. There's another on Broadway. There are plenty of buses, and cabs are easy to get. And, of course, you have the park."

They began to climb the stone staircase to the raised front entrance.

"Around the far corner there is a supermarket. There's also a cleaner's nearby and a hardware store."

Allison digested the geography lesson as Miss

Logan smiled broadly, Allison's look of satisfaction having added fuel to the impending sale.

"We've become slaves to convenience," said Allison.

"New York does that."

"Unfortunately."

"Shall we?" asked the renting agent as she opened the heavy front door and stepped into the rectangular hallway.

Allison followed, admiring the soiled wood paneling that completely covered the walls.

She glanced at herself in a hanging mirror, then leaned against a bicycle rack in the center of the hallway.

"You can keep a bicycle here," said Miss Logan, standing at the base of the wooden staircase, "although the basement is probably more convenient."

Allison nodded thoughtfully. Eyes darting. Feeling a rapport with the building's personality.

With the renting agent leading the way, they began to climb the stairs. Halfway up, Allison stopped, grabbed the banister and shook it firmly. It was sturdy. Reassured, she continued to the first landing, forty-two steps from where she had started.

The second floor was paneled like the first with long strips of worn, soiled pine. However, at the junction of the landing and the second-floor hallway there was a segment of wall that had been completely refurbished. It began about four feet off the ground, ran to the ceiling and was approximately eight feet wide, reaching from the stairwell wall to the door of the B apartment that stood at the top of the landing in the beginning of the hallway. Allison inspected the fine new pine closely, touched it and thought of a pearl in an oyster, an isolated addition to an otherwise homogeneous surrounding. She shrugged, dismissed its presence and stepped away.

The lighting was extremely poor; the texture of the air was thick, almost filamentous, making it even harder to see. But she continued to follow Miss Logan,

relying more on the agent's exemplary progress and
her own non-visual senses than on her eyes. They
wandered down the hall past the A apartment and
climbed the second staircase to the third landing,
which was easily as dark and forbidding as the second.
The small yellow wall lights, one at each end of the
hall, provided the only illumination. Miss Logan
removed the chain of keys from her pocket and inserted
one into the door marked 3 A. It opened and they
entered.

The apartment, as advertised, was a floor through.
The living room, which lay directly beyond the entrance, was large, rectangular and generally well pre-
served. The furniture was eye-catching, the style Vic-
torian, the condition old. A treasure chest of antiques,
from the smallest ashtray to the two large grandfather
clocks that stood on either side of the mantel. She
particularly liked the sofa that set the general tone
and mood and stood in the middle of the room between
two old granny lamps and before a low-standing bookshelf. Across from the sofa was a fireplace bordered
in marble. It was clean; obviously it had not been
used in some time. Scattered around the room were
delicate chairs with arching backs and exquisite hand-
sewn fabrics. She noted their position and thought
to herself that the chair in front of the middle window
belonged by the chair near the side wall. Perhaps
she could buy a coffee table to place between the
two, thereby establishing a separate personality to
that little corner of the living room. The idea pleased
her; she smiled to herself as she crossed the Oriental
rug, glancing at the handsomely papered walls and
hand-wrought mirrors.

Miss Logan followed and stuttered. "The old
furniture fits it perfectly, I'm sure you'll agree."

She did. But no response. Instead, a continued
walk around the room. Attention to details. The many
small objects. "I assume all of this will come with
the apartment?"

"I think so," said the agent, "but I can check before either of us makes a final decision."

"I'd appreciate it," Allison acknowledged, opening the window draperies, admitting the soft muted light of late afternoon. Looking out the third-floor window, she nodded her circumspect approval, closed the draperies, then turned back to the impatient renting agent and asked whether she could see the bedroom.

"Of course," answered Miss Logan.

She led Allison down a narrow hallway approximately fifteen feet long, which was bisected lengthwise by two opposing doorways—one leading to the small kitchenette, the other leading to the bathroom. Allison peeked in—they were standard, no more, no less—listened to Miss Logan's inane commentary about the utility and workmanship of each of the items, including the toilet bowl, then continued down the hall and walked into the bedroom. She sat down on the four-poster and looked about the room at the antique furnishings. The burnished walls. The gold-leafed metalwork. The ceiling. It was hand-carved. "Who put it in?" she asked, glancing upward.

"A prior tenant."

The ceiling was certainly an unexpected find in a rented apartment. Not the type of addition one would include without an interest in the building or a long-term lease. "Did you know the people?" Allison asked curiously.

"No," replied the agent.

Allison shrugged. She patted the quilted bedspread; little bits of dust billowed into the air, dancing in the gray light, settling into the darkness. She stood and walked back through the hallway; Miss Logan followed nervously.

"I want the apartment," Allison declared when they reached the brighter confines of the living room. The grandfather clocks struck the hour, then resumed their frantic ticking. She turned. "It's exactly what I need. Exactly."

"I was sure that you would feel that way."

"How much did you say the rent was?"

"I didn't," said the agent. The modulation in her voice increased in intensity; she appeared overly anxious. "The rental is four hundred and fifty a month. I'm certain that's within reason."

"Interesting," remarked Allison after a long pause, "but I'm afraid we have different standards of reasonableness."

Miss Logan smiled. "The apartment is large and it's furnished."

"And it's in the West Eighties," said Allison. "Not one of the up-and-coming neighborhoods in the city."

"I wouldn't say that," challenged the agent as she sat down on the sofa and leaned forward.

"I would. Four hundred and fifty is out of line. If you can't bring it down by at least one hundred, we might as well thank each other for the other's company and call it a day."

Miss Logan bit her lip. "You want the apartment?" she asked rhetorically.

Allison nodded.

"Frankly, three hundred and seventy-five a month is not excessive in New York."

"You said four hundred and fifty."

Miss Logan wrinkled her brow. "Did I? Careless of me. I do that all the time."

"I'm sure," said Allison with an amused grin. She opened her pocketbook and removed her checkbook. "Do you have a pen I could borrow?" she asked.

Miss Logan withdrew an expensive ballpoint from her jacket and laid it in Allison's outstretched hand. "A fifty-dollar deposit will be fine."

Allison scribbled in the figure and handed her the check.

"You've made an excellent choice," declared the agent.

"I'm sure I have," said Allison as she followed Miss Logan through the door and began the descent toward the lobby, which they reached quickly and left immediately, stepping from the brownstone into the fading light of dusk.

Miss Logan leaned against the abutment. "I'll see about improving the lighting in the halls. I'd hate to have you fall and break something, and I'm sure the landlord will be most concerned about it."

"Thank you."

"As to the landlord, remember that your occupancy must be passed on and accepted by him. He hasn't liked anyone yet, but who knows, maybe he's decided to stop being so picayune. The apartment is no good to anyone empty."

"I hope you'll be able to get back to me quickly. I want to get settled as soon as possible."

"I understand. I'll let you know one way or the other by tomorrow evening."

The two women shook hands and descended to the street.

"Can I give you a lift back to the East Side?" asked Miss Logan.

"No, thank you," replied Allison. "I'm going to browse around the neighborhood before I go back."

Miss Logan smiled and began to walk toward the corner.

Allison stepped back and reappraised the building. "Miss Logan," she called moments later.

The agent turned. "Yes?" she asked.

Allison continued to stare at the last row of windows.

"Yes," repeated the agent.

"Unless I'm mistaken," Allison began, "someone is staring at me through the curtains in one of the fifth-floor windows."

"I'm sure you've been stared at before." The agent laughed.

"Yes," replied Allison, "but—"

"That's Father Halliran," interrupted Miss Logan. "Matthew Halliran. In five A. A priest. He's been here for years. As far as I know, he doesn't leave his room—kind of senile and blind. But he's harmless. He usually just sits by the window."

"Sounds ominous," said Allison, somewhat amused by the image she drew of this barely visible character.

"Speak to you tomorrow." Miss Logan saluted and briskly sauntered toward the corner.

Allison watched until the agent had disappeared. Then she tilted her head up again. Perhaps she could see more of the priest. No, the angle was too sharp, the curtains too thick, the light too weak. She crossed the street to get a better view. That proved no better. Whatever light was left caused a dull reflection to hang on the glass, obscuring the image beyond recognition.

She stood for a moment watching for movement. There was none. She hailed a cab, satisfied that she had had a fruitful day.

3

The light at best was only adequate; it crept through the glass inconspicuously, like a burglar.

Allison glanced at the window. "What do you think?" she asked and sipped from a cup of instant coffee.

The electrician walked slowly across the bedroom and looked out the window. There was no view; the rear wall of the opposite building stood no more than six or eight feet away. And the overhanging roofs of both buildings created an inaccessible shaft topped by a narrow opening into which the daylight could only enter obliquely.

"I can put another socket in the wall," he said with a heavy Germanic accent. "And I will wire the ceiling for an overhead light." He paused, scratched his balding head and glanced along the walls. "Of course, it may already be wired. Sometimes they remove the fixtures but leave the leads. That would be of great help."

"Anything you can do," Allison declared, "but please be careful of the carved wood." She slipped a leather vest over her blouse and carried the empty cup into the kitchen. "I'm not used to having so little light in the bedroom. In my old place I had an east and west exposure. There was plenty of sun all the time. In fact, I could even tell the time of day by watching the rays cross the design on my rug."

She heard a grumbling in the other room.

"Get a clock," the man said without suggesting any offense. "And Thomas Edison will take care of the light."

She laughed softly and dumped a loaded dustpan into the garbage.

The electrician walked past the kitchen into the living room; Allison followed.

"You'll wire the closets?"

The man nodded. "And I'll put in new sockets where you marked."

"Good!" Allison put on a fur-lined jacket and grabbed her black portfolio. "Just close the door when you're ready to leave. And thank you."

The man turned to pursue his work; Allison stepped from the apartment with a smile and descended the now familiar staircase.

She stopped in front of apartment 2 B. She could hear voices. They were female; two women were arguing. She leaned closer, listening. They were arguing over dessert. One wanted to make a chocolate-iced vanilla cake for dinner while the other wanted plain angel food, claiming that it would be far less fattening. It appeared that the first woman had little concern for the size of her waistline; it also appeared she would win.

This was her first significant contact with the neighbors. Peculiarly, she hadn't met anyone in the hallways as yet, though several days before she had heard someone walking up the staircase on the landing above. Yet, if anything, her isolation was her own fault. She had kept to herself since she had moved into the building. All she would have had to do would have been to ring one of the doorbells and announce her presence. But she just hadn't been in the right frame of mind. Perhaps soon. Or perhaps she would continue to rely on circumstance.

She left the brownstone and strolled past the adjoining buildings and through the Park entrance on Ninetieth Street, heading downtown. It was cold. Overcast. A good day for walking. And she couldn't have been in a better mood; she was going back to work.

She had been looking forward to the click of the camera all week, though she had been far too busy to do anything beyond stopping at the agency, announcing her return, prodding the bookers and fetching her portfolio from a locked cabinet. That was accomplished Monday morning, an hour after Miss Logan had called to confirm the apartment and an hour before she had piled her clothes and belongings into two taxis, directed them to the new apartment and begun what was to become a week—today was Monday, so it was exactly one week—of toil. She had expected Michael's help but he had called Sunday night, sheepishly explaining that the transaction would take longer than expected, perhaps another few days. He then demanded to know why she insisted on renting another apartment when she could just as well have lived with him. Disappointed as she was, she was in no mood to reargue the already mutilated subject of marriage. Rather, she agreed to talk to him on Thursday—which she did—only to discover that he wouldn't be back until next Thursday—a week later than promised.

Paradoxically, his absence proved helpful. Without him around she was able to concentrate on the apartment. Not that she was dissatisfied with the furniture or the layout, but there were so many possibilities for creative decorating that she couldn't resist the temptation. Her first purchase was a dining room set made of heavy oak, which she substituted for the present table and chairs—without Miss Logan's approval. Then came a picture, framed in carved wood. Strangely, though, she cared a great deal more for the frame than she did for the painting. She realized, after she had brought it home, that it very much resembled Michael's Napoleon Bonaparte. Of all things! Panicked, she immediately determined to replace the canvas, but until then the bedroom closet was the ideal place for storage. After the picture she was slightly more careful. She bought a clock for the bedroom, several decorative pieces for various tables and dressers, two new "antique" lamps, a pirate's chest, which she spent all Friday refinishing, and a slew of utensils and gizmos for the kitchen and bathroom.

There were other items she had wanted, especially a coffee table for the living room, but she had decided to give the matter more thought. She did not want to rush and buy the wrong piece. It would be her most important acquisition. It could wait until Michael had returned and the painters had finished the bathroom, kitchen and doorways.

The other notable event of the week was the news of the booking. She had learned of it on Friday. She would be working with her favorite photographer, Jack Tucci. And her best friend, Jennifer Learson. She had tried to contact Jennifer all week, but only on Thursday did she remember to call the agency and ask for her whereabouts. They told her that Jennifer was out of town on a job and would return late Sunday night. It seemed as if all her close personal friends had fled New York in prospect of her return. Undaunted, she had called Sunday night, found Jennifer at home, talked for at least an hour and arranged to meet for lunch the next day before going down to the studio.

So she was justifiably excited as she exited the Park near the Plaza Hotel, walked to Third Avenue and entered the restaurant just as Jennifer was sitting down at the table they had reserved in the front room next to the door.

"Allison," screamed Jennifer unabashedly as she ground her cigarette into an ashtray.

Allison maneuvered through the crowd, embraced her friend and sat. "Still smoking too much," she admonished, noticing the smoldering butt.

"Too much for tuberculosis," Jennifer replied, smiling, "but not enough for cancer or a heart condition." She laughed, leaned back in the chair and asked if it felt good to be back.

"Excessively," said Allison as she removed her coat.

Jennifer took another cigarette from the pack that lay on the table. "I give you two weeks and you'll be complaining that you're overworked and underpaid, that the photographers are lechers and the agency executives are dullards and that you must find something more creative and stimulating to do with your time." She laughed. "I've never known a model whose sense of commitment didn't resemble the flight path of a punctured balloon."

"I don't doubt you're right," agreed Allison, "but for the time being let me indulge in my fantasies."

"I wouldn't conceive of introducing a note of reality. You've every right to delude yourself for as long as you can." Jennifer looked up as the waiter leaned over the red and white checked tablecloth. "Two Bloody Marys," she ordered, glancing at Allison who nodded accommodatingly. "And strong on the Worcestershire," she added.

Allison grabbed Jennifer's portfolio and began to

thumb the pages. "New pictures?" she asked after a pause.

"The product of off-season hysteria."

Allison pulled out a contact sheet and held it to the light. "You worked hard."

"My lot in life."

"Didn't you know?" Allison smiled. "Everyone works hard."

"The butcher, the baker and the candlestick maker?"

"Yes."

"Even Michael?"

"So I've been told."

"So have I."

"By whom?"

"Michael."

Allison shook her head. "He's looking for sympathy."

"Do you give it?"

"I haven't had the chance. I've been away—remember?"

"Will you give it now?"

"Depends."

"On?"

"Just depends."

"Will he give it to you?"

"I don't want any."

Jennifer nodded. "It's very romantic," she said.

"What?"

"Separation. It makes the head grow fonder."

"Wrong organ."

"The liver?"

They laughed.

The two drinks soon arrived and sat untouched for some time as they rehashed much of their telephone conversation of the night before. Then they ordered, finished quickly, left the restaurant and hailed a cab on Lexington Avenue, headed downtown. The taxi crawled through the traffic to West Twenty-sixth, a crumbling block of commercial tenements. It stopped

halfway between Fifth and Sixth. They stepped out
and entered a dilapidated loft building. Another model
was standing in front of the elevator. They introduced
themselves—the model's name was Lois—walked into
the elevator and scrambled out on the seventh floor
in front of Jack Tucci's studio.

They had been working several hours.

"A few more," Tucci finally announced in a clipped
English accent that was tarnished by a slight New
York inflection.

The Hasselblad clicked—one, two, three.

He shifted, altered his position, brushed the
perspiration from the perfectly barbered goatee that
hugged his chin, then shifted again. His slender body
moved like a breaking wave. Practiced. Sure. Egocen-
tric.

"A little to the left," he ordered. He motioned
with his hand to emphasize the command. "Raise
your chins—too much—good!"

The camera responded.

"Okay," he declared, "let's break for dinner. Then
we'll do the black and whites."

Shielding their eyes from the hot lights, they stepped
away from the backdrop and carefully negotiated
the wires and light stands to the lounge area in the
rear of the studio.

Jack placed the camera on a tripod and followed.

"Have a cigarette?" asked Jennifer.

Jack removed a pack from his shirt pocket and
tossed it on the formica-topped bar.

Allison eased into an old armchair.

"Anybody else?" Tucci asked, holding out the
cigarettes. Receiving no reply, he placed them back
in his pocket, circled the bar, reached into a cabinet
and removed a stack of photos. "Tell me what you
think of these," he commanded, handing them to
Jennifer before disappearing through an open doorway.

He returned a moment later carrying a tray which
held several sandwiches, some Cokes and a bottle

of white wine. "The dark bread is tongue," he announced. "The rye is roast beef." He smiled and began to distribute the food. "Allison?" he asked after the other two models had chosen.

"In a moment," she replied submissively, her arms dangling limply over the supports of the chair, her legs stiffly extended.

"Well?" he prodded, gesturing to the pictures.

"Quite good," answered Jennifer. She removed a pair of glasses from her purse—wire rims—placed them on her fine-boned nose, held the pictures to the light and re-examined them closely. "Who is the girl?"

"You don't know her."

"A model?"

"No. Just a friend." He winked suggestively.

"I admire the quality."

"Natural?"

"Very. How did you get it?"

"Ah," he exclaimed lasciviously. "Natural light and voyeurism. The camera is a remarkable voyeur. With nudes, the texture of the subject is most important but with the knowledge of the camera's presence, the normal serenity of the body is lost. Look at her face. I could never have achieved the subtlety you see there if she had known I was shooting her. The narcissism wouldn't be as clearly stated." He lifted one of the photos and held it to the light. "Remarkable realism," he declared with a note of self-acclaim.

He began to discuss the visual ramifications.

Then it happened.

Allison had remained seated in the chair, casually thumbing through a copy of *Vogue*. The headache came first. Almost instantly, as if it had been there all along but had been held back by a dam whose ramparts had suddenly been torn away. It was centered at the base of her skull. Her initial reaction was surprise, then consternation. She had felt fine all week. In fact the last headache had occurred the morning Miss Logan had called with the approval. And that really wasn't a headache, just a dull pressure that she had attributed to a residue of tension. And now? There seemed to be no logical explanation other than a reaction to the long hours under the hot lights. Yet, if it had just been a migraine, she would have dismissed it summarily. There was also a sensation of constriction along her back that made her skin prickle as if a slab of dry ice had been jammed against her body. Unnerved, she sat up, threw the magazine on the chair, walked to the closed skylight and looked over the rooftops. There wasn't much of a view. A few chimneys. The moon in its last quarter. She shook her head in a vain attempt to drive away the pain, then she turned back toward the bar and listened. "Are you sure you couldn't achieve the same effect with the right model?" she heard Lois ask. But was "hearing" the right word? The sounds were muffled as if the vibrations were being projected through a sonic sponge.

Then they ceased altogether.

She stumbled back against the glass panes. They vibrated noisily; several cracked.

Everyone turned, shocked, watching.

"I . . . I," Allison mumbled as a tingling sensation coursed along the insides of her arms toward the shoulders. Quickly she felt it spread through all her extremities and then give way to a far more alarming perception: a total deadness. Frantically, she began to rub her hands together.

Jack hurled himself over the bar, grabbed her as she was beginning to fall and carried her over the wires to the armchair. Jennifer crushed her cigarette and squirmed in pursuit.

"Allison," Jack shouted, "what's the matter?"

"I don't know!" Allison stammered in garbled tones, terrified.

"Get some ice!" said Jack.

Lois pulled several cubes from the ice bucket, wrapped them in a silk scarf and handed them to him;

he pressed the bundle against her forehead after wiping off the beads of sweat.

Allison lifted her hands to her neck and rubbed the flesh. Her pulse slowed. She looked around the room and blinked unsurely as the shapes that had decomposed during the onslaught of the pain began to reassume coherency. She leaned forward in the chair and gripped her knees. She remained silent for several minutes, unresponsive to Jack's prodding. Then she looked up, breathed deeply and sat back. "It's gone."

"What's gone?" Jack asked.

"I'm not sure," she replied with a look that implied an absence of total consciousness. Yet, some of her color had returned and her eyes had steadied. "I had a migraine," she said, "and this sensation, as if the sense of touch had left my hands and legs."

Jack regarded her inquisitively. "Can you hold the ice?" he asked.

She nodded and laid her hand over the scarf.

"Do you want to lie down?"

"No," she said, shaking her head deliberately. "I feel better."

"Are you sure?" asked Jennifer as she nervously leaned over the arm of the chair.

"Yes," Allison answered. She did feel better. Almost a complete reversal of her condition just moments ago. She was understandably skeptical. Could the migraine and deadness have disappeared that quickly? It seemed impossible. Yet the pain had arrived almost instantaneously. Surely it could have left the same way. That is, assuming there really was a headache and a polarization of her sense of touch and not a psychological mirage brought on by the heat or excitement.

"I want you to sit for a couple of minutes more," said Jack.

"Yes, I think I will," Allison said.

She did, during which time Jack hovered over her,

occasionally going over to the broken skylight window to comment on the excessive heat in the studio.

After several minutes he asked how she felt. She said, "Fine." He asked if she had eaten. She said she had nibbled a hamburger at lunch. He concluded that food would do her good and pulled her to the bar, where she began to eat one of the remaining sandwiches.

She chewed slowly. She wasn't hungry. Strange! She hadn't eaten since lunchtime. And her appetite had seemed perfectly normal. Perhaps she was coming down with the flu. You could always count on the flu to arrive at the most inopportune time and bring with it the most peculiar set of symptoms imaginable. That might explain everything. Still she should have started slower. An hour booking instead of a long session. And a staggered schedule rather than consecutive commitments. She had a major commercial to shoot the next day, a national spot, which would probably require a few days' work. Then she would have to shop and cook dinner for Michael. There were several still sessions scheduled for Wednesday and a fashion show for Thursday. Rest? She doubted she would have much time for that until the weekend, providing she didn't become sick, in which event everything might have to be canceled.

Jack cleaned up the cellophane and napkins and placed the tray and discarded bottles under the bar. He walked around and gently laid his hand on her shoulders and massaged the delicate but tense muscles with the tips of his fingers. She lowered her head. He ran his hand up her neck and over the back of her scalp, following the wave of her fine-spun hair. "You're a right pretty thing, you know," he said reassuringly.

She smiled.

"I want to be sure that you feel all right before we begin. If not, we'll wait."

She swiveled around and kissed him on the cheek. "I'm fine," she said.

He pulled her from the seat, slapped her on the rear and led her back toward Jennifer and Lois, who were back on the set.

Allison watched Lois and Jennifer turn the near corner onto Fifth Avenue and disappear.

She glanced at her watch; it was late, eleven o'clock. The session had lasted longer than she had expected. She was tired. Yet apart from the "fainting spell," it had been a good first booking. A triumphant return of sorts.

She picked up her duffel, stepped out of the doorway and looked toward Sixth Avenue, now a blotch of light in the distance. She began to walk slowly, acutely aware of the darkness, shadows, and dirt. She felt curiously uneasy. Strange, she had walked this neighborhood at night many times over the past few years. And she had learned to accommodate the terrors. But tonight, for some unexplainable reason, she felt threatened. Perhaps she had been away from New York too long.

Halfway down the block she stopped. She could hear footsteps echoing between the grotesque overhanging buildings. Turning quickly, she strained her eyes, but there was nothing visible; the footsteps died. She squeezed her fingers into fists. The feeling again. It returned with the same suddenness with which it had hit her in the studio. She felt a surge through her arms, then a lack of sensation, as if all the nerve endings had been cauterized. Nervously, she looked for the source of the footsteps, hoping to see Jack appear, explain away the intruder and reassure her as he had done before. Then, suddenly, the dull tingling was gone. She kicked at the ground, angered that she would let the strain of past weeks do this to her.

Steadying herself, she took several steps and stopped again. Footsteps echoed once more. Quickly, she crossed the street, huddled in the shadow of a garment factory and looked back. The footsteps continued, but they sounded different now. They were no longer coming toward her; they were either moving away or turning into one of the side alleys. She remained frozen in place, sensing that she was still in danger, praying that the horrible tingling sensation would not return to her arms. Then she bolted through the refuse toward the corner. Running, gasping frantically, arriving under the streetlight just as an arm wrapped around her chest and pulled her to the side.

"Hey."

She looked around, panic-stricken; there was a man behind her.

"Slow down, my child; you'll kill someone," he said softly.

She stood shaking, holding on to a muscular arm that held her securely. She panted wildly, wound her fingers into the little tufts of white hair that dotted his freckled skin and focused on the diminutive nun who stood close to him, holding her rosary and using his body as a buffer against the cold night wind.

The priest released his grip, raised his heavy white eyebrows and regarded her sympathetically.

"Are you all right?" asked the nun.

Allison nodded and turned.

"What happened?" questioned the priest.

She hesitated and, as a gesture of regained composure, tried to tidy her wildly scattered hair. She was relieved. Of all people to run into, a priest and a nun. How lucky could she have been? She quickly grabbed her crucifix—in deference to something—and held it tightly.

Turning, she glanced down the block. There was nothing. She looked back at the priest, embarrassed. "I'm terribly sorry, Father, I thought someone was behind me. I was trying to get off the street."

"Let me see," said the priest. He stepped away and looked down the barely visible sidewalks. "I don't see anything," he said, shaking his head. "Stay with the good sister for a moment."

The priest began to search the doorways.

"Sister, I'm so sorry."

"There's nothing to be sorry about, my child," said the nun. Her cheeks glistened under the shower of light from the streetlights; her eyes reflected her warmth and sincerity. "If something scared you," she continued, "that is not your sin. You shouldn't walk alone here at this hour of the night."

"But this has never happened before," Allison protested.

"Something bad need only happen once." The nun reached out and took her hand. "Calm yourself, my child. No one will hurt you now."

They stood together under the streetlight for two or three minutes.

At the sound of footsteps they turned; the priest stepped from the shadows.

"Nothing," he said as he wiped some dust off his authoritative hands.

"I'm sorry," Allison repeated once again. "I don't know what got into me."

"I wouldn't concern myself, my child. It's very dark and every sound echoes no matter how slight. It's certainly understandable that you would become frightened."

"Where are you going?" asked the nun. "If it's near, you can walk with us."

"No, thank you. I have to go uptown to Eighty-ninth Street. I'll hail a cab, but I would appreciate it if you could wait with me until one comes. I'm still a little unnerved."

"Of course," said the priest. "We'll stand on the other corner."

They crossed the street and waited for several minutes until a taxi passed.

"Thank you again," Allison said as she stepped into it.

"Don't mention it," replied the priest. "Just stay off dark streets." He closed the door.

She turned and looked out the back window. A car was coming toward her, partially illuminating West Twenty-sixth Street. She watched the car's prog-

ress until it reached the corner. Seeing nothing, she
laid her head back on the poorly upholstered seat.

"Eighty-ninth and Central Park West, please."

The cab jolted forward.

She lifted her head once again and peered out the
dirty back window. The priest and nun were walking
slowly up the block. She smiled, thankfully, but the
smile quickly faded. She was furious with herself.
Silly! Cowardly! Paranoid! The epithets ran quickly
through her head. She couldn't believe how she had
just acted. She had to get control of herself. The
tactile strangeness. The sensation of footsteps. The
headaches.

All nonsense.

She promised herself it would not happen again.
And she promised herself she would say nothing to
Michael.

4

"Damn, it's hot," she cried as she emerged from
the confines of the tiny kitchen.

She hustled down the corridor carrying two round
porcelain bowls. Cautiously, she set them on the dining
table, blew on her singed fingers lifted the lids to
check the condition of the vegetables, then stepped
back, surveyed the fruits of her considerable labor
and realigned the mirrored settings at either end of
the white tablecloth. She lifted two long-stemmed
wine glasses and placed them next to a tear-shaped

decanter and a bottle of French wine, finest vintage, that had been selected earlier in the day according to Michael's strictest instructions.

Quickly noting the time on the grandfather clocks, she squeezed her hands nervously, scurried back into the kitchen and re-emerged with a hot plate. She skirted the end of the table, placed it on a portable bronze heater, applied a match, and stood back to admire the bright blue flame that shot up to singe the bottom of the metal casserole. She was satisfied. There was still more to do, but she was beginning to create some order out of the previous two hours' chaos.

The doorbell rang. She jumped up and quickly glanced once more at the clocks. They read nine-thirty; Michael was half an hour early. How could he have done this to her? He had never been early for anything in his life.

"Coming!" she shouted.

She ran to the mirror and straightened her pants suit. Not that it needed straightening, but a woman surprised is a woman unkempt, and the first thing she invariably does, whether the feelings of dishevelment are illusory or not, is check her clothes and makeup. She tossed her hair, frowning slightly at the sight of a few loose ends, and placed the dangling crucifix inside the top of her jacket. The bell rang again.

"I'm coming, Michael!"

She grabbed the latch, pulled the chain guard, started to turn the knob and then stopped. Michael hadn't rung the front buzzer. How had he gotten in? Maybe one of the neighbors had been coming through the foyer at the same time. With a quick twist, she opened the door.

"Chazen's the name. Charles Chazen," said the little man. There he stood, all five feet six of him, slight of build and substance, with an elongated head and comically unmatched features emphasized by thinning gray hair that curled over his ears, an enormous pair of warped bifocals which sat precariously on the bridge of his sharply pointed nose, and sunken but ruddy cheeks that smacked of an Irish background or an extreme and constant state of embarrassment. The rest of his face was a composite of lines, crags and crevices, all appropriately aged and asymmetric. But though it much resembled a prune his immediate smile was ingratiating.

"I'm your neighbor in five B," he said.

Mr. Chazen was dressed in an old gray suit that was frayed around the edges and creaseless. The top two buttons were missing, as were the buttons on his sleeves, though the threads still remained. In his lapel was a shriveled flower.

"This is Mortimer," he said, nodding to the green and gold parakeet that sat on his right shoulder.

The bird chirped an opinion.

"Yes, she is," Chazen answered.

Allison eyed him queerly as the bird hopped about his shoulder.

"A most sagacious bird. Extraordinary. Unfortunately he cannot speak a word of English, so if you're not proficient in the language of the species, I'm afraid, you will miss a stimulating exhibition of erudition."

"I . . . uh . . ." she stammered. "I'm afraid I'm not."

"Tut, tut, my dear. In good time I shall teach you. It's quite simple, you know." He paused, glanced at the bird and continued. "I trust you like birds?"

"I do."

"He's from Brazil. Have you ever been there?"

"No."

"I hear 'tis a lovely country."

"Yes, I have also," she said as she shifted unsurely in place.

Chazen stood erect, almost at attention. His left arm hung at his side while his right arm hooked in front of him, forming a cradle in which sat another animal, a silly-looking black and white alley cat with limpid green eyes and the most frazzled, unkempt coat she had ever seen.

Chazen held up the cat.

"And this is Jezebel. She speaks perfect English," he announced, looking into the cat's eyes. "Say hello to the nice lady, sweetheart!" The cat said nothing. "Come on." Still nothing. "Well, she's not been too talkative tonight. Perhaps she has a bit of indigestion."

Allison stood nonplused. She had expected Michael, but instead here appeared a strange man with his mini-menagerie—a cat and a bird—her upstairs neighbor.

"My name's Allison," she said.

Mr. Chazen smiled broadly and extended his hand. "Glad to meet you. Yes sirreee. Glad to, glad to." He chucked the cat under the chin. "Aren't we? of course we are, my little angels."

The cat sneezed.

Chazen frowned. "Is my little baby catching a nasty cold?" He felt the cat's nose, then each of her paws; satisfied, he wiped the look of parental concern from his face and smiled at Allison once again.

"Yes, I'm happy to know you too," she said while extending her hand to join Chazen's. "I was wondering when I was going to meet some of the neighbors."

"Oh, yes. I'm sure." The little man bounced into the apartment with the animals. "Come, my children," he said affectionately. He had a funny little walk, Chaplinesque in manner; his feet pointed in opposite directions, his legs remained stiff and extended as his body swayed from side to side. All that was missing was the black bowler, a set of tails and a cane.

The cat bobbed merrily in his arm as he walked, her head mimicking the movement of his body. She seemed comfortable; she had obviously been carried like this many times before.

"What a lovely apartment," he said, scurrying about like a bargain hunter at a rummage sale. Within moments he had examined every piece of furniture in the room. "Mortimer finds the decor stimulating," he added after a brief discussion with the bird.

"Thank you," Allison replied.

Chazen wobbled to the fireplace, quickly examined it, then turned his attention to the grandfather clocks, which he studied judiciously.

"Magnificent timepieces," he said as he ran his eyes along the mantelpiece; it was covered by cameos and ferrotypes. He reached out, removed one and held it up. "Herbert Hoover," he declared. "A noble President."

As far as she knew, she had neither a picture nor a cameo of the man. Curiously, she walked over and looked at the antique.

"It doesn't look like him."

"Of course it does. Unquestionably so." He nodded; then, oblivious to the fact that she had claimed ignorance of its presence, added, "I admire your patriotism. I remember the man distinctly." He puffed his chest proudly. " 'I shall go to Korea,' he said. Got him elected."

"That was Eisenhower."

"Eisenhower? Was it?" He pondered momentarily. "I guess it was. Funny. I thought it was Hoover. Now what did Hoover say?"

Allison shrugged.

"Ask not what your country can do for you, ask—"

"No."

"No?" He wrinkled his brow and challenged, "Who said that?"

"Kennedy."

"Really?"

"Yes."

He glanced at the parakeet. "Hoover must have said something!"

"I'm sure he did."

"What could it be?" he asked himself.

Allison smiled. "Give me liberty or give me death."

"That's it," he screamed. "A great man."

She shook her head incredulously.

He returned the cameo to the mantel, roamed to the center of the room, listened to some rapid commentary from Mortimer, then leaned on the couch and rubbed his chin. "My dear, your taste is exquisite. I should like you to help me redecorate my apartment someday."

She protested. "Thank you, but I can't accept the credit. Most of this was here when I arrived."

"Tut. Tut. Immodesty is not a virtue when one's abilities are genuinely laudable. Aristotle said so."

She laughed. If Aristotle had said so, it was probably right. But then again Aristotle had said that the earth was the center of the universe.

Chazen continued to move about the apartment, displaying an intense curiosity about every object within reach, re-inspecting everything a second time. Suddenly he stopped.

"Oh," he said in a self-reprimanding tone, "I've interrupted your dinner."

She looked at the exquisite table setting. "No," she corrected, "I haven't begun yet."

"That's reassuring! I would feel so contrite if I had barged in. Ingestion and digestion must progress without interference of idle chitchat. Don't you think?"

"Why yes," said Allison. "I'm waiting for a gentleman to join me for dinner. His name's Michael," she continued, trying to think of a way to politely induce her neighbor to leave.

"You're married?"

"No."

"Engaged?"

She shook her head.

"Ah, just friends," he concluded. "But friendships often blossom into bliss." He smiled. "Definitely so!"

She frowned. She hadn't heard such corn in years.

Chazen continued to smile broadly as he walked around the table. He studied several of the bibelots with the aplomb of an antiques expert. Then he sat down at the head of the table.

"Thank you for offering," he bellowed.

"Offering?" she responded, not quite knowing what he was talking about.

"Oh, yes, yes. I know when someone's going to offer me a chair. From experience; I'm no youngster, you know. So I merely saved you the effort by thanking you in advance." Chazen paused, petted the cat and continued. "I've been meaning to pop in for the last three days, but between this and that I first had the chance now."

"I'm so happy you were able to find the time."

"So am I," Chazen declared, adjusting his unadjustable bifocals. "I so love new neighbors. I like the old ones too. But new neighbors are so much fun. They remind me of my first apartment back in the twenties—or was it my second back in the thirties? Well, whatever. It was so long ago I really don't remember accurately, but I had so much fun with the new neighbors."

"Can I offer you anything?" asked Allison, interrupting the confusion. "Some wine or food?"

"Oh, no, it's way past my mealtime and at my age I must keep a careful regimen."

"And the animals?"

"They eat with me," stated the old man definitively.

She stifled a laugh. She couldn't believe the conversation. But he was entertaining and she immediately felt a pleasant affection for him. She sat and petted Jezebel's neck; the cat purred.

Chazen smiled contentedly. "Mortimer likes his stomach rubbed," he declared.

Allison reached over and caressed the bird's breast.

"A hedonistic bird." Chazen giggled, his cheeks reddening. "Hedonism and sagacity. A rare combination in any animal—human or otherwise."

"I would suppose," Allison surmised.

"So would I," announced Chazen. "So would I."

Allison smiled, bemused.

"Do you know any of the other neighbors?" she questioned.

"Of course," he answered. "I know them all, such nice people, except—" He motioned Allison to lean in so that he might whisper in her ear. "Well, there's a priest on the floor with me who belongs in a mental institution! Crazy as a loon!" The old man looked up at the ceiling as if he were repentant for having uttered such an insinuation. "God forgive me," he begged. "But he's really nuts. Sits in his apartment all day looking out the window."

"The renting agent mentioned him."

"She did?"

Allison nodded. "He was watching us as we were leaving the building."

"I see." Chazen paused. "But don't worry, he never comes out and he's very quiet. Well, anyway, there's that apartment four A!"

"Who lives there?"

"No one. That's the point. They've never rented it. And it really is nice. Now all of the rest of the people are quite pleasant and I— No, wait, I almost forgot those two women on the second floor. There's something evil about them. Worthy of damnation!"

"That's a harsh judgment," she cautioned.

"Oh, tut," he responded.

"Excuse me?" questioned Allison, not quite knowing the meaning of his remark.

"Tut! Tut! Never you mind. Evil, I said."

She was duly chastened. She sat back in her chair and waited for his next revelation.

"Now what was I talking about?" puzzled the old man. "Let me see."

"The neighbors?" suggested Allison.

"No, it was something else. Before that. No. Ah, marriage. That's it. Marriage! Never indulged myself. Confidentially, I've always been somewhat afraid and suspicious of women. No offense, my dear."

"I'm sure none was intended."

"No, no, of course not. Let me see. Yes, I must admit that I have some terrible foibles. When I was just a child, my mother, the dear soul, tried . . ."

She glanced over at the clocks as he continued to drone like a broken record. It was already ten, time for Michael's arrival. But she knew he would be late as usual. This annoyed her. Couldn't he have come on time to rescue her from this discourse on Chazen's life history?

The old man spoke dramatically. Each momentous event of his life was announced with a humph in his voice and a barreling of his chest, produced to allow a great intake of air so that he might continue without pausing to breathe. Fortunately, she heard very little. Her mind was elsewhere and his voice encouraged her stupor.

Sometime in the midst of his dissertation she rejoined the flow of words. She again looked at the old grandfather clock to the right of the mantel. She could not believe that she had been listening for forty-five minutes. And she had heard almost nothing. There was some stuff about the Bronx, a few parables about the Depression, a list of his life's accomplishments and a survey of the numerous jobs he had held over the years. But not much else. She was concerned. What if the old man asked her to comment on the highlights of his life. It would be impossible and she could never face him again. Then she thought that that might not be so bad, if speechmaking was his favorite pastime.

"So you see, my dear Allison, Jezebel and Mortimer are my only true companions. Sure, Mrs. Clark in four B is an attentive acquaintance, but only they can truly sympathize—or should I say empathize. I share my most intimate moments with them, and as you can well guess, there are many intimate moments in an old man's life."

He sat back and smiled. His story was finished. He looked at the clock. "My God," he murmured, "it's well past their bedtime. Do you know that lack of sleep ruffles a cat's fur and curls a bird's feathers?"

"You live and learn," said Allison a little sarcastically.

"How true! How true! Well now, I had only intended to stay for a few minutes, but I've gone and jabbered on for an hour. How selfish of me! Anyhow, I know you have to prepare for your friend so I'll be going." He lifted the cat off the table. "I've enjoyed this little chat. It's a shame Jezebel wasn't more talkative. Maybe next time."

"I'm sure," she said.

He stood and walked to the door. "You needn't help me out. I'll do just fine. If you ever need anything or any help, just knock on my door at any time."

"Thank you for the offer," she said as she followed him.

"Tut, tut, don't mention it. It's my pleasure."

"Mr. Chazen, there is one thing. Might I use your phone in an emergency? The telephone company still hasn't installed mine."

"If I had one, it would be my pleasure, but I don't. Who would I call?"

Allison nodded sympathetically.

Once again he extended his hand. "Good night, my dear," he said and then warned, "Eat and drink with moderation."

"Good night," she answered affectionately.

"I almost forgot." He balanced the cat in the air. "Say good night, Jezebel." The cat said nothing. "I don't know what's gotten into her tonight. Maybe she does have a cold." He shook his head, shrugged, stepped out and closed the door.

She was alone again. She set the chain lock, turned the latch, then stepped away from the door and walked back across the rug to the table, where she sat, looked at the candles, which had already burned a quarter of the way down, and concluded that though utter confusion had reigned in Chazen's head, she had enjoyed his visit.

She lifted a fork and began to tap it against a plate. Slowly, she brought the percussion into unison with the ticking of the clocks. She continued as she surveyed the elaborate setting before her. Suddenly she stopped and leaned over the table. Next to the salt shaker was a small four-by-ten picture inside a simple, unadorned frame. She lifted it and brought it close. Chazen stared at her from the black and white glossy. He was dressed in a dated black tuxedo with a black bow tie; he held a bouquet of roses in his hand. The picture was adorable; he was smiling. She held it away and then closer, gauging which way it looked better. Strangely, she hadn't seen him leave it, nor had he said he was going to. Maybe it was a house-warming present. Maybe it was his calling card. Whatever, she liked it. She walked to the mantel and placed it squarely in the middle. When Chazen returned he would see it there and be pleased.

Then she turned away scowling. She was losing her patience. Where was Michael?

5

"Hysteria can make you physically ill," Michael declared after she had finished describing the discomfort she had experienced during the funeral.

"I'm not the hysterical type!" she protested.

He straightened the sleeves of his shirt and jiggled the polished gold cufflinks that read MSF, Michael Spencer Farmer. They were special. Fourteen-carat gold. A birthday present that past July. "Outwardly no," he agreed, "but we know better, don't we?" He looked for her reaction.

She sat back and watched the candlelight flicker against his sharp olive-toned features. His eyes were alive, deeply brown, almost hypnotic; his expression was intelligent, probing. He seemed open and reachable, yet between Charles Chazen's exit and his arrival, she had catechized herself into insensibility. Had he changed? she had asked over and over. Had she? Even as he had stepped through the door, the questions had continued to gnaw at her. She had greeted him silently. That was the best way to begin, she had thought to herself. And realistically, she had reasoned, she'd have every right to have been annoyed. He had been an hour and a half late, after a week and a half of delay. He didn't deserve an affectionate welcome; he deserved indifference. So what if the indifference had also served to insulate her insecurities. But now, after an exchange of gifts, a tour of the apartment, a pleasant dinner, it appeared that her anxiety would be eased. She had started to feel reasonably comfortable and secure.

"I've always found pressure to be very internalizing," he declared. "You start to reject external stimuli and focus on your own minor discomforts to the point where they can become exaggerated into actual illnesses, or symptoms of imagined disorders." He leaned forward and lifted a half-filled glass of wine, glancing at the cluttered table which held the remnants of their dinner. "You could have had worse than migraine."

"Perhaps."

"What did the doctor say?"

"Nothing."

"You've been all right since you've returned?" he asked pensively.

"Yes," she said, passing over the brief episode at Jack Tucci's. She glanced toward the windows and reminded herself that the far wall was still in

desperate need of additional furniture. Tomorrow—after spending the night with Michael—she would
be in an extravagant mood, the proper mood for the
proper acquisition.

He leaned back and yawned, reclining his head
as if his body had been dispossessed of its strength.
He raised his hands and drew them over his face.

"Tired?" she asked.

"No, but contentedly high," he admitted, stroking
the wine bottle affectionately. "And emotionally
drained."

"By what?"

"The atmosphere, the candles in particular, the
apartment." He caught her smile in the corner of
his eye. "And you. I'm not invulnerable, you know."

"I know," she agreed as she grasped his hand.
"I planned it this way. It takes a little extra effort
to make you melt."

"How much?"

"Very much."

He smiled. "You know me well."

"I've known you long."

He kissed her hand, the milk-soft skin. "Too long,"
he finally said.

"How long is that?" she asked.

"Long enough for you to be able to manipulate
my emotions."

"Can I do that?"

"It seems you can."

They sat quietly. The clocks ticking. The fire crack-
ling.

"It's strange," Allison began. "From the moment
I stepped off the plane, I couldn't bear to think of
home. But tonight I've been reliving the entire four
months. And not uncomfortably."

"That's understandable."

"Why?"

"As you said, you're comfortable. And I'm recep-
tive."

She closed her eyes. "When I read your note, I

was angry and disappointed. I had built this grand illusion of reunion. Very romantic."

"And cathartic. All the tension would have dissipated quickly."

"Yes . . . but then you weren't here."

"I'm sorry . . . I had no choice."

"Business." She muttered resolutely.

He nodded. "It might prove fortunate that I was away. It might have given you time to think, rather than dismiss."

"About what?"

"Your life."

She didn't answer.

Coldly he added, "The significance of your father's death!"

She then looked away, freezing. "I've done enough thinking!" There was a long pause. Then she cried, "It's over!" She raised her arms over her head. Her eyes opened sharply; she smiled, displaying an intense self-satisfaction. "Over! All of it."

He regarded her thoughtfully, sitting motionless. Then his mood began to darken; she could see the change settle over his face.

"Is anything wrong?" she asked. The visual answer had prompted the question.

Yet he said, "No."

"One thing you've never been able to do, Michael, is lie to me. What's wrong?"

He glanced at her. "All of it?" he asked.

"I don't understand," she countered.

He stood, lifted his glass, walked unsurely to the fireplace and jiggled the burning logs with the poker. He watched the embers rekindle and burn brightly. "It's a good fire," he said, then leaned down, threw in another log and remained crouched for several minutes. She asked him what he was thinking. "Things," he replied, "people and places and the key to your total resurrection." He noticed her look of confusion. The clock behind him struck the hour, then the clock to his right repeated, about six seconds behind. He noted the discrepancy. "Your father is dead," he declared intensely, almost as if the statement was revelatory. He paused. "I want you to answer a question." He walked back to his chair, sat and stared at her silently.

"Ask it," she said. She knew it was coming. She was surprised he hadn't started to prod her before. She had been prepared for it all evening.

"Why did you leave home?"

She looked up questioningly.

"You know what I mean!"

She glanced about the room, avoiding his eyes. "I wanted to become a model, and New York was the best place for that." She nervously toyed with her hair, her cheeks noticeably drained of their color.

"We've been through that before." He leaned forward. "I want to know the real reason. There was something else. A reason why you *had* to leave home. Why for seven years you never visited your family. Why you refused to let me go home with you in July. Should I go on?"

"I wanted to become a model," she repeated hypnotically.

He sighed, frustrated. "Your father made your life miserable."

"Yes, you know that."

"And you left home because of it."

"If you insist." She turned away. "All right. That helped make my decision to leave easier. I've admitted that before."

"There's more. Something traumatic. And it's time you told me." He crumpled his napkin and threw it into the salad bowl. "Your father is dead now and there's no reason why you shouldn't." He paused, waiting for a response. She sat stone-faced, and he added, "Something made you frigid! We've been able to conquer the problem physically, but we've never really gotten at the source of the problem."

She bit hard into her lip. "For the thousandth time, I wanted to be a model," she replied with strained softness, not quite understanding why she didn't come out and tell him the real story; but then again, after lying for so long the lies assumed the status of truth. She winced; for the first time the inability to reveal hurt her. She owed him more after all he had done to break the psychological noose that had choked her ability to enjoy normal relations with a man.

"All right, if you won't, you won't," he said.

"I don't understand why you keep badgering me about this."

"Yes, you do. Until you can tell me what happened, there'll be something between us and there'll be that slight doubt in your own mind that you've completely beaten your past. But until you're ready, I'll accept the fact that you wanted to be a model, but with the proviso that I really don't accept it."

"Ever the lawyer," she said, restating what she had known for so long, that he rarely was able to engage in any conversation without becoming litigious.

"It's amazing that an attorney can look at a set of facts, put them together, add some salt and pepper and then deduce that the main ingredient, the key to the entire entree, is missing."

"Or invent something that isn't there." She lifted a stalk of celery and began to break it disgustedly into sections.

"Never," he sternly replied, sitting back in the chair and tapping his fingers on the tablecloth. "No speculation. Just pure deductive reasoning."

"And ninety per cent of the time overanalyzation."

"I don't overanalyze." He reached into his pocket, removed a thin filter-tipped cigar, placed it in his mouth, applied a match, and tilted back his chair. He stared at her, his right eyelid twitching, reflecting the tension, and then said, "I don't like to see you lie to yourself."

"Michael, I—"

"Yes? Say it."

"There's nothing to say." She countered defiantly. "Please, no more questions. No more pressure."

He sat back and stared again for several minutes. Then he grabbed her arm, his expression softening. "Forget I said anything," he pleaded. But his tone still seemed accusatory.

"Yes, Michael," she replied. She looked away.

"I mean it," he said. He picked up the bottle of wine, tipped it to see if anything remained, then, disappointed, pivoted and ambled down the hall to the kitchen. He returned with a new bottle of Bordeaux and a corkscrew. "Do you know what time it is?" he asked as he wrenched out the cork.

"No," she replied, refusing to glance at the grandfather clocks.

He poured the wine. "Three o'clock, according to the clock on the right." He grinned apologetically. "Approximately two fifty-nine and fifty-four seconds according to the one on the left." He drank from his glass and fell silent.

"I don't know why, but I love you," she whispered as she rose mechanically from her chair, walked to him, placed her arms around his neck and sat gently on his lap. "Damn you!"

His eyes glanced toward the bedroom; she stared, smiling with anticipation, then stood and walked toward the hallway.

He gathered the wine glass and bottle, rose from the chair and walked to the fireplace to spread the burning logs so that they would burn independently and die quickly. "Who's this?" he asked as he removed a frame from the mantel.

"Herbert Hoover's brother." She laughed.

Looking closely at the glossy, he shook his head and observed, "Don't be ridiculous. This isn't Hoover's brother!"

"That depends on the perspective of the viewer," she answered as she continued to pull at the buttons on her blouse.

"Who is it?"

"Charles Chazen."

He raised his brow.

"My neighbor from upstairs. Apartment five B. He stopped in with his cat and parakeet before you arrived."

Michael puzzled over the picture. "I saw a cat in the hall," he stated, leaning against the mantel for support.

She looked at him questioningly.

"Black and white," he asserted. "It was running up the stairs."

"That's Jezebel," she said. "I wonder why Chazen would let her run around the halls alone. He was very protective about her and the bird."

Michael shrugged.

"I like him very much," she said, remembering his clothes, walk and manner.

"How old?"

"I'd guess about eighty, give or take four or five years."

"Lucid?" he asked.

She shook her head pityingly.

He looked at the picture sideways and upside down. "He looks like a prune."

She strode indignantly across the floor. "Very funny," she chided as she grabbed the picture and held it up; the glass flickered with the reflecting dance of embers. "I think he's kind of cute."

She placed the picture on the mantel.

"He sat there for an hour giving me his whole life history. None of it made any sense. He was pathetic, a little old man with no one but his cat and bird and nothing to do but to sit around all day reminiscing."

"He's better off than most."

"I never want to end up like that, to wake up in the morning with nothing to look forward to but the next bedtime. Or a conversation with my animals." She reached over his shoulder and pulled a cameo off the marble mantel. "He thought this was Herbert

Hoover. And I couldn't convince him otherwise." She ran her hands over the carved ivory. "In a way I'm glad I failed."

He cupped his hand under her chin and kissed her on the bridge of her nose. "Why don't we talk about him later?" he suggested. He began to unbutton his shirt.

She smiled and followed him expectantly to the bedroom.

The room was dark. He could see very little as he stood facing himself in the full-length mirror that hung opposite the bed. The reflection was almost motionless, a combination of inert objects and dark, heavy shadows, only punctuated by the glimmer from one of the wall sconces and the graceful movement of her body. He watched as she folded her blouse over the clothes horse to the right of the bed. Her figure never looked more sensuous and inviting than it did in the semi-darkness of the mirror.

He pulled his shirt from his shoulders, placed the sleeves together and threw it on the chair. Turning from the mirror, he walked to the window and grabbed the shade.

"Don't," she said softly. "There's no one to see in."

Bending down, he looked out, nodded, and released the small metal ring.

She lay down, rolled back onto the pillows and smoothed the quilt that lay extended beneath her.

"Are you happy?" he asked.

"Very."

He removed the last of his clothing, a pair of dark brown socks, and carefully found his way to the bed. Wrapping his arm around her shoulders, he pulled her close, gently kissing her ears, and pressing against her breasts. Then he stopped. He switched on the reading light, reached out and wrapped his fingers around the crucifix. "What's this?" he asked, breathing heavily.

"A crucifix."

"I know that. Where'd it come from?"

She paused to catch her breath. "From my father's room."

"I didn't know you were Catholic."

"No?"

He shook his head. "Since when?"

"Since ever." She paused, squinted at the shining bulb, reached up and turned it off. "You don't need light to speak to me."

"Allison, you never—"

She interrupted. "I haven't had much to do with it for the last few years. In fact, nothing at all."

"That's self-evident."

"But I did as a child."

"Why'd you stop?"

"Michael, let's drop it. We can discuss it another time."

He shook his head determinedly and repeated the question.

"Let's just say I began to *not* believe in it," she answered, knowing he would not let it slide. She sighed audibly.

"Does this have anything to do with your leaving home?"

"No." Her voice was soft, yet her annoyance unmistakable.

"It doesn't become you," he said after a pause.

She held the crucifix up and pressed it against her lips. "I think it looks just fine."

"It looks lovely. Catholicism does not become you."

"Why don't you let me be the judge of that?"

"I'm only voicing an opinion."

"Because you can't admit the existence of anything that's alien to you!"

"You don't believe that."

"You're making it obvious."

"I can very well accept any religion. Unless my memory fails me, you're the avowed atheist."

"People change."

"So it seems."

She turned away. "I resent being cross-examined at a time like this. You're in my bed, not in a court-room."

"I'm not cross-examining you."

"You've been doing it all night. From the moment you stepped in the door."

He sat up and laid his head on his knees. "Let's cut it," he said angrily. "I don't want to argue over something this ridiculous."

"You started it. I haven't said a damn thing. All I did was put on an old crucifix my father gave me. So what?"

He nodded. "I'm sorry." He reached out and touched the chain once again. "If you want to wear it, fine. Or go to church on Sunday, fine. I was just surprised."

Surprised! she thought to herself as she realized that she had been equally as surprised the day she had retrieved the crucifix.

They stared at each other. There was little com-munication between their eyes. Then Allison grabbed the crucifix and leaned back into the pillows, looking away.

"Please close the light," she asked.

He continued to stare, unresponsive. She turned back to him and glared. Then she reached up and flicked the switch.

Very surprised, she thought to herself.

6

Allison raced up the stone staircase laden with packages of groceries purchased at the supermarket on Columbus, located right where Miss Logan had indicated. It had been a tiring day, even though it was still early afternoon, what with a trip down to Foley Square to see Michael begin a defense in Criminal Court, two hours at *Cosmopolitan* to inform all the fashion editors in person that she had returned to New York and finally, the supermarket—by far the worst part of the day, since she hated shopping with a passion.

The sun was shining brilliantly, the warm day having materialized unexpectedly in the midst of what had been an unusually bleak autumn. Since early October the weather had been cold and wet, and that strange listlessness so characteristic of winter had enveloped the city. But not today. She was guardedly optimistic. There might still be an Indian summer after all.

She checked her mailbox and, finding nothing, stepped through the front door and over the soft woven carpet which deadened the sound of her shoes on the otherwise cold and unprotected tile; she started to climb the staircase. Halfway up she stopped and shook the banister, a ritual she had unfailingly observed since the day she had first entered the brownstone with Miss Logan. The banister didn't move; it was still sturdy.

She climbed to the first-floor landing and started down the hall.

The door to apartment 2 A stood ajar; a beam of light extended vertically into the hall. She stopped and curiously peered through the slit. She could see very little. Moving closer, she squeezed into the narrow space, pushed against the door and edged it open, exposing the living room.

She stood motionless, reluctant to enter without an invitation.

"Hello, is anybody home?"

She waited for a response.

Nothing.

The apartment seemed empty. Stupid to leave the door open if it was; the tenants could return and find everything gone.

She stepped into the room and glanced at the furniture, which appeared well kept and well used. The air seemed terribly still, the room unsettlingly quiet. She blinked apprehensively and tilted her head. "Hello," she repeated unsurely, tightening her grip on her packages. "Is anyone here?"

Continued silence.

She regretted her honesty. If she were a bit of a kleptomaniac she could make off with some interesting floor pieces that would fit perfectly into her apartment, more so than into this eclectic setting. Just one granny lamp. Or the wicker chairs. Who would know? But then again the fire hadn't set itself; the logs were intact, relatively new. Someone had just been in the apartment, probably had left for a few minutes and would return soon.

She scanned the heavy window shutters. They immediately struck her as permanent and explained why in the week she had been there she had never seen an unobstructed view from the outside.

"Is anybody home?" she repeated one last time, encouraged by the brightly burning fire that spit red-hot embers against the black fire screen.

Again there was no answer.

She turned to leave.

Standing directly behind her was a woman. About five feet five. Wearing no makeup. Yet her features were striking, perfect, uncompromising in their presence.

Allison could not help but admire her.

Another woman stepped into the doorway. She was taller by perhaps one or two inches. She had very sharp features, accentuated by heavy makeup. Her skin seemed to cling to her bones as if she'd had her face lifted. But she couldn't have been that old. Allison's first thought was thirty-five. Maybe thirty-eight. But no older. As soft as the other girl seemed, this one seemed hard.

Allison was puzzled. How had they come up behind her unnoticed? She studied them apprehensively, noted their nondescript though acceptably styled clothing, then focused on their feet. Both were wearing black ballet slippers. She glanced at the paintings and posters she had seen on the walls—some picturing ballerinas, others reproducing displays of Royal Ballet performances. And then back at the slippers. Ballerinas? Maybe that's why she hadn't heard them?

Embarrassed, she stammered, "I . . . uh . . ."

"How may we help you?" asked the taller woman, her voice cold and distant.

Allison shifted awkwardly.

"Speak up," demanded the woman with little flexibility in her angular jaw, almost as if her words had been supplied by a ventriloquist standing unnoticed elsewhere in the room.

"I was carrying my packages up to my apartment—I just moved in—and I saw the door open so I thought I'd introduce myself." She paused, noted their lack of response, and added, "I assure you that I had no other intentions."

She could barely get the words out of her mouth.

The two women, unsympathetic, continued to stare.

"My name's Allison Parker," she declared, which,

in view of the tense confrontation, was a remarkable recollection.

The taller woman inched a step closer and stood eye to eye. Then she broke a slanted semi-smile. "You must forgive us," she said while moving past Allison and into the room.

The sudden change was surprising. Allison watched the slipper-clad feet cross the rug. There wasn't a sound. She certainly was or at least had been a dancer.

"We don't get too many visitors. I'm Gerde. The name is Norwegian." She pointed to the other woman. "And that's Sandra."

Allison gestured toward Sandra, who remained silent and motionless.

"Do come in. You'll find the place very comfortable." Gerde removed her red scarf and placed it on the mantel. "Especially the fireplace. It's warm and relaxing. And you'll have some coffee with us." She turned and waited for a response.

"Well, I shouldn't—"

"No. I insist!"

Allison puckered her mouth to protest; she was uncomfortable. Even the words of invitation were spoken in a totally uninviting tone. But though she wanted to leave, she could not. Something kept telling her to get acquainted with these obviously difficult people, if only to avoid another such uncomfortable incident.

"Hospitality is a virtue that one has little opportunity to exploit in New York," said Gerde. "It runs against the grain of the city. People are too suspicious and jealous. And self-serving." She paused, lifted a cigarette from a silver dish, and motioned toward Allison.

"I don't smoke."

Gerde nodded with an expression that indicated admiration. "Put your packages on the table and sit down," she said, walking down the short hallway to the kitchen. "I put the coffee up a short while ago, so it should be ready. And I'm boiling some water, if you'd like tea."

"Coffee will be fine," said Allison as she sat down across from Sandra, who had moved to the faded brown couch.

"Have you met anyone else in the building?" echoed Gerde's voice.

"Yes, Mr. Chazen from upstairs. He dropped in to say hello two nights ago with his cat and bird."

"A nice man."

A nice man? she thought to herself. They obviously hadn't heard his opinion of them. "He mentioned you to me," she replied.

"I trust he said good things."

"Of course," answered Allison.

"We don't spend too much time with neighbors. New York inhospitality, as I said before. People living right next door to you might just as well be living in Siberia. And I don't wish to be exonerated; we're just as guilty."

"I don't think things are that bad. Mr. Chazen's visit proves otherwise right here in our own building." She smiled. "It's a matter of actively seeking communication."

"How courageous," replied Gerde with a note of sarcasm.

Allison frowned and turned to Sandra. "Have you lived here long?" she asked. She fidgeted while waiting for a response. The girl sat frozen.

"Don't be alarmed if Sandra doesn't speak," boomed the deep voice from the kitchen. "She never does except to me—and only if we're alone."

Allison puzzled that one out, then sat back on the ottoman and resolved to forgo any attempt to communicate with the mute. She turned away from the girl to see Gerde reappear with a cluttered tray.

"Help yourself," Gerde offered as she set the tray on the glass table.

"Thank you."

Gerde removed the dangling cigarette from her

mouth and ground it into an ashtray. "I meant to ask you," she said as she coughed.

"Yes," replied Allison.

"The crucifix you're wearing. Where did you get it?"

Allison looked down. The darn thing was exposed. She preferred to have it hang under her clothes. "From my family," she replied.

"Where was it made?"

"I don't know. It was a gift." She placed it back beneath her sweater.

"It looks French."

"It just might be. As I said, I don't know."

"I see," said Gerde curtly. "I admire beautiful things, especially crucifixes." She reached inside her blouse and removed one of her own, slightly larger than Allison's and by appearance ancient, belonging to an era of more mystical opulence. "I acquired it in Hungary. It was made in the eleventh century by Slavic monks."

Allison leaned forward. "It must be worth a fortune."

"Perhaps, but more than monetarily, as you might guess. Are you religious?"

She paused, then answered, "No."

"We are, so we find it difficult to reduce the meaning of a Christ to dollars and cents."

Sandra nodded slowly.

"I'm sorry," said Allison apologetically.

"There's no need to be. Religious sentiment in this day and age in New York is like hospitality and the word 'neighbor.' Virtually extinct." She stared at Allison intently. The cross dangled from her neck.

"May I take some coffee?" Allison asked, nervously licking her lips.

"Of course. That's what it's there for."

Allison leaned forward, selected a cup, poured the coffee, added a tablespoon of cream and three lumps of sugar. Though her concentration focused on cup and urn, she kept one eye on the two women.

"We've lived here several years," said Gerde, responding to Allison's earlier question. "Three, or maybe it's four now."

"How nice," observed Allison

"Yes, how nice," Gerde repeated slowly.

"Where did you live before?"

"In Europe. Paris for nine fantastic years and before that in Oslo, where I was born."

"I like Paris too," Allison interjected.

"You do? That's surprising. Most Americans don't."

"Why?"

"They find the city beautiful and the food excellent, but they don't like the French." Gerde paused, running her tongue over her lips. "And vice versa. You know the French are not particularly fond of Americans. Once de Gaulle had rekindled French nationalism, the inherent antagonism toward America surfaced. I saw this happen while I was there," she concluded obviously proud of the fact that she had been a witness to history. She leaned forward and poured a cup of coffee—no sugar, no cream. "But on the other hand, I can see why you'd like Paris. You're a beautiful girl and Frenchmen are gallant." She sipped from her cup and smiled. "The coffee is good," she declared.

"Did you meet Sandra there?" asked Allison.

"No, she's American. Never been to Europe." Gerde glanced at her friend, who responded by nodding slightly. "I met her in New York soon after I arrived. She had been living with a man for some time who had treated her very badly." Gerde patted Sandra's knee maternally. "I convinced her to get rid of him. She did. Then she moved in with me here and I've taken care of her since." Gerde and Sandra exchanged furtive smiles, their lips hardly breaking.

Allison sipped her coffee, watching them intently, trying to gauge and comprehend the disturbing tenor of the woman's words and their seemingly unnatural interdependence.

"Men are sadistic," cried Gerde with intensity.

Allison swallowed hard and countered, "I think that's an immoderate generalization. Most of the men I know are gentle and kind."

Gerde's eyes narrowed. "I see," she said, a nebulous smile crossing her lips. "The gentleman who left here yesterday morning in a brown sport jacket, is he your boy friend?"

Allison looked askance.

"Is he?" Gerde repeated.

"Yes."

Gerde sipped her coffee slowly, eyes on Allison; then she placed the cup down and folded her hands in her lap. "He looks like an adequate lover."

"I don't think that's any of your business," Allison declared.

Gerde lowered her eyes, a gesture which feigned self-castigation. "Please excuse me again. I'm quite frank, but also forgetful of common etiquette." She looked at Sandra and smiled, a strange grimace that stretched a pair of reluctant lips. "You see, Sandra and I are very open with one another and it has become a practice—or should I saw a deeply ingrained habit."

"I . . . uh . . . understand." Allison, lost for words, tried to change the subject. "I like the way you have your apartment furnished. I also prefer a combination of various styles."

"We're glad you approve," Gerde said, just as the telephone rang in the bedroom.

Gerde quickly excused herself, stood up and went to answer it. Allison watched her lope across the room, then reluctantly turned back toward Sandra.

In the fleeting moment she had looked away, there had been a change in Sandra's expression. It was now relaxed. The muscles were loose, the lips were parted and the blank expression now whispered a hint of life.

Allison examined Sandra's face and body. Then she blanched. Sandra's hand was inside her pants, massaging herself in a gentle circular motion. Her legs stiffened as the euphoria spread throughout her body. Harder and harder she rubbed, totally oblivious to Allison's presence, totally absorbed in her sexual ecstasy. Allison watched, both repulsed and fascinated. The girl's breathing deepened; her lips shook violently. Sighing deeply, she reached orgasm.

Sandra withdrew her hand, inhaled deeply once and then assumed her prior pose, as if what Allison had just seen had not happened. Again she was cold, distant, motionless.

Allison's stomach churned. She stood, wanting to get out of the apartment quickly. But something pinned her to the ground, like a counteracting force of opposing gravities.

Gerde loped back to the room and sat on the couch next to Sandra.

"We're quite proud of our apartment," she said to Allison, who was still standing mesmerized. Gerde had an amazing ability to seize upon unfinished conversations and questions after an interruption and continue as if the line had been unbroken. "It took us a long time to furnish it properly. No expense spared."

"That's the best way." Allison sat down on the ottoman, curiosity superseding her desire to run from the apartment.

"You know," Gerde continued, "we found many of these pieces lying about in the strangest places. If one keeps their eyes open, one can find veritable treasures."

Allison and Gerde began to drink their coffee, while Sandra slowly sipped at a steaming cup of tea. Her efforts were an accommodation. Her interest in the tea was minimal. The conversation, whatever there was, died. All three just stared at one another.

Slowly, Sandra inched her way closer to Gerde and slid her hand down her side and into her room-mate's. Allison fidgeted nervously with her cup, spilling much of the coffee into the saucer. Again the silence. She watched the sensual movement of Sandra's hand in Gerde's, the intertwining of the fingers and the pressing of the palms. Sandra's entire body experienced another euphoric relaxation; the distant look disappeared, the sallow expression brightened. Gerde remained impassive. Sandra reached orgasm again.

"Do— What do you do for a living?" Allison was clutching.

"Nothing," replied Gerde curtly.

"You must do something to earn money."

Gerde shook her head, looked at her entwined hand, glanced back up to Allison and tightened her grip, causing Sandra to wince in excitement.

Allison, now visibly disturbed, still tried to avoid the impending confrontation. "Then you must get quite bored. What do you do to keep busy?" she asked.

"We fondle each other."

Allison stared, her mouth open.

"Fondle! Caress!" Gerde was very direct, very curt and very piqued.

Gerde leaned over and touched Sandra's breast, and Sandra's body responded with convulsive jerks.

Allison shot to her feet. "I think I'd better be going," she blurted. "I have to put away all the groceries and then I have an appointment."

"I think it's rather rude to eat and run," said Gerde.

"First of all, I didn't eat, I drank," Allison blustered, flushing. "And how dare you call me rude! After this demonstration of sickness! Masturbation and lesbianism. Right in front of me! I've never seen anything like it."

Gerde's eyes narrowed like a threatened cat. She slowly rose to her feet. "You little bitch," she mouthed deliberately.

Allison rushed by her and began to gather her

packages; the largest fell to the floor. She bent down to pick it up only to find Gerde's foot pressing it against the ground. She grabbed Gerde's leg and tried to move it off the bag. It wouldn't budge. She pulled out the package, upsetting the woman, sending her sprawling to the rug. Gerde struggled to her feet and grabbed Allison by the hair as she dropped her packages and grasped Gerde's wrist, digging in her nails. Gerde winced in pain and released her hold.

Allison ran to the door, threw it open, and stumbled into the hall. When Gerde followed, Allison pressed against the rail and turned to defend herself.

Suddenly Gerde stopped, her eyes turning to the third-floor staircase. Allison jerked her head in that direction. Charles Chazen stood at the base of the stairs stroking Jezebel. Mortimer hopped from shoulder to shoulder, chirping frantically. Gone was the pleasant smile. His shriveled face was impassive, the old eyes strangely dilated.

Gerde trembled. Quickly, without looking at Allison, she stepped back into the apartment and closed the door.

Allison swayed, exhausted, her breathing almost convulsive.

"I warned you! Yes, I did. From now on, you should avoid them. They're evil." The little man stepped off the staircase and took Allison gently by the hand. "Now come, I'll walk you up to your apartment."

Allison followed Chazen up the staircase. He said nothing, neither did she. Thoughts raced through her mind. About Gerde. About Chazen. Why did the woman stop the way she had when she saw the old man? She was obviously afraid of him. Why? She didn't know. She didn't ask.

"I suggest you take two aspirin and get some sleep," advised Mr. Chazen as he watched Allison fumble for her key. "Sleep would be most therapeutic. Tsk, tsk, what a terrible incident. I hope you've learned your lesson. Listen to Chazen from now on."

Allison nodded as she inserted the key into the lock. "Thank you. I don't know what I—"

"Don't mention it. Just get some sleep."

She kissed the old man on the cheek and closed her door.

7

"We're about ready to start," said the pencil-thin fashion coordinator with the clipboard. "Is anybody unsure of the order of appearance?" She poked her hairpiece nervously with a nineteen-cent Bic as she waited for a reply. "Then I trust everything will go like clockwork."

Allison adjusted her pants suit and took a quick sip from the cup of coffee she had placed moments before in front of the dressing mirror. She was ready.

"Vicki, if you will? Allison, please."

Allison was surprised she had gotten there on time. She hadn't wanted to do it; it had been two years since she had done live fashion work. But she had promised and it was for charity.

She had slept very little the night before. Gerde and Sandra had seen to that. She lay in bed for hours, afraid to close her eyes. Afraid to dream. She knew she reacted badly to nightmares; she had known that since her childhood. There was nothing she feared more. And she had a feeling that— Well, she wasn't sure, but she sensed the same kind of dizziness that she had experienced so often as a child, the dizziness that had invariably preceded a night of terror.

She tried everything to fall asleep. First, she sipped tea, then hot milk. Then she took a hot bath. Nothing relaxed her. She tried to read, but she was so nervous that she couldn't hold the book steady; it fell to the floor. She wondered if the two women below had heard the sound. And what were they doing? Were they in bed together making love? She cringed, got up from the bed to retrieve the book and placed it on the night table. She bent down, her hands extended. Her head swimming, she fell to her knees and buried her face in the blankets. If only the dizziness would go away. She was so tired. All she wanted was some sleep, just like she had wanted so many times when as a child she had knelt in a similar position, her head spinning, her nerves shattered. She lifted her head slightly and clasped her hands in front of her. The position was strange; it had been years since she had crouched this way.

"Angel of God," she prayed. "My Guardian Dear, To whom God's love, commits me here, Ever this day be at my side." She stopped abruptly. This was ridiculous. She was twenty-six years old. She hadn't been in a church in seven years. And what good would this stupid little chant do?

"To light, to guard, to rule, to guide. Amen," she concluded.

Soon she was asleep.

The alarm buzzed at ten. Five and a half hours' sleep. Her head ached, her eyelids were heavy and her face was drained of color. But she hadn't dreamed. She smiled as she moved the bright green toothbrush over her gleaming teeth. No banshees. No monsters. No horrors. No matter how bad the night before had been, the fact that she had not dreamed made it quickly fade from her mind.

She left the apartment at eleven fifteen, giving herself just enough time to hail a cab, scoot downtown and join Michael for an early lunch. She raced down the third-floor staircase, portfolio in one hand, duffel bag in the other, and stopped at the base. Apartment 2 A was ten feet away, the door closed; she walked slowly, measuring the length of each step. Carefully placing her feet so as not to make any noise. Carefully watching the door. Would it be like this every time she had to pass? Maybe, but she was primarily concerned with this one time—the morning after.

Having crossed the ten feet without so much as a squeak, she stopped, listening for any evidence of life. There was none; she felt relieved. A small bead of perspiration rolled down her cheek. She wiped it away, walked to the top of the landing, started down the staircase, tested the banister and halted abruptly at the sound of rustling below.

The basement door opened. Out stepped Charles Chazen, catless, birdless, holding a large box awkwardly between his two hands and chin.

She walked down the stairs to meet him.

He chugged around the banister post. "Good morning!" he cried. "Lovely morning."

"How are you?"

"Fine, my dear. And yourself? Have you forgotten about yesterday's unfortunate incident?"

She hesitated, then answered, "Yes."

"Good. So be it." He started up the staircase. "It's nippy outside. I think I might have gotten a chill this morning. Be sure to keep your jacket on."

"I will."

He fidgeted. "Can't talk now. I'm very busy."

"Spring cleaning?"

"No. I'll tell you about it later."

She stepped onto the hall floor as he raced upward.

"Mr. Chazen?"

He stopped and pivoted. "Yes?"

"I'd like to ask you something."

"Quickly. Quickly."

She bit her lip. "Why was that woman so frightened of you?"

The smile disappeared; his eye glinted. "Evil, I said."

"That doesn't answer my question," she said sternly.

"Evil."

"But—"

He put down the box, raised his arm and curled his hand into a fist. His cheeks reddened. "I gave them this before," he said, shaking his hand like a pummeling hammer, "and I shall smite them again if they bother my friends."

She looked at him queerly. "I see," she said.

"Stay away from them. Tsk, tsk." The smile returned to his face. He leaned over and picked up the box. "I must be off. Speak to you later."

He sauntered up the stairs.

Moments later she emerged from the building, hailed a cab and joined Michael—on time.

"Sounds familiar, a bull dyke and her lover," Michael said, his mouth full of ice cream. "When you walk into the lion's den and play with the cubs, be prepared to get bitten."

"That's a lousy analogy."

"Why?"

"I didn't play with any cubs."

"All right, but you know what I mean. You know how vicious a dyke can be if provoked."

"Yes."

"Just stay out of that apartment and keep away from them and you shouldn't have any trouble."

"It's not just them that bothers me. It's what happened in the hall. You had to have been there to have seen Gerde's reaction when she saw the old man. I never saw anyone register so much fear. And I can't begin to figure out why."

"You said the old man told you they were evil. Maybe he's had it out with them already."

"Maybe."

"It's logical."

"Yes, but—"

"But?"

She thought for a moment. "I met him in the hall this morning. He said he gave them this." She shook her fist to illustrate.

"There you have it. He beat the shit out of them. And if that's the case, no wonder the woman was frightened."

"I don't know. There's something more."

"Allison!"

"What?"

"Just Allison," he said, focusing his eyes on her severely.

"Okay, I promise. I won't dwell on it. You're probably right anyway."

"It wouldn't be the first time." He laughed.

She glanced at her watch. "I'd better get out of here."

"What time is it?"

"Twelve forty-five."

"I have to go too. I have to finish a brief." He motioned for the waiter.

"Want me to help later?"

"No."

"What about the trial?"

"Adjourned until tomorrow."

"You'll win."

Michael smiled. "Why don't you go ahead. I'll wait to pay the check."

"Okay." She leaned across the table and kissed him very gently on the forehead. "I love you," she said softly.

He nodded affectionately.

She grabbed her portfolio and duffel and stood up. "Did you call the phone company for me?"

"I forgot."

"Michael, please. I've got to get a phone into that apartment."

"All right. I'll call this afternoon." He paused and thought for a moment. "But only if you promise to forget about last night and leave those two women alone."

"I promise." She blew him a kiss and hurried out of the restaurant.

Half an hour later she stepped through the curtain and closed her eyes to avoid the blinding glare of the high-powered spotlights. She heard a few whispers and the high-pitched voice of the gay announcer. Then, opening her lids, she squinted. Five or six seconds passed in whiteness as her eyes adjusted. She slowly moved about the stage and eventually disappeared behind the curtain. She hustled into the dressing room, tore off the outfit, changed clothes and went back in time to make her second entrance.

"Allison again, this time wearing a floor-length chamois dress," lisped the announcer.

She walked to the runway and turned about in place. A sharp pain jolted her head. She stumbled slightly but retained her balance and continued to walk in front of the crowd. She was dizzy again. Perhaps it was the recurrence of last night's disability. Or maybe the lack of sleep.

Then the rush, the lack of sensation in her arms and legs. And a new terror: the loss of sight and sound.

She stood in the middle of the stage, unable to move. The faces in the audience blurred; her vision darkened. She reached out. Into a long dark room. She walked. Faster. Faster. She heard a mumbling, something unintelligible. She listened. Then the image and sounds faded and she fell to the ground before the horrified audience.

8

"The white pills are supposed to relax me," said Allison. She held the receiver against her shoulder, closed the folding door and waited for Michael's response. Damn the phone company, she thought to herself angrily. If they had installed her phone as promised, she would not have had to search the streets for nearly half an hour in order to find a street phone that was working. The one on the corner of Eighty-ninth was out of order, someone having broken the mechanism while trying to pry loose the coin box. The nearest in service was six blocks uptown on Columbus Avenue. Expectedly, it too had been battered. The casing was dotted by deep gouges and long scratches; the coin return was stuffed with Baby Ruth candy wrappers, cemented in place by a foul-smelling clump of red licorice. But fortunately it had survived.

"The others are just sleeping pills," Allison replied to Michael's next question.

She had spent the last six hours in Roosevelt Hospital, where she had been taken after her collapse. They had run a series of tests. Primarily neurological and vascular. Apart from a slightly elevated blood pressure, the results were negative. She was released, given medication and advised to consult a neurologist if there was a repetition of the incident.

Instead of going to the apartment, she located the

phone booth, told Michael of the seizure and now stood jiggling the door, trying to close out the cold air.

"I'll be all right. You don't have to come." She listened intently then added, "Yesterday's episode didn't help!"

No, it hadn't. Obviously Gerde and Sandra had contributed to the tensions that had caused the blackout. Hadn't the incident kept her up much of the night? Surely that was enough. She listened again while trying to reconstruct the impressions she'd had just prior to her collapse. The dizziness and darkness. The long room that stretched into eternity. The noises. It made no sense.

"I'll call you if I don't feel all right," Allison concluded. She placed the receiver on its hook, stepped out onto the darkened street, turned downtown and walked along the rows of middle-income housing that had sprouted like mushrooms during the past few years, fertilized by federal subsidies.

She alternately counted the rows of lighted windows and the slabs of concrete that skidded under her feet until she turned off Columbus onto Eighty-ninth Street and walked into the darkness.

A note was taped to her door. She pulled it off. It was the bill from Slapen's Appliance Mart. Her television had arrived.

Excited, she entered the apartment.

There it stood, twenty-four inches' worth, full color, attractive frame, nestled right into the space she had marked against the wall.

She tossed her jacket on the sofa, walked into the kitchen and turned on the water. She placed two vials on the sink, one with a white top, the other blue. The white one was marked "Tranquilizer" and listed elaborate instructions. The other was marked "Sleeping Pills." She read the tranquilizer label carefully, removed two oval pills, popped them onto her tongue, then filled her mouth with water. She had never been good with pills. Unsympathetically, they squeezed down her throat.

She placed the covered vials on the formica counter and returned to the living room.

Kneeling in front of the console, she turned on the set and adjusted the color. Then, standing with her eyes glued to the screen, she unbuttoned her long-sleeved blouse and exchanged it for a white tee shirt that lay on the sofa. She examined herself in the mirror, approved the change, noted that her breasts looked extremely full under the tight-fitting pullover, and smiled as she caught the reflected image on the television screen.

She sat on the sofa to watch. That seemed like a good way to spend the evening. At least she knew the ending would be happy. And this had not been a very happy day.

She placed her feet on the hassock; she was exhausted. She licked her lips with a sensual swipe of the tongue; she was beginning to feel the effect of the pills. The images on the screen blurred; their movements slowed.

Then the doorbell rang. She jumped to her feet. She knew it wasn't Michael; he was working late. And it was no one else from outside. If it had been, they would have buzzed to get in. Chazen? The two lesbians? The other neighbors?

"Who is it?" she asked loudly as she approached the door. There was no response. She bit her nails nervously. "Who's there?" she repeated. Silence. She paced back and forth in front of the door, the ticking of the large grandfather clocks counterpointing the thump of her footsteps, her shadow mimicking her progress.

"It's me," came the high-pitched voice.

"Mr. Chazen?"

"Yes, of course."

She caught her breath, relieved. She opened the door, careful to keep the safety chain on. Peeping out through the opening, she saw a little man dressed in a rumpled black tuxedo. It was Chazen. Jezebel and Mortimer were markedly absent.

"Come, come, open the chain so I can come in."

She slipped off the chain catch; Chazen stepped in.

"Why are you so nervous?" he asked.

"I'm not nervous," she replied.

"You are," he scolded.

"Well, yesterday's experience—"

"Oh, that," he interrupted. "Forget it ever happened."

She smiled. "That's a lovely outfit you have on, Mr. Chazen."

"Yes it is." He adjusted the old-fashioned bow tie that hung loosely from his neck and pressed the front of his jacket to smooth out the rumples.

"Do you like my flower? I grew it myself in my window box."

"It's lovely."

He grabbed her by the hand. "Now, my dear, I have a surprise for you."

"A surprise?" she replied, concerned. She'd had enough surprises recently.

"Yes, a lovely surprise. Come with me to my apartment."

She squeezed his hand gently. "No, thank you."

"Now Allison," he said sternly.

She interrupted. "I've had a very trying day and I don't feel too well. Besides, I've just taken two tranquilizers and I'm really out of it. Maybe next time."

"I insist," he demanded. "My surprise will make you feel a thousand times better. And it means a great deal to me!"

"But—"

He raised his hand. It was hopeless. The little man was not going to leave the apartment without her. There was nothing she could do but say yes. And maybe his surprise would make her feel better. She shrugged.

"Okay, but only for a few minutes."

He smiled, pleased with his success. He whipped his right hand from behind his back and produced a large top hat with a rumpled brim, which he proceeded to place gently on his head, tipped slightly to the side. She looked at his clothes.

"Never mind these," he said. "Just come as you are. You look lovely, simply smashing."

She smiled again. "By the way, thank you for the picture," she said.

"The picture? Oh, yes, the picture. My welcoming gift. But then, it was somewhat presumptuous to assume you would like a picture of me in my Sunday best."

"Not at all. It's absolutely adorable. I put it on the mantelpiece. Next to Herbert Hoover."

"Allison, you are most considerate. It warms an old man's heart to be received this way." He stared at the picture. "I do think that's my better side, don't you?"

She nodded.

"Now, now!" he said, his grin receding into his weather-beaten face. "Let us go. My surprise is waiting."

She reached over, grabbed the key off the convenient nail, shut the door and walked up the long flights of stairs. The little man bounced joyfully, several steps behind her, humming an unidentifiable tune. They reached the fifth floor and stood in front of his door. At the base was a mat that read "Welcome." On the door was a Christmas wreath.

"Allison," he cried excitedly, "I want you to close your eyes and promise not to peek until I tell you that you may!"

"I promise," she agreed reluctantly.

"Stand right there," he commanded as he opened the door. He grabbed her arm and pulled her over the threshold. "Now!" he yelled.

She opened her eyes.

Chazen's living room was decorated for a celebration. Streamers hung from the ceiling; helium-filled balloons floated next to the walls.

The living room was the same size as hers, except in the reverse, hers being an A apartment, his a B. There was no bedroom, only a sleeping alcove. The furnishings were dilapidated. Along the wall next to the entrance were bookshelves, partially filled with books but mostly covered by tiny plants, which made up only a small part of Chazen's collection. The apartment, apart from the furniture, resembled a botanical garden. In each of the corners and on either side of the kitchenette were baby palm trees that stretched from floor to ceiling, spreading their leaves and branches along the walls. Various shrubs were interspersed among the chairs and tables; almost everywhere stood flowerpots and boxes containing assortments of colorful plants. And raised above all the others on a marble platform near the window was Chazen's prize fern, an award winner. Picked off a mountainside in the high Andes in Central Peru, cultivated in New York under the most unfavorable conditions, but thriving under his care. Beneath the plant was an engraved plaque detailing the history and relevant characteristics of the prized Filicale. And there was another sign which warned "Hands Off."

"Surprise!" shouted Chazen, flinging a streamer into the air.

Everyone turned to look at the new arrival.

The large table in the middle of the room was covered with a white tablecloth. Scattered among the plates were noisemakers and party hats; there were several bottles of wine, some soda and a large bowl filled with potato chips. In the center of the table was a big black and white birthday cake with seven candles, topped by fluffy cone-shaped tufts of sugar. Jezebel, bedecked in a tasseled birthday hat and red silk scarf, sat at the head of the rectangular table on an elevated chair facing the guests: three elderly women, a younger girl of about thirty and a man of thirty-five or perhaps forty.

"It's Jezebel's birthday, so I thought we'd cele-brate."

Chazen led Allison through the jungle to the table.

"Here's your hat, two noisemakers, some streamers and your chair."

"Thank you," she said, smiling. She certainly had not expected this. A birthday party for a cat! Maybe Chazen was right, maybe his surprise would make her feel better.

"Mortimer," he cried.

The bird chirped from high on a fern branch.

"Come to Papa," he commanded sternly.

The bird fluttered its wings, flew off the shrub and landed on his shoulder.

"Say hello to Allison."

Mortimer arranged several feathers on his right wing and chirped at Allison with a dignified arch of the head befitting a host.

"Hello, Mortimer," she said awkwardly.

"Good," Chazen cried proudly. "I've been planning this party for a long time. Caught Jezebel completely by surprise while she was shuffling in the litter. But I wouldn't have considered it a success without you."

"That's very sweet of you, Mr. Chazen," Allison said appreciatively.

Jezebel purred.

"She says hello, also, but for some reason she's been reticent to speak the King's English. I do think she has a cold. I hope you understand."

"Of course."

"I want you to meet my other guests." He placed his hand on her shoulder. Everyone, this is Allison Parker. She just rented apartment three A."

Allison looked down the table.

"This is Mrs. Clark from four B," Chazen continued, nodding at a woman of seventy, hunchbacked, gray-haired, wrinkled and unsmiling.

Allison looked at her closely; she couldn't detect any makeup.

"Happy to meet you," said the old woman.

Chazen continued: "Miss Emma Clotkin and her twin sister Lillian. They live in apartment two B."

"Nice to meet you," greeted Allison. She grabbed Emma Klotkin's right hand, noted her size, the bosom that had been lost in the general accumulation of blubber, and the small eyes that peered out above her puffed cheeks.

"My pleasure," laughed Emma.

Lillian was her "little sister." And tiny compared to Emma. Emma was about five feet eight. Lillian five feet two. Emma weighed three hundred and fifty; Lillian two hundred and ten.

Allison couldn't help but smile as she greeted "tiny" Lillian.

"Glad to have you," squealed Lillian. "Charles told me about you." Lillian's heavy New York inflection was strangely missing in her sister's voice. Maybe they had been raised separately. Or perhaps Emma had taken voice lessons.

"Malcolm Stinnet," stated the man at the end of the table. "The Klotkins' cousin. This is my wife Rebecca."

Allison nodded. A strange couple. Mutt and Jeff, except that the taller of the two was Rebecca, by at least three inches. Malcolm wore a smart black tuxedo with a very wide bow tie that paralleled the generous brown mustache that twirled around the corners of his mouth in Zapatian fashion. There was something very English about him. She pictured him sitting behind the wheel of a Rolls-Royce, chauffeur's cap on head, eyes glued diligently to the road, ever mindful of his station and destiny.

"How long have you been in the building?" asked Rebecca.

"A little over a week," said Allison, watching Rebecca smile. The woman had bad teeth, discolored and set poorly in place, yet there was something about her that was extremely feminine and attractive. "Which apartment do you live in?"

"We don't, at least not here," answered Malcolm. "We live on the East Side in Murray Hill. Rebecca likes it better. It's cleaner and safer."

"It seems safe here."

"Here, yes," interrupted Rebecca, "but not toward Broadway, especially at night. Anyway, we visit our cousins so often, it seems like we live in the building."

Allison smiled. "Murray Hill's a good place. I stayed there when I first came to New York."

"Where?"

"On Lexington, between Thirty-seventh and Thirty-eighth. The big apartment."

"That's not too far from us," said Rebecca excitedly.

Lillian twirled a noisemaker about her head. The cat coughed. The bird chirped.

Allison placed the blue and gold party hat on her head. The rubber-band chinstrap barely fit around her jaw. It must have been fifteen years since she had last worn one of these things. Maybe even longer. She looked in the full-length mirror that hung on the wall. She looked ridiculous, but no more so than the collection that sat around the table.

She lifted a blower and placed the reed in her mouth. Looking over the frilled end, she noticed everyone staring at her. She stared back, unsure, then blew, sending out the long snaking arm with an ear-piercing buzz.

Everyone clapped and cheered.

"Some music to liven the party," cried Chazen. He skipped to the nearby victrola, vintage 1920, and placed a record on the turntable. After some vigorous cranking, the old rusted mechanism began to spin slowly, picking up velocity until it reached the necessary speed. He lifted the ancient metal arm, blew on the timeworn needle and placed it down on the spinning disk. The speaker crackled with static.

"The polka," cried Chazen, his voice lilting. "I used to dance it at the Foxland Casino in the Bronx every Friday for ten years."

"I remember," shouted Emma over the loud dance music. "Lillian and I used to go up there also. But it must have been some years later."

"It brings back memories," added Lillian, who was bouncing in her seat to the rhythm of the music. "Everyone used to pile into the place at one time. Remember? The girl's would sit on one side, the guys on the other."

"Then the music would start, any one of the three bands," added Chazen.

"Right! The girls would charge the guys and pull them out on the floor. Those polka bands were great. I really miss them."

"Those were the days," said Chazen forlornly, as if the memory of his youth pained him. "It's a shame we can't relive them."

Allison looked at the old man sympathetically; she was touched. "They sound like they were good days," she said.

Chazen smiled and returned to the table. Jezebel lifted her head in short jerky movements, almost as if she too were keeping time to the music. Chazen sat down next to her, puffed his chest with air and sang the first note in a series of off-key attempts at music. He buried his jaw in his neck and waved his arms in front of him like an operatic baritone. With a smile that stretched from one ear to the other, he recorded his self-satisfaction with his virtuoso performance.

"Everybody sing," Chazen declared between chords.

Emma joined, her massive body producing loud, full notes. She too was off-key, though Chazen sounded worse. But together their contrasting dissonance produced a strange combination of sounds—certainly not melodious or harmonious, but interesting. Like a Stravinsky concerto.

Cousin Malcolm pounded his knife against the top of his wine glass and then danced in his chair while his wife, Rebecca, spun in concentric circles behind him, trying, single-handed, to reproduce the effect of dozens of partying Bavarians.

"What polka is this?" asked Malcolm.

"The 'Beer Barrel,' " replied Chazen.

The enthusiasm was contagious. When Chazen stood and beckoned Allison responded to his outstretched hands by grabbing them securely and spinning onto the floor. Around and around they went; she was concerned lest he overtax himself. But, surprisingly, he was a good and seemingly tireless dancer.

Finally Allison pulled away to catch her breath. Looking about, she saw Mrs. Clark near the kitchen entrance disinterested and exceedingly bored. Her complexion had waxed sallow, her lips drooped toward her crooked mouth and her eyes glared.

The intensity of the woman's attention was disquieting. There was something familiar about her. She had seen or met her before. But she couldn't remember. One strange bird, she thought to herself and turned away.

The record ended and everyone clapped. Chazen lifted the arm and removed the old warped disk from the turntable. He placed it to the side and grabbed a stack of possible selections. He nimbly thumbed through the pile and placed those he liked on top of the table next to the victrola and those rejected back on the shelf.

"I'd love to hear a tango," cried Emma.

"Tango!" bellowed Chazen. "Perfect! The dance of the caballeros. I remember Valentino dancing in *Blood and Sand*." He placed a new record on the turntable reset the arm and cranked the machine. It sputtered, coughed and vibrated; the turntable began to revolve and once again the room was filled with music. He sat down next to the cat, looked over his shoulder and motioned Mrs. Clark to her seat. The woman hesitated, then walked to the table, glanced at him and sat down.

"Some champagne?" asked Chazen. He removed the open bottle of Piper Heidsieck from the ice bucket.

Everyone enthusiastically assented. He leaned over and filled Allison's glass, then he stood and marched around the table like an experienced wine waiter.

"I propose a toast," said Malcolm as he rose from his chair, glass raised high over his head. "To Jezebel, may she have nine fruitful lives."

"To Jezebel," they all responded, raising their glasses in unison. The cat purred as if she had understood that the toast was directed to her.

"Emma, don't you think it was nice of Allison to join us for Jezebel's birthday?" prompted Lillian after sipping her champagne. Her sister nodded. "Allison, you must come down to our apartment sometime soon. I'd love you to try some of my cookies. Emma and I are expert cookie makers, as you can probably tell just by looking at us." Emma laughed boisterously.

"I would love to," said Allison as she recalled the cake argument. "I love homemade cookies; my mother used to make them for me all the time."

"Good, it's settled. You'll come by tomorrow."

Chazen stood, turned the record over and sat down again to the accompaniment of a different tango. He turned to Allison and lifted his champagne to his mouth. "Do you like my little party?" he asked.

"Yes!" She glanced quickly at Mrs. Clark, who sat with a noticeable frown on her face.

"And hasn't it made you feel better?"

"Yes, it has. Much."

"Trust to Chazen!"

She smiled, leaned forward and kissed Chazen on the cheek.

He jumped to his feet. "It's time for the cake."

"Good!" cried Malcolm from the far end of the table, his eyes ravenously devouring the triple-decked birthday cake.

Chazen quickly snatched the record off the victrola and put it to the side.

"Happy birthday to you," he screamed as he returned to the table and kissed Jezebel on top of her head. He pulled the cake toward him, whipped a cake knife from under his napkin, and cut deep into the frosting.

"That's the first black and white birthday cake I've ever seen!" said Allison, smiling.

Mrs. Clark smacked her plate against the table.

Allison turned.

The idle table chatter ceased abruptly.

The graying woman slowly unclenched her teeth, lifted her head and looked directly at Allison. "Black and white cat—black and white cake," she said with directed animosity.

What was that all about? Allison shrugged. A strange bird all right. Now, where did she know her from?

Afterward she lay in her darkened bedroom, half asleep. For two hours she twisted and turned, unable to get comfortable, unable to unwind. She'd had a little too much champagne and a little too much cake. Her head spun and her stomach ached. And when she finally fell asleep, she was taunted by nightmares. Chazen! Emma! Lillian! Malcolm! Rebecca! They all danced about singing "Happy Birthday" to the cat. What a terrible noise that had been!

She dreamed of Mrs. Clark. Uncomfortably, she rolled in the bed, beginning to sweat, remembering the uneasiness she had felt around the woman. She would certainly try to avoid her, as she would avoid the two lesbians. Yet she could not keep them out of her subconscious. She saw Gerde naked, full-breasted and suppliant, lying on her bed. And she envisioned Sandra gliding with ballerinalike grace across their darkened bedroom to the bedside and with extended hands stroking her lover's smooth skin.

The tension continued to build. She writhed, her skin glistening with perspiration. The party. Mrs. Clark. The lesbians. The visions began to fuse, to revolve about one another accompanied by continuous pounding and the sound of clashing metal.

She sprang up in bed, awake, frightened. She felt the flesh contract about her body; her nightgown was soaking wet.

The images were gone. But the noises remained. She listened carefully, flicked on the small reading light and looked up at the ceiling. The pounding? Footsteps! She was positive. They were coming from an apartment that was supposedly empty and had been so for many years. She shivered and looked at her alarm clock. It was four fifteen in the morning.

Someone was in a place where no one should have have been, pacing back and forth methodically, like a soldier on guard.

Then the walking ceased, but the sound of clashing metal continued.

She threw on her robe, bolted into the living room and rushed to the door. She checked it; it was locked.

She stood panting, terrified. The footsteps, the noise; something was wrong.

She turned her back to the door. She was exhausted. She shut her eyes. Her mouth closed and arms dropped, Exhausted, she slid down the door and fell unconscious to the floor, her hand wrapped tightly about the crucifix.

9

"There's something peculiar going on in that house!"

Allison turned to Michael and waited for a response. Behind them a large ape dangled from the crossbeam in his cage, arms and legs extended over the bars, poised as if he were listening to their conversation. Every several seconds he rumpled his heavy jowls and grunted his disapproval.

Michael walked away from her, stopped in front of the next cage and leaned over the rail to get a closer look at the Bengal tiger that paced behind the heavy iron bars. His study was brief, his interest minimal; he turned away and leaned in his French-cut suit against the hand railing.

"I'll admit that Chazen is a little weird and that those others who live there are also a bit odd, but so what? This is New York, and weirdos are not a species in danger of extinction."

"You're being flippant?"

"I'm not."

"You are, and I don't like it."

"How serious can you expect me to be? Look what we're dealing with. An old coot with one foot in the grave, an alley cat and a squawking parrot."

"Parakeet!"

"Parakeet. Not very sinister. I think it's funny."

"Ha, ha," she said bitterly.

"And then there's Mrs. Clark, a hunchback, hardening after years of loneliness and pain. Doesn't smile. Doesn't talk much. Rude. What do you expect?" He waited for an answer but, receiving none, added, "she sounds as if she's done all right. If you or I had been born hunchbacked we would have put ourselves in a box and locked the lid. The two fat women? The only frightening thing about them is the thought of them falling on you. And let's take a look at what's his name—"

"Malcolm."

"Yes, Malcolm and his wife. Now there's a pair! They're absolutely harmless. So look at what we have: a group of nonentities souring in their old age. I think you're making too much out of your geriatric friends. So what if they're odd!"

"It's more than that, Michael. The pieces don't fit together properly!" She scanned the brick walkway, observed that the area seemed more deserted than usual, then said, "It's as if someone mixed three different puzzles together and then tried to fit the parts into one big picture—for example, the fear that dyke showed when she saw Chazen."

"We have the probable explanation for that."

"Or the sound of footsteps above me last night?"

"Mice!"

"They were human."

"How do you know?"

"I know!" Her voice was stern.

"Okay, so someone was in the apartment last night."

"But it's supposed to be empty."

"Whoever it was walked in by mistake."

"At four fifteen in the morning? Michael, let's be rational about this. No one accidentally walks into the wrong apartment that time of night, and if he does he certainly doesn't go to the bedroom and pace back and forth for an hour."

Michael bit his lower lip, turned to the animal cages

and tossed several pieces of popcorn to the waiting chimpanzees.

"I'm not concerned about bogeymen or phantom footsteps." He looked straight into the cages, trusting his voice to hold her attention. "I *am* concerned about your fainting spell. The way you're constructing fantasies from the antics of a few old fools and a pair of perverts. The way you're beginning to fold under the pressure. I grant you, the last few months were tough, but still, Allison, you're no child. This worries me."

"I fainted because—"

"Because?"

She paused. "I don't know," she murmured.

"Fatigue."

"I feel fine."

"Nervous tension. Lack of sleep. Any number of other things. But mostly an overactive imagination."

Her lips tightened; she was annoyed at his simplistic conclusions. She knew that something was peculiar about that house. No matter what he said, he couldn't convince her otherwise.

"All right, Michael, I'm not going to argue any more. I can't seem to get through to you."

"That's where you're wrong. But I'm not hearing what you think I'm hearing."

"Then what?"

He pulled her away from the animal house and toward the pool that occupied the center of the Central Park Zoo. They walked to the railing and silently watched the seals.

He ran his hand through her hair. "I want you to go to the doctor and get a complete physical examination."

"The doctors examined me in the hospital."

"They were interns. I want you to go to a specialist or two, doctors who won't let you out until they know what's the matter or that there is definitely nothing wrong. And if you have to go away for a while, fine.

You need a rest. You should have taken some time before you returned to work."

She shrugged.

"Maybe you should even go see a psychiatrist."

She glanced at him angrily. "You're a damn fool," she cried as she pulled away.

Michael leaned back against the cold metal railing and watched her climb the stairs to the zoo exit. Dejected, he clapped his frozen hands together, held his breath for several seconds, then let the air out of his lungs; a vapor trail extended for several feet. It was cold. Damn cold. And overcast. There were few spaces of blue in the sky, which was gradually becoming grayer. Winter was not far away. Soon the zoo would be empty, the trees completely bare, and the ground covered with snow.

He surveyed the area, decided that she'd had enough time to cool off, and walked slowly in the same direction. He found her seated under an aging maple, her back flush against the trunk, her feet extended before her. She was carefully counting the sections of a leaf as she pulled them out. Soon the last picking fell to the ground and she was left with the narrow twisted green stalk. She closed one eye and held the stem in front of the other, trying to block her vision. Then she laid her hand back on her lap.

Standing over her, he watched her fingers tremble. The last time he had seen her so tense and disturbed, aside from the period prior to her return home last July, was the week before her attempted suicide during the "Karen Farmer" investigation two and a half years ago. Could she be in a similar state? Might something cause her to reach for the barbiturates once again? He wouldn't be surprised. He had suspected her father's death might disturb her badly. And he had realized that he might have to face the consequences directly.

She looked up as he kneeled down, but her eyes avoided his.

"Mind if I keep you company?"

She shook her head.

"What are you doing?"

She held up the stalk; he grabbed it, rubbed it between his thumb and forefinger and laid it back in her palm. "She loves me, she loves me not," he declared. "Which one?" he asked.

"I don't know."

"You didn't keep count?"

"I wasn't playing the game."

"I see."

She lifted her legs and pulled her knees under her chin. "I was stripping away the beauty to see what it was really like underneath."

"Did you find out?" he asked as he sat back.

"Not yet."

He nodded, raked his fingers along the sod and said, "There was no reason to walk away."

"If you say so."

"All I did was suggest some help, if you feel you need it. There was nothing else intended."

"If you say so."

He lowered his eyes. "I remember the last time a woman ran away from me. When I first met her. She wouldn't talk at all. So I chased her like a fool. But it was worth it."

"That's very romantic, Michael," she said coldly.

He lowered his head. "But I caught her and everything worked out all right."

"Everything?"

"Yes, everything. And now I've caught her again."

"So everything will work out fine again?"

"Right, if you do what I tell you."

"And if I don't?" He didn't respond. "Do I wind up like Karen?"

He slapped her across the face. Her head spun back; a welt raised on her cheek. Stifling a cry of pain, she rubbed the bruise with her hand, trying to massage the sting away.

He had never hit her before. If he had thought,

even for a moment, he would have held back. But Karen's name had stabbed him like a machete.

He looked at his open palm. He looked at Allison. "I'm sorry." He grabbed for her hand; she pulled away. "You've got to believe me. I don't know what came over me. I don't understand. I just don't. Why Karen? Why now?"

"Because."

"Why resurrect something that should remain buried?"

"Should it?" Her voice was meek; her mouth barely moved.

Michael leaned forward and placed his hands on her shoulders. "Forgive me."

"I've heard that before."

"What do you mean?"

"Nothing."

"Bullshit. You said it because you meant it."

"Every once in a while you remind me of someone."

"Who?"

"No one."

"Let's cut the riddles."

"Why do they bother you? I thought you liked riddles."

"Not particularly."

She stood up. "I don't want to talk about . . ." she said.

His eyes intensified. "Perhaps we should talk about your frigidity. Or why you left home."

"No."

"Or the crucifix?"

"No."

"Or why suddenly Karen is such a hot topic?"

"I don't want to talk about anything."

"Just throw out little puzzle pieces for me to play with."

"Call it what you will."

He stared.

"I forgive you," she said perfunctorily. But her voice was cold and shallow.

"I don't want you to mention Karen again. There's no reason why we should torture ourselves."

She tossed the stem of the leaf on the ground. "Can we go back to your office?"

He nodded.

Michael's office was typical. Rows of law books filled the hardwood shelves; two diplomas hung on the wall. There were pictures of a famous judge, several caricatures of early English judicial proceedings and a reproduction of the Magna Carta. A rectangular desk filled much of the floor space. Two chairs, a couch and a carved wood table occupied the rest. Having been purchased within the last several weeks, they sparkled with newness.

Michael leaned back in the desk chair and lit an imported cigar. "If it will make you happy, fine," he declared. "Call Miss Logan. There's no harm to be done!"

Allison sat down on the edge of the desk and removed a piece of paper from her purse. "It will make me ecstatic." She pulled the receiver from the desk phone, glanced at the paper and dialed the listed number.

Michael began to blow smoke rings, oblivious to her presence.

In a moment Allison greeted Miss Logan and, without being specific, asked if they could meet. They agreed on twelve o'clock. In the coffee shop across from the rental office.

"Do you want me to come?" Michael asked as she lowered the phone.

"No."

"Do you want me to say I'm sorry again?"

"No."

She walked around the desk and kissed him on the forehead. There was little in the kiss other than goodbye. The incident in the park was still fresh in her mind, the red welt still visible on her left cheek.

"Michael."

"Yes," he said expectantly.

"I'll speak to you later."

Disappointed, he replied, "I'll be here."

She turned and hurried out the door. He sat blowing smoke rings, thinking. Should he get up and go after her? He wasn't sure. He decided not to. Instead he reached across the desk and grabbed his phone book. He opened it, flipped a few pages, found a number and wrote it down. He looked at it momentarily, picked up the phone and then dialed. "Brenner," he said after a pause. "This is me. I've got something for you."

10

It was noon; the restaurant was filled.

Allison walked past the counter into the dining area, sighted Miss Logan in the corner and approached her table.

"I hope this is not an inconvenience," she said apologetically. She took off her jacket and placed it on the coat hook attached to the booth.

"Not at all," answered the agent as she fidgeted with her dated hairstyle.

"I was afraid it was."

"No. We couldn't meet at the office because my

associate is interviewing this afternoon. And you know how small the room is."

Allison slid into the booth. "This place is fine." Before her stood a cup of coffee.

"I took the liberty," said Miss Logan. "I hope it's not cold."

Allison lifted the cup and sipped slowly. "No. It's just right. Hot coffee is good on a day like today."

"Yes, it is getting cold. But then again, we had that warm day two days ago."

"You never can predict how the weather's going to turn—or when."

Miss Logan nodded approvingly.

Allison sipped her coffee; Miss Logan cleared her throat.

"How have you been, Miss Parker?"

"All right, and yourself?"

"Splendid. Renting apartments by the dozen."

"I'm glad someone is making a living."

"Why? Are you having trouble with your career?"

"Not exactly. I haven't slept much lately and I haven't felt that well, so it's having an effect on my work."

"That's too bad. I hope it's nothing serious." Miss Logan appeared genuinely concerned.

"I hope not," Allison replied.

Miss Logan missed the innuendo. She lifted the cup of tea in her right hand and sipped. Miss Logan was a tea drinker. Allison had known that instantly. There are some people who look coffee, some who look tea, and Miss Logan's preference was obvious.

"Well now," Miss Logan began, "what seems to be the problem? I hope there's nothing wrong with your apartment?"

"No."

"The workmen were there?"

"Yes and they did a good job."

"And the painters?"

"They did a fine job too."

"You like the color I suggested?"

"Yes, but—" Allison stopped, looked at Miss Logan and sipped more of the coffee.

"Yes?"

"Everything's . . . uh, perfect." Allison kicked herself. Tell her! There was no reason not to. Criticizing neighbors is not a crime. And she had never before shied away from saying what was on her mind.

"Come now, Miss Parker, obviously something is bothering you," chided Miss Logan.

Allison took a deep breath. "To be frank, Miss Logan, something is. It's not the apartment but the occurrences of the last few days in the building."

"Like what?"

"Well . . ." she stammered once more.

"I warned you about the old priest."

"No, it's not him. I haven't seen or heard him at all. It's the other tenants."

Miss Logan looked at Allison blandly. "The other tenants? Which ones in particular?"

"Mr. Chazen in five B. Those two young lesbians in the apartment below me. The taller one—you know, Gerde—attacked me. And there's that strange Mrs. Clark in apartment—I don't remember which. Those immense Klotkin sisters are nice, but you must admit a little strange. And last night I heard footsteps pacing back and forth in that supposedly empty apartment above me. And then clanging. Now, it's getting a little unnerving. And to be honest, I'm afraid of those two perverts in two A. Every time I walk by their door my skin crawls."

She sat back waiting for a response. Miss Logan just stared.

"I see," the agent finally said. Then suddenly she stood up, pulled her coat off the hook and began to put it on.

"Where are you going?" Allison asked, puzzled.

"I said before that this was not an inconvenience, but it has become so. And I am a very busy woman."

"I don't understand."

"Don't you?"

"I really wish you'd explain."

"My dear Miss Parker, aside from the old priest, and now you, no one has lived in that building for three years!"

Allison blanched. She looked up at the renting agent, her lips quivering. Surely Miss Logan was joking! She had been with these people. Talked to them. Touched them. And now to be told that none of them existed. It was impossible!

"What do you mean, no one lives there?"

"Just what I said!"

"But I saw—"

Miss Logan interrupted. "If you've seen tenants, I'd suggest you consult a psychiatrist."

"But I saw them, talked to them." Allison's voice was hardly audible.

Miss Logan looked down at her. "Three years ago the landlord decided not to rent out any apartments—for what reason I don't know. The old priest was the only one living there at the time, and he'd been there for many years. And that's the way it's been. No renting, no tenants. Our agency has literally taken care of the building."

"Why didn't you tell me this before?"

"You didn't ask."

Allison lifted her cup. It shook violently in her hand, most of the coffee spilling onto the table. Finally she sipped slowly, as if she were trying to find hidden ingredients in the fluid that might help her to comprehend what she had just been told.

She set the cup down and looked at Miss Logan. "I'm telling you," she snapped, "there are people living in that building!"

Miss Logan resumed buttoning her overcoat.

Allison jumped up and grabbed her by the arm. "Please don't go," she begged. "Please."

Miss Logan pulled away. "I do not appreciate being addressed in that tone of voice."

"I'm sorry." Allison was determined to keep the renting agent there, at least until she could find out something more, anything that might help explain away the experience of the last few days. "As you can tell, this has me rather upset."

"I realize that, but don't take your frustrations out on me."

Allison looked at Miss Logan with pleading eyes. The agent paused, studied Allison's grim expression, then sat down once again.

"Believe me, no one lives in the other apartments," she said.

"When was the last time you looked into one of them?" Allison asked.

"About a month ago."

"Are you sure?"

"Of course I'm sure."

"Has anyone else checked the apartments in the interim?"

"Not that I know of."

"Maybe these people got in since then. Maybe they're squatters. If no one has checked, it's certainly feasible."

Miss Logan shook her head. "Impossible," she declared. "If we were talking about one person, okay. But five or six in different apartments! No, I can assure you that it is out of the question."

"Then how do you explain what I've seen?"

Miss Logan shrugged.

"Could you let me into those apartments?" Allison asked.

"It can be arranged."

"Now?"

"I'm afraid I—"

Allison interrupted. "I must get into those apartments."

"But—"

"Please? Now?"

Miss Logan stared at her. "Yes, if it will convince you that nobody lives there."

The two women stood.

"I wish you would take my word that—"

"I can't," said Allison. "If I did I would be rejecting my own senses. Would you expect me to do that?" She took the check, slipped into her jacket and walked through the crowd to the cashier's counter. She paid the bill, then followed Miss Logan out the door.

11

A note was placed under a light and examined.

It was headed "ALLISON PARKER." The address of the brownstone was written across the upper right corner. It described the events of the last few days in the brownstone and reviewed certain other incidents that had occurred over the last two years. It detailed a long list of instructions that were to be scrupulously followed and closed with a simple direction to destroy.

After Brenner had finished reading it several times, he tossed it on the desk, next to a gold nameplate inscribed "William Brenner, Private Investigator." He grabbed an envelope denoted "By Hand Delivery," tore it in half and threw it into the wastepaper basket.

Then he turned off the light.

Allison sat silently in the rear of the cab as it crossed the Eighty-sixth Street transverse road through Central Park. Her head tilted downward, her face lay partly against the glass and her eyes, carefully avoiding any contact with the renting agent who sat impassively next to her, scanned the top of the gray stone wall that bordered the road and set off the branching maples and elms which intermittently erased the encroaching skyline of high-rise apartments.

From the moment Miss Logan had denied the existence of the other tenants, Allison had been in a daze. She kept telling herself that the renting agent was wrong; there were people living there. She had seen them. She wasn't mad. Logan was wrong, whether she knew it or not.

"To light, to guard, to rule, to guide," she said in a barely audible whisper.

"Excuse me?" asked the agent.

Allison did not respond.

"Miss Parker, did you say something?"

"Me?" asked Allison, turning her head. "No." She turned back to the window and pressed her nose against the pane.

Miss Logan humphed once or twice and looked ahead toward the rapidly approaching exit from the park.

The taxi left the park, skirted the intervening streets, turned into Eighty-ninth Street and stopped in front of the brownstone.

Allison continued to stare out the window.

"Miss Parker, we're here," announced Miss Logan.

Allison smiled meekly but didn't move.

Miss Logan leaned toward her, jerked the latch and opened the cab door. "I have no time to waste!" she said indignantly.

Without reply, Allison stiffly slid out the door.

Miss Logan paid the fare and joined her at the base of the stone staircase.

"Shall we?" asked Miss Logan.

Allison continued to look upward. Then she reached out and pointed to the fifth floor.

The curtain in the middle window was open; in the frame was a man.

Unfortunately, the outside light and shading made it difficult to define any features. The image resembled a picture negative, discernible, but unspecific. The figure seemed to be in a sitting position. Allison was sure of this; if he had been standing, more of him would have been seen. His arms were crossed meeting below the waist, where his hands were probably clasped. Perhaps he was holding something. It was impossible to tell. But there he was. Clearer than ever before. The old blind priest.

"The old man," said Miss Logan matter-of-factly.

"This is the first time I've seen him so clearly."

"And it won't be the last. He, I can assure you, exists."

Allison scowled at the renting agent. "So do the others," she said as they climbed the staircase.

Miss Logan touched Allison's forearm to gain her attention. She pointed to the rust-covered mailboxes; they were set into the wall just inside the vestibule.

"I know," Allison said irritably. "But there's no name tag on the priest's mailbox either."

Miss Logan shrugged and opened the front door.

They walked down the dimly lit hallway and climbed the first-landing staircase. As usual, Allison tested the banister, then she stopped in front of apartment 2 A. She placed her ear next to the door and listened.

"This one belongs to the lesbians," she said.

Miss Logan snapped her tongue against the upper bridge of her mouth, producing a tiny audible click which implied her doubts. She removed the master key from her purse, opened the door and motioned Allison into the apartment. "Be my guest," she said, secure in the knowledge of what they would find.

Allison walked through the door and into the living room.

The place was filthy. The layer of dust on the floor was thick. So too was the accumulation on the furniture, which she had not seen there before. But the furniture was familiar; it was strikingly similar to what she had in her own apartment. In fact, once she discounted the effect of the dust, she realized that the furniture was identical, from the smallest bibelot to the two great grandfather clocks that guarded the fireplace. She sniffed the thick heavy air and walked to the couch, leaving a distinctive track in the dark-gray dust. She patted the fabric, causing billows of dirt to rise into the air.

"The furniture is exactly like mine," she said, biting her lip.

"Yes. The old landlord, the person who furnished the building, did all the A apartments alike and all the B apartments alike. I can't say that I approve, but I guess it saved him money."

"There was different furniture here before."

"Oh, come now, Miss Parker, you can't expect me to believe that. These pieces haven't been touched in years!"

Allison smiled wanly, walked to the mantel and ran her hand along the top. It was covered with dust. She wiped her palm on her jacket, turned and began to inspect the furniture and closets, looking for anything that might help explain what had occurred there. But there was nothing. Then why? Maybe she had been in another apartment. She entertained the idea momentarily and then shook her head. No, she had been in this room.

She walked into the kitchen and then the bedroom. More of the same. Dust. Furniture identical to her own. The musty smell of mildew.

She returned to the living room. Miss Logan was standing by the door with a smug look on her face. "Find anyone?" she asked.

"No," said Allison quietly. She walked to a chair, sat briefly and rubbed her eyes. The caustic air hurt them. "Open four A for me," she demanded, and then stood up.

Miss Logan nodded and, after watching Allison walk through the door, closed it.

Apartment 4 A offered no new surprises. The furniture was identical, the dust equally in evidence and the air similarly stale. Allison quickly surveyed the

living room and then carefully examined the bedroom.
There was no sign of life. Certainly, if someone had
been in this room the night before, there would have
been some indication. But there wasn't.

She was disturbed and frustrated as she followed
Miss Logan up the staircase to the fifth floor and
into Chazen's apartment. Except for a chair that stood
in the middle of the living room and a series of bookshelves along the wall, there was no other furniture.

"I thought you said that the B apartments were
furnished identically," Allison claimed.

"I did. The furniture was removed from here about
a year ago. Most of it was falling apart."

Allison grabbed the solitary chair and flicked off
the cobwebs. "A memento of better times?" She
studied it carefully, trying to remember if it had been
one of the chairs that had stood around the birthday
table. She wasn't sure.

She sat down and cleared her throat. "Happy birthday to you. Happy birthday to you. Happy birthday,
dear Jezebel. Happy birthday to you." She listened
to the echo of her song reverberate throughout the
apartment.

"Where's the cake?" asked Miss Logan, her face
betraying her perplexity.

"That's what I'd like to know."

"Well, if we can find it, I'd like the first piece."

Allison was annoyed. "You know what I like about
you best?"

"What?"

"The endearing nature of your cynicism."

"I trust you don't expect me to pretend that a bunch
of people have been running about these apartments?"

"No, I guess not," said Allison. She stood up and
walked to the cobweb-lined bookshelves that adorned
the wall next to the front entrance. They were filled
with musty old volumes, their covers disintegrating,
their titles faded. She examined several of the titles.
The Decameron, Hobbes's *Leviathan,* Euripides'

Hippolytus, The Iliad, Canterbury Tales, Beowulf, and books by Aquinas, Bacon, Shakespeare, Milton, Spinoza, Kierkegaard, Dickens and Stendhal. Whoever had assembled the collection had a well-developed appreciation of classical literature, from ethical philosophy to metaphysics and political philosophy.

"Believe it or not," said Allison, "I attended a birthday party for a cat here last night."

"How quaint," said Miss Logan.

"The cat—her name was Jezebel—was here and so were a lot of other people. Charles Chazen, Mrs. Clark, the Klotkins and Cousin Malcolm and his wife. And there was a parakeet named Mortimer. We danced and sang till almost midnight. There were streamers and balloons everywhere. Everyone had a good time. And now all are gone—except for myself—and so is any hint or indication that they were ever here or even existed."

"I'm sorry I missed it," said Miss Logan skeptically.

Allison continued to examine the books. "You probably think I'm going mad."

"Did I say that?"

"I can assure you that I'm not."

Had the bookshelf been in the room the night before? Allison couldn't remember. She reached up to the top shelf and removed a book. It was inordinately old. In fact, several of the pages had almost disintegrated, the pulp rubbing off the paper onto her hands.

It was written in Latin; she couldn't decipher the title or any of the contents. She thumbed through the pages curiously. As she was about to close it, she noticed something peculiar. All the pages were identical. She flipped several back to verify the fact.

Miss Logan cleared her throat. Allison reached up, placed the book back on the shelf, turned and scanned the room once more.

"I must be getting back," announced the renting agent.

"Yes, I'm sorry I'm taking so long," said Allison. She stepped toward the agent while brushing the adhesive dust from her blouse.

"Is there anything else?"

"Yes," declared Allison pointedly. "The old priest."

"It's a waste of time."

"The old priest," she repeated.

Miss Logan nodded reluctantly. The old priest was just down the hall. The worst that could happen would be the waste of a few minutes more. Miss Logan turned, opened the door and ushered Allison through.

"You know what I think," Allison said as she passed Miss Logan. "I think someone is playing a little game—or should I say engineering a practical joke—and I'm not so sure that the joke's not supposed to be on me."

Miss Logan declined comment. She walked up to the old priest's apartment and knocked. There was no response. Again. Still no response.

"The old man probably can't hear," said Miss Logan.

Allison stepped up to the door, and rapped several more times, her knocks being applied with greater force. Again there was no answer.

"Have you ever met or spoken to him?"

"No."

"Has anyone?"

"I wouldn't know."

"Somebody must."

"Perhaps, but I wouldn't know."

"Has he ever been out of the apartment?"

"I wouldn't know that either."

"Look, Miss Logan, if he doesn't go out or see anyone, how does he live?"

"I don't know. You should ask him yourself."

"That's exactly what I'd like to do."

Miss Logan turned from the door and confronted her. "All I care about is that his rent is paid on time."

"Has it been?"

"Yes, without fail."

"Who pays it?"

"The Archdiocese of New York."

Allison paused, then said, "I'd like to get into this apartment—now!"

"I'm sorry," said the renting agent, shaking her head.

"Why not?"

"Because I cannot let someone into an apartment that's occupied, especially when the occupant is home." Her reply indicated that no further argument could change her mind. "Shall we go?" she added.

Allison walked slowly to the staircase. "Don't you find it peculiar," she asked, turning, "that the man should exist in such isolation?"

"No," replied Miss Logan. "I establish no criteria for the manner in which another should live his life." Dispassionately, she began to descend the stairs with Allison trailing behind.

They stopped in front of apartment 3 A.

"I hope you're satisfied that no one has been in these apartments?" stated Miss Logan.

"Thank you for taking me around," said Allison, ignoring the question. She inserted her key into her apartment door.

"Perhaps—"

Allison interrupted. "I must apologize again for having been an inconvenience."

Miss Logan nodded icily, remaining silent.

Allison opened the door. "If you'll excuse me, I must make an urgent phone call."

"If you have any other problems, call me."

"Other problems? I think the one I have right now is more than enough!"

"I suppose I—"

"Thank you," said Allison. "I'll let you know if I see any of these people again." She smiled unconvincingly, entered the apartment and slammed the door.

She leaned against the door frame. She felt weak and tired and frightened. She closed her eyes and rubbed her forehead with her hand. Her head had begun to hurt; perhaps another migraine was beginning.

She walked into the hallway and down to the kitchen. After groping momentarily for the light switch, she flicked it, grabbed the vial of tranquilizers off the sink, removed three, one more than the recommended dosage, and downed them without the aid of anything to drink. They stuck in her throat. She choked and gulped frantically to force them down. In desperation she turned on the tap and gulped a mouthful of water. The pressure on her throat eased and the pills went down.

She walked into the living room, bolted the door securely and sat down on the sofa to think. But she could not. Instead, she cried.

12

It was dark outside. The rain that had started about seven o'clock splattered against the glass walls of the phone booth, obscuring the view. Everything was blurred, the colors undefined and muted. She was uncomfortable, disquieted by the oppressively small space, the wet umbrella that continually dripped on the floor and the choking feeling she had experienced since early that afternoon when Miss Logan had questioned her sanity.

Thank God they had fixed the corner phone. The

thought of walking to Ninety-fifth Street in the freezing rain had appalled her.

She held the receiver to her ear, dialed Michael's office and waited, licking her lips nervously; they were chapped and cracking. The rest of her face had fared no better; her complexion was sallow and her eyes were red from crying and fatigue.

Since early afternoon she had been terrified, and if necessity hadn't forced her to call Michael she would have locked herself in the apartment, secured the shutters, gone to bed and buried herself under the protection of her knitted quilt. But she had needed the comfort and assurance of his presence. And she needed his calm, logical mind.

The telephone rang in his office. Once, twice . . . ten times. No one was there. She angrily slammed the receiver, fished out the dime. She dropped it in the slot and dialed; the phone rang, this time in his apartment. Again no one answered.

She turned around in the cramped booth, wiped the clinging fog off the glass and looked through the window at the tree-lined street that stretched before her and the now ominous brownstone that stood half-way down the block. West Eighty-ninth Street seemed darker than she had ever seen it. The shadows longer. If it had been this threatening the day she had first seen the brownstone, she would have looked elsewhere for an apartment. As it was, she wished she had.

She left the booth, opened the umbrella and walked up the street through the deepening puddles, invoking the resolution she had made several nights before on a similarly threatening street and listening to the splashing beneath her boots intermingled with the distant buzz of automobiles on the avenue behind her. She stopped, momentarily closed her eyes, laughed nervously, then climbed the stone staircase and looked up toward the fifth-floor windows. They were black and uninviting.

She had eaten supper behind securely fastened doors. To settle her nerves she had gulped an additional

tranquilizer between the Russian-dressed salad and
the mushroom-covered TV steak. And for an apéritif
she had opened a bottle of rosé.

Sipping from a wine glass—the clocks ticking quietly
in the background—she walked across the carpet and
kneeled beside the portable phonograph that sat in
the corner. She selected the opening act of Verdi's
La Forza del Destino, placed it on the turntable and
set the arm.

The speakers cracked noisily as the needle settled
into the grooves. She watched the record circle about
the little knob that held it in place. An important
invention, the automatic record player. A great advance over the hand-cranked gramophone. She would
lend her machine to Mr. Chazen the next time he
had a party so that he could spend more time on
the dance floor.

She turned back to the sofa, lay down and listened,
rejecting any sounds that might have interfered with
the music. Gradually, her eyes began to close. Soon
she was asleep.

She opened her eyes. Without lifting her head,
she glanced at one of the grandfather clocks. The
hands lay on top of each other; it was a quarter past
three. In the background the phonograph rasped noisily; the record had failed to reject.

She fumbled to the machine, shut it off, walked
out of the living room and swayed down the darkened
hallway to the bedroom.

She dropped her blouse at the doorway. Next her
dark blue jeans fell to the floor. Ring and watch were
placed on the night table and her stockings were thrown
on the clothes horse.

She stood naked before the fourposter at the end
of a trail of clothes. The bed was inviting, so much
so that her body slipped effortlessly between the sheets.
Within seconds she was sleeping again.

The rain continued to fall heavily on the darkened

street. As the wind increased in velocity, it drove
the torrent of water diagonally into the brownstone,
pounding the walls. The drains ran at floor level;
the water poured over the sides in cascades and spiraled
downward, challenging the high winds that buffeted
its descent.

The street was deserted. The night was black, the
street-lights rendered ineffectual by the blanket of
water that deadened their effect. A torrential stream
punctuated by swirling eddies ran along the gutter
toward the drains at either intersection.

A pair of feet sloshed through an alley where even
from the rearmost point the stone staircase of the
brownstone was visible. The figure remained in the
dark, avoiding any possibility of detection. Slowly
it moved among the shadows until it reached the
alley entrance, where it stopped and raised a covered
hand to ward off the wind and rain. It stood motionless
for quite some time, watching, waiting. There were
no lights burning in any of the immediate buildings.
There were no cars. No unexpected sounds.

A pair of eyes glanced up and down the street.
Satisfied, the figure hunched its shoulders and hurried
across the flooded road into the protected abutment
under the stone staircase where it shook the water
off its shoulders before turning to the heavy iron gate
that guarded the entrance to the basement. A rusted
padlock sealed the gate. The figure jostled the lock
with its gloved hand, then fumbled in the large pocket
of its raincoat and removed a set of keys, the largest
of which was forced into the keyhole. The lock would
not open. Again the figure fumbled in the pocket
and this time withdrew a small tube, after which it
removed the key, squeezed some fluid into the hole,
reinserted the key and tried again. It turned. The
figure entered the cellar and closed the gate.

Once again her sleep was pained and uncomfortable, though at first not with the same intensity

as the night before. She lay in bed completely nude, rolling from side to side, clawing at the pillows.

The visions of the previous night reappeared—Chazen, the lesbians and the other members of the party. She felt their presence, heard their voices. The singing. "Happy birthday, dear Jezebel, happy birthday to you."

The sheets dampened from the perspiration. The blanket fell off, propelled by a compulsive kick; the pillows followed.

And she heard the pounding.

At first it was barely audible, then almost ear-splitting.

Still sleeping, she raised her palms to her ears and tried to close out the noise. But the pounding increased in magnitude. Louder and louder, then mixed with the clanging sounds of metal.

She awoke disoriented, terrified. She switched on the bed light and glanced quickly around the room. There was no discernible movement. Her tense muscles relaxed; her spasmodic breathing subsided.

"No," she muttered, resting her head in her cupped hands. "What have I done? What have I done to deserve this?" She dried her eyes with her palms. "What have I done?" Her voice trailed off to a whisper. She looked up.

The slow, methodical and uneven advance of two pacing feet sounded overhead—left to right and then back across the floor. Once again she covered her ears. She couldn't stand it any more.

She jumped from the bed, picked up her clothes, quickly put them on, then pulled the shade on the rear window so that the bed light would remain undetected from above.

She moved hesitantly down the hallway to the kitchen, flicked on the small oven light and scanned the formica counter. The remnants of the TV dinner sat on the edge of the sink, the drained bottle of rosé lay sideways on the meat board and a sheet of aluminum foil lay on the refrigerator. She reached out, clasped the bottle of tranquilizers and popped off the top; a little white pellet fell into her hand. Should she take it? She had to steady her nerves! More important, she had to summon as much courage as she could from her frail body. But the tranquilizers would not do that. Nor could they prime her for what lay ahead. She was determined to uncover the secret of the disappearing tenants, and she knew that whoever was upstairs probably held the key to the entire puzzle. In the soft yellow light that bathed the kitchen she weighed the alternatives. There were none; she had to go up to apartment 4 A and get in. The tranquilizers? Useless. She replaced the top and returned the vial to the counter.

She opened the drawer below the formica table and removed a butcher knife; it gave her comfort and protection. She would not be going upstairs alone.

From the utility pantry she withdrew a flashlight and pressed the button. The light fluttered and went out. She shook the flashlight violently; the beam flicked on and off. Determined, she unscrewed the back knob and jostled the batteries. She closed the flashlight and pressed the "on" button once more. It worked perfectly.

The wall light off, she walked to the living room, barefoot, and flashed the beam about. There was no one there. Nothing out of the ordinary. Turning toward the bedroom, she listened carefully. The footsteps continued. She took a deep breath, switched off the flashlight, stepped into the hall and shut the door.

The landing was dark; both the third and fourth stairwell lights were out. She inched her way along the wall to the staircase and twisted the solitary bulb. It remained dead. She jiggled the bulb violently, then turned away and began to climb. Slowly. The steps squeaking horribly. The sounds of the contrasting storm outside filling the air.

The perspiration poured from her body; her brain ached from the unrelenting strain.

Then, suddenly, she recoiled, smashing her head against the wall. She covered her mouth with the back of her palm to prevent an outcry. She whimpered, eyes closed, horrified. She had stepped on something.

Shaking violently, she tried desperately to pull herself together. She flicked on the flashlight and panned the steps at her feet. There was nothing there. She ran the light up the staircase, completely covering each step. The light came to rest on the edge of the fourth landing. In the full flush of the beam sat the cat, Jezebel, the cat that didn't exist. The frazzled body was motionless; the green eyes fixed. In her mouth was the parakeet, its head torn open and its feathers shredded from the tiny body, its once delicate form now battered carrion, dripping blood onto the floor.

Allison shook uncontrollably.

She was angry. That fool Miss Logan hadn't believed a damn word she had said. But here was incontestable proof! Jezebel. Spitting and ominous. Mortimer. Dead.

The cat showed her fangs over the shattered body. Allison steadied the knife and took a step upward. The cat put the bird down, arched her back and hissed. Another step. The cat arched her back even further; Allison took two quick steps. The cat shot out her paw, backed away with a menacing hiss, picked up the bird and ran off into the darkness.

There was silence again.

Allison turned off the flashlight; breathing deeply, she climbed the remaining steps to the fourth floor and slowly walked along the corridor to apartment 4 A. She leaned, immobile, on the door frame for several minutes, then tried the knob, expecting it to be locked. Surprisingly, the latch clicked and the door swung open. She looked behind her. There was no sign of Jezebel; the hall was empty. She squeezed her way through the small opening into the living room. She studied the darkness. It was too dark, unnaturally so. Almost as if she were looking through an infinite tunnel in an unmapped dimension. She could not even see the flashlight held ready in her left hand or the steel knife that she held tightly in the right. And if not for her highly tuned senses, she might have doubted her own existence.

The room was silent; there were no footsteps.

Turning on the flashlight, she flicked it over the walls. The furniture was as she had seen it earlier that day when Miss Logan had taken her through the apartments. She sniffed the air and recoiled. The musty odor was stronger than ever. She wiped her nose to kill the sting and turned toward the grandfather clocks. The faces were clogged with dust; the hands lay still. The fireplace was empty and the living room closets were open. Except for a tattered old umbrella, they too were bare.

She angled toward the bedroom hallway. The footsteps echoed again. She shut the flashlight, cowered against the wall and held her breath, fearing that even the sound of her heaving chest might be heard. The living room seemed to shrink around her, the walls converging and the ceiling lowering. Frantically, she turned. She had left the front door partially open. Every muscle begged her to break for safety. Yet she knew she could not. The bedroom lay a mere twenty feet down the short hallway. And in it the source of the footsteps, the key to her nightmares and, perhaps, the solution to the mystery of the missing tenants.

Brandishing the knife before her, she moved deliberately down the corridor, shoulder touching the wall, one step at a time.

The footsteps ceased; there was a squeaking.

She reached the open door to the bedroom and extended the knife before her. At first there was no indication of life. She waited, then turned toward the faint outline of the bed. A soft rustling drifted out of the darkness. She pressed the button on the flashlight, it didn't work. She shook the cylinder violently; the batteries jiggled but still no light. There was movement; a figure slid through the darkness and stood, back to Allison, against the outline of the rear window.

"Hello," she called, her voice choked and frightened. There was no answer. "Hello," she repeated.

The figure stood silent—motionless.

"What do you want from me?"

There was no reply.

She slowly moved toward the form, calling to it in a high-pitched voice. The knife was fully extended; she shook the flashlight in desperation. Never before had she known such fear, such restrained hysteria.

Reaching the figure, she touched its shoulder. It turned, but in the darkness of the room she could only see the outline of a head. "Who are you?" she begged, tears rolling down her cheeks. The figure stood silent, immobile. She jiggled the flashlight once more. It burst on, a powerful beam of white shattering the darkness and shining directly into the eyes of: Her father!

He was pallid white, a death mask covering his face. The lips and eyelids were swollen and hideous. Blue veins criss-crossed the crusted skin. His hair was shriveled, his eyeballs opaque. The cobalt scars that coursed along the right side of his face, down the neck and onto the right arm were festered; colorless pus oozed on the surface. And he was naked.

Her hideous scream fractured the night.

Lurching backward into a chair, she fell against the wall, still screaming, then stumbled back and forth, swinging the flashlight wildly in ever-widening arcs. The beam sporadically fell across her father's charred body as he painfully moved toward her, his right leg partially paralyzed and dragging behind. She ran backward, colliding with the furniture. The light continued to spray the room. It caught the bed and framed two fat naked women lying in an obscene position. Then darkness.

She ran into the living room, fell over an armchair and sprawled across the floor, losing her grasp on the flashlight. It flickered out. The sound of the approaching footsteps rang in her ears.

The chair had fallen on her; she pushed frantically to get it off.

The partially opened door slammed shut. The figure was standing in front of her only means of escape. She screamed hysterically, shot to her feet and charged toward the door. He grabbed her by the hair with one hand, by the crucifix chain with the other. She swung the knife into the darkness. It dug into the heavy chest. A bloodcurdling scream shook the apartment. Again and again the knife plunged downward as a trickle of blood curled down her arm. More screams—a cry of death. Then a body dropped. She ran toward the door, threw it open and sprang into the hallway.

The front door of the brownstone burst open; Allison rushed out, screaming, and tumbled down the wet stone steps. She no longer had the knife. Lights switched on in the surrounding buildings in response to the cries; curious heads emerged from open windows. Pulling at her soaked hair in terror, she tumbled through the puddles, falling every few steps from the force of the wind and her own imbalance. Running—falling—she managed to make her way down the block to the corner.

High above the street the old priest—awake, but still motionless—sat at the window, hands braced in front of him.

The rain continued to fall.

The wind blew fiercely.

The house stood dark and silent.

13

"This way, ma'am."

"I hope this won't take too long."

"I wouldn't know, ma'am."

"I'm anxious to see her."

"That's up to the man inside."

The detective opened an opaque glass door.

"Thank you," said Jennifer Learson as she walked by the man and into the room.

The detective looked at the lettering on the door. It was marked "Bellevue Hospital—Police Interrogation." "Just take a seat on the bench," he said officiously.

The room was small, sparsely furnished. The walls were discolored; chips of paint hung from the plaster or already lay on the gray cement floor. The furniture was plain, splintered and untended—a long brown bench along the right wall, a simple square unpainted table to the left.

Jennifer sat down on the bench.

The detective closed the door.

A squat little man with an angular face was seated behind the table. He possessed a pair of black eyes, a long nose with a bump on the bridge, and two unnaturally thin and colorless lips. On his head was an old fedora which blended perfectly with his oversized suit. His shirt was covered with ashes that had fallen from a short chewed-up cigar that hung from his mouth and bobbed about as he ruminated.

He smiled at Jennifer, revealing a beaverlike mouth of teeth that stretched across his face and left the impression that the lower part of his head was a huge dental bridge. He held the smile and said nothing. She fidgeted on the bench, unnerved by the unprotected, sterile surroundings and the piercing nature of the little ferret's ambivalent grin.

"My name's Gatz, Detective Gatz, with a Z." His voice, a low-pitched twang, was irritating to the ear. The sound emanated from deep in his throat and took much of its form from the unnatural tucked-in position of his jaw, which caused the muscles to constrict and the vocal cords to compress.

"Yes, sir," she replied as she watched the misleading smile recede from his face.

"I'd like to talk to you."

"Yes, sir," she repeated. Her fingers ran nervously along the pleats of her blue skirt.

"Your name is Learson, Jennifer Learson?"

"Yes."

He held up a piece of paper. "Home: Three eleven East Fifty-first Street. Profession: Model."

"Yes."

"Good."

"I wanted—"

He interrupted. "I trust detective Richardson filled you in?" he asked, glancing at the tall, unresponsive detective behind him.

She paused, then replied, "Vaguely."

"I see. Well, we'll try to clarify the picture a bit more. You know Miss Allison Parker, I presume?"

"Yes, sir, but—"

"When's the last time you saw her?"

"About four days ago. Look, I'm very upset! Can't you tell me what happened?"

"In a moment." His voice implied more command than explanation. "When was the last time you spoke to her?"

"Also four days ago."

"What did you talk about?"

"Clothes."

"That's all?"

"Yes, well, she talked about a party."

"What party?"

"A housewarming party she was going to have."

"When?"

"She didn't say. She just said she was going to have one and asked me for suggestions on who she should invite."

"And you gave them?"

"Yes, sir."

"I'd like you to make a list of the names you mentioned."

She nodded. "They were all her friends."

"Good. What else did you talk about?"

"That's it. Clothes and the party."

"And she said nothing out of the ordinary?"

"No."

"Nothing strange or disturbing?"

"No."

"You're positive?"

"Yes."

He held up another piece of paper, read it and declared, "She's been in the building on 89th Street a week."

"Almost two," Jennifer corrected.

Gatz added a notation to the paper. "Have you seen her apartment?" he asked. "Or been in the building?"

"No," she replied.

"Has anyone you know?"

"Her boyfriend."

He grinned. "I see," he said with a peculiar note of anticipation in his voice.

The door opened once more; Michael entered the room. He nodded at Jennifer, then walked, unaware of Detective Gatz's presence, to the bench and sat down.

Seeing Gatz, he shot to his feet, his cheeks a deep crimson.

Gatz sat grinning coldly, his right foot beating slowly on the cement floor. "Sit down!" he ordered, his eyes revealing a hatred that matched Michael's virulent expression. "Sit!"

"What the—"

"Sit down I said!" commanded the detective angrily.

Michael reluctantly did so.

"What are you doing here?" Michael said at last.

"It's my job, isn't it?"

"There are other detectives in the city!"

"How true! But this case interests me. You see, I was sitting in Division Headquarters when the call came in. Sounded like the usual nut case murder. So I was just about to assign one of the third-grade detectives. There's just something about psychos that don't intrigue me. I like murders that are products of evil minds. But you know that already. So as I'm saying, I was about to do a disappearing act when I heard the name of the broad and the guy whose calling card was in her pocket. And what do you know? I came flying out of my office faster than hell, because I knew that with you involved it had to be a pretty dirty matter."

"What happened to Allison?" asked Michael, ignoring the insult.

Gatz scowled. "What was the name of your wife—the poor kid—Karen?"

Michael gripped the underside of the bench. It was all he could do to restrain himself from leaping at Gatz and smashing him through the wall.

Gatz smiled. He enjoyed watching Michael torture himself.

"What happened to Allison?" repeated Michael through gritted teeth.

"Allison Parker?" Gatz was taunting him.

Realizing the detective's purpose, Michael released his grip on the bench, relaxed the taut muscles in his face and sat back calmly. "Yes, sir, Allison Parker."

The game was over. Gatz reclined in his chair and gathered his thoughts. "The Karen Farmer case." He had spent six months digging and probing until his superiors had forced him to close the file. Then he was transferred to another division and busted in rank. He would never forget it—nor the fact that he was sure he had been right and everyone else wrong. And here right in front of him was Michael Farmer, but as much as he wanted to, he couldn't dig back into the past. At least not yet. Right now he had the "Allison Parker case," and he had to get to the bottom of it first. Then, if his luck held, discover the truth about the death of Michael Farmer's wife.

"I haven't got much of an idea as to what happened. So as far as I'm concerned, nobody's suspected of anything yet. And that includes you too, Farmer. Like I say, a man's innocent until proven guilty."

"Did you think that up all by yourself?"

"Don't start, my friend," cautioned Gatz, standing up. The sheriff's chair rocked behind him, squeaking. Detective Richardson leaned over and stopped the seat. Gatz glanced approvingly at his assistant and began to pace the floor.

"It seems we had a rather strange incident last night. One Allison Parker was found roaming the streets, hysterical, screaming she had just stabbed her father to death."

Michael gasped. He sat frozen in place as did Jennifer, and then he blurted, "That's impossible! Her father died of cancer weeks ago!"

Gatz frowned. He leaned forward and pulled a clipboard off the table. Simultaneously he picked up a pair of horn-rimmed glasses and, after placing them precariously above the bump on his nose, examined his notes with deepening interest. "Are you sure?" he asked.

"Absolutely! You can call her mother if—" He caught himself midway through the sentence. "No, you had better not," he corrected. "I don't think she could handle this. Call the police authorities in her home town. They'll confirm."

Gatz removed a cheap pen from his shirt pocket, leaving behind a dark ink stain; he shook the pen violently to force the oozing ink down toward the point where it belonged. The paper crackled as he carefully crossed out the name and address of Allison's father and inscribed the word "deceased." Returning the amended paper to the table, he once again sat back in the chair and stared at Michael.

"Let me review some facts. Your relationship with Miss Parker is?"

"Friend."

Gatz gritted his teeth, indicating his displeasure.

"Boy friend," Michael corrected.

Gatz smiled impolitely. Satisfied, he turned his eyes toward Jennifer. "And you're her friend?" he asked.

"You already know that."

"And you two know each other." It was a statement rather than a question. He had observed their silent greeting when Michael had first entered the room. Nodding, Gatz stood and once again began to pace the floor. The cigar which continued to hang from his mouth was somewhat shorter now; he had bitten off a portion of the chewed-up end.

He stopped and leaned against the wall below the sealed windows. He regarded his two captives suspiciously.

"We found some blood on her clothing, but it turned out to be her own—from a cut on her forearm. Type AB, Rh negative. Then we searched the apartment in the building where she said she killed the old man and we found no blood, no corpse."

"Which apartment?" asked Michael.

"Four A. Ever been in there?"

"No."

Michael looked at the floor, Apartment 4 A. The

one Allison had complained about. A shiver ran down his spine.

"Not only that, but we found no evidence to indicate any kind of struggle."

"In the apartment?"

"In the entire building!"

"Did you talk to the old priest?"

"The old coot's deaf and blind and useless."

"And Chazen? And the other tenants?"

"Who?"

"The other tenants in the building! Charles Chazen, Mrs. Clark, a pair of fat sisters—I forget their name—and a few others."

"I'm warning you, Farmer. No games."

"Now you wait a minute, mister. I'm trying to find out what happened to my girl friend, and I don't think it's being too demanding to assume that the police—especially a detective as diligent as yourself—would have talked to the other neighbors who just might have seen or heard something relevant."

Gatz sucked in his stomach and whipped the cigar up and down angrily.

Michael looked at the detective, puzzled.

"I've been through every apartment in that building in the last six hours," said Gatz, "and there's no evidence that anyone's been living in any of the apartments in years except Miss Parker and the priest!"

"What?" Michael cried, having received his second major surprise. "That's impossible! Allison met them all. Spoke to them. Spent some time with them in their apartments."

"Did you?" asked the unimpressed detective.

"No."

"Did anybody else you know?"

"No!"

"That's interesting."

Gatz pivoted away, removed the cigar from his mouth and spat a wad of tobacco into his ashtray. Jennifer cringed; Michael stared at the detective's back, awaiting his next pronouncement. Gatz stood relatively still, thinking, and then turned to the silent detective who stood patiently to his right.

"Tell Rizzo to get a rundown on Charles Chazen and that Mrs. Clark." He looked to Michael for help.

"The sisters—Klotkin, that's it—and there are a pair of lesbians—I don't remember their names."

The assistant hesitated. "No one could have been living in those places."

"I know, but we'll check on these people anyway. They might not live there, but, for some reason or other, hang out in the building."

Richardson nodded.

"What is the landlord's name again?" asked Gatz.

"Caruso. David Caruso," replied Richardson.

"Have Rizzo try these people on him."

"Yes, sir," he said as he went out, leaving the three alone.

Gatz adjusted the position of his fedora and began to pace the room once again.

"When can I see Allison?" Michael asked.

"The nurse will let us know. Until then we'll continue our chat, just like in the old days."

Michael restrained himself. "You said that there's no evidence anything occurred there, right?"

"I did?" Gatz smiled sadistically and turned toward Jennifer. "How long did you say you know Miss Parker?"

"Two years."

"Have you ever seen her hysterical like this before?"

"No. Allison is a very rational and controlled person."

"Is she?" Gatz asked skeptically, his tone suggesting that he knew otherwise.

"She's been under a great deal of strain lately," said Michael.

"What kind of strain?"

"Her father. The illness dragged on for almost four months. Since his death she's been tense and unsettled. She's been eating and sleeping badly. She had a couple of nightmares. And then she fainted at a fashion show two days ago."

"I see. That might explain it. A nightmare. Hallucination. Whatever." There was a long pause. "But then again it might not."

"You might try finding a corpse."

"If there's one to find—and I think there is—we'll find it. And when I do, I'm going to see to it that it's pinned around someone's neck. And I'm not going to miss a second time."

Michael remained unmoved.

"Where were you last night from three to five in the morning?"

"Home." He flushed with rage.

"I'm not so sure," said Gatz vindictively.

Michael exploded. "Now wait a minute! I don't like the tone—"

"No, *you* wait a minute! A woman is brought in claiming she murdered her father, hacked him to death with a knife. The facts, I like facts, say that that's impossible. But maybe she killed someone who she thought was her father. That seems a little more probable. Or maybe she has a screw loose and belongs in a funny farm. But something keeps telling me that the limburger sitting in the mousetrap is smelling and might catch a big fat rat. Now wouldn't you ask a few questions if you were me? Especially if the parties had been involved in a suspected homicide once before. And especially if the rat might be the famous Michael Farmer."

Michael sat, silenced. Gatz was right, at least as to the investigation. Any cop would do the same. But Michael knew what really was on the detective's mind. No matter how fair and honest Gatz tried to appear, no matter how impartial, Michael knew.

"As soon as I'm able to, I'm going to get some information out of Miss Parker so that this thing will start to make some sense."

Gatz chewed another piece of tobacco off the stunted

cigar; he was satisfied. Until he could find a body and until the woman in room 211 was lucid enough to make some sense, there was little else he could do. But it was also possible that there would be no body and no evidence of a crime. Then Farmer would walk away from him again. And his chance to get something on the lawyer after his previous failure would be gone. No, it couldn't be. No matter how senseless this whole incident seemed, it certainly made more sense than assuming that one man could be involved in two suspicious homicides and have nothing to hide. Gatz's years of experience told him that. And so did the sharp, stabbing pain in his gut. No, Farmer had murdered his wife and now he was up to something else. He would play it smart this time—out of necessity. He would go slow and steady; and when he got the facts he needed, he would pounce like a leopard. He smiled.

The wall phone rang. Gatz pulled the receiver off its cradle. "Yah, Gatz." He listened intently and returned the receiver to its place.

"She's awake," he announced. He sat back and examined his notes. "You can go see her now."

"Is she all right?" asked Jennifer, who had watched the exchange between Michael and Gatz with fascination.

"Ask the doctor," Gatz said curtly. "She's in two eleven. Go down the hall and take the first left. And after you're done, we'll continue with our little discussion."

"I can't wait," said Michael as he stood up.

"I'm flattered," replied Gatz.

Michael turned and walked Jennifer through the door.

"What was that all about?" she began as they started down the hall.

"Nothing."

"I'm not so sure; he obviously has something against you."

"I'm telling you, it's nothing. And it's too far in the past to be worried about."

"How far?"

"Before you came to New York."

"How long before?"

They walked several steps silently.

"Long enough," he said after a pause. He was getting irritated. Jennifer shut her mouth and quietly followed him into the side corridor.

Unlike the main hallways, it was practically empty. A large desk stood at the entrance. A policewoman sat behind it.

"Can I help you?" she asked.

"Yes," answered Michael. "Room two eleven."

"Your names?"

"Michael Farmer and Jennifer Learson."

Her expression remained neutral. But she said, pointing, "Go down to where the policeman is sitting. That's two eleven."

Michael grabbed Jennifer's hand and led her down the hall. The woman turned and waved to the seated cop who had looked up to her for instructions. He stood and opened the door behind him.

A nurse stepped into the doorway.

"How is she?" asked Michael.

"She's heavily drugged, so she's very groggy. But other than that, I think she's doing fine."

"Can she be taken home?"

"Not yet."

"Could you be more specific?"

"You'll have to speak to the doctor. He can tell you more than I." She paused, then smiled reassuringly, suggesting that she could supply some additional information. "I'm sure she'll have to stay here at least two or three days until the effects of the shock and the exposure wear off. She has a severe sore throat. The infection is not that serious, but we do want to prevent unnecessary complications. I'm sure you understand."

"Yes."

"You can only have five minutes. The doctor wants her to get as much rest as possible."

"Thank you," said Michael.

"If you'll excuse me," said the nurse, smiling. Michael nodded and stepped into the room; Jennifer followed, closing the door. Inside, they stood in stunned silence, staring at the hospital bed.

Allison lay under a blanket. Her face was colorless. Her lips were swollen and her eyes unresponsive. Her body was extended, rigid and motionless. She seemed more frail than he had ever seen her. Almost lifeless.

They approached the bed on different sides.

Michael reached down and took Allison's wrist. She did not react.

"Allison," he whispered.

Her eyes continued to stare at the ceiling. He called to her again, louder, but she remained unresponsive.

"Allison, it's Michael and Jennifer," said Jennifer leaning over.

Allison's lips parted. A tiny bubble of saliva emerged, hung over her lower lip for several seconds and then burst. Her jaw moved slightly downward; she was trying to speak. Her eyes moved slowly to Michael and widened with recognition. The pupils reflected the pain; they told nothing about what had happened.

Jennifer pushed herself farther over the bed, her mouth near to Allison's ear. "Can you hear and understand me? Can you?"

Allison moved her hand. Again she tried to open her lips without success. No words were formed, just another bubble which soon burst silently like its predecessor.

Michael glanced at Jennifer. "It's senseless to ask her questions," he said. "She can't respond."

Jennifer didn't agree. "Allison," she called, "I want you to answer me." Allison's focus withdrew from Michael and moved to Jennifer. "Allison, what happened last night?"

Her eyes widened in terror; a gurgling moan surged up from deep in her throat and the colorless lips parted, futilely trying to form the proper words.

Michael tried to imagine what had happened.

The door opened and Detective Gatz stepped inside. He shut it and leaned against the wall.

Michael flinched uncomfortably.

"A rather sorry-looking sight," commented the policeman. "Even worse than when she took all those pills." He looked at Michael severely. "Remember that? The loving wife 'committed suicide' by slicing her wrists; then, soon after, the mistress tried to drown her guilt with pills. Messy stuff."

"Can't we be alone?" asked Michael, scowling.

The detective shook his head. "I suddenly became curious. You don't mind if I listen and perhaps offer some expert medical advice."

"There's nothing to listen to," said Jennifer contemptuously. "She can't speak yet."

Gatz shrugged. If that was the case, that was the case. But he would remain just to make sure. Patients like this were more likely to speak to someone with whom they were familiar. It was a fact. And there was nothing he liked more in the entire world than facts.

"You know," said Gatz, "Miss Parker looks a little like your former wife. Yes, Parker really reminds me of her. Fortunately there's a difference. Miss Parker didn't die when she tried to kill herself. And she isn't going to die now." He looked at Michael. "Did Karen Farmer commit suicide? Some said yes. Nice neat letter saying goodbye to everyone. It was rather sad. I said no. Everything told me different. It was no suicide."

"Are you through?" asked Michael, restraining his fury.

"You don't like my story?"

"I'm warning you, Mr. Detective. The past is dead and buried, and if you try to resurrect it, I'll see to it that you get thrown off the force."

"How violent," said the cop benevolently. He pulled the cigar from his mouth, studied the chewed end and returned it to its spot between his teeth. He had said enough; he could only push Farmer so far, because Farmer was right. He could pull strings and could get him booted in the ass. He had done it before. If he was going to sniff back into the Karen Farmer suicide, he would have to do it through the present investigation. And do it very quietly.

The door opened once again and the nurse re-entered.

"Five minutes are up and Dr. Bleifer is strict with his rules. Miss Parker needs as much rest as possible."

"Where can I find the doctor?"

"He should be in the hospital in fifteen minutes."

"We can continue our little chat while you wait for him," said the detective.

"Must we?" asked Jennifer, already annoyed with Gatz's persistence.

The man smiled stolidly.

The nurse walked to the bed and felt Allison's head. Then she measured Allison's blood pressure and took her pulse while Michael and Gatz exchanged antagonistic glances.

"Let me take you all to the waiting room," declared the nurse. "When the doctor arrives, I'll ask him to come down."

The nurse lifted the chart off the end of the bed and recorded the readings. After replacing it, she walked to the door and motioned the visitors outside. Michael and Jennifer were the first two out. Gatz stopped a moment to look at Allison, shook his head, then followed the nurse as she moved down the corridor.

As they turned the corner into the main hall, a sound crept through the door of room 211. Nearly inaudible, it was the sound of someone weeping.

Twenty minutes later Michael and Jennifer exited the main elevator with Gatz on their heels. They walked past the reception desk and into the outer hall of the hospital.

"Remember, don't leave town without letting me know."

Michael didn't bother to turn. Instead, he locked his arm through Jennifer's and stepped outside.

Gatz ambled to the entrance. leaned against the glass doors, and watched them walk to First Avenue and hail a cab. He removed the cigar from his mouth for the thousandth time that day. He studied the little stub and the chewed-up end. It had had enough. He had worked hard; he deserved a new one. He tossed the butt into the bushes near the "No Littering" sign, dug into his coat pocket and removed a new six-inch panatela. Carefully, he peeled the cellophane and then, with the precision of a diamond cutter, examined the tobacco wrapping, approved its form, and enjoyed its scent.

Placing the cigar in his mouth, he turned and re-entered the hospital.

14

The night of horror remained imprinted in her mind. Over and over she relived the tense moments on the staircase, the confrontation with her "father" and the lunging knife that continuously pierced his rotted flesh and was discolored from the trickle of blood. Again and again she challenged her recollections, doubting, hoping, yet in the end acknowledging what she knew had happened. It was a traumatic exercise to face a reality which was unreal, to force one's thoughts to the unthinkable. And in the end exhaust oneself for a totally inconclusive conclusion that could only breed more terror.

She lay propped in Michael's bed, covered to the waist by the linen quilt. The table to her right was cluttered with an assortment of vials and jars containing a variety of medicines to which she had been subjected. Most were only half filled. Around her neck hung the crucifix, clenched in her right fist. The stereo played softly in the background.

Michael entered with a bed tray and forced an unconvincing smile. He tipped down the legs, laid it on her lap and uncovered a bowl of steaming chicken broth, two pieces of buttered toast and a little copper tea kettle.

"Where is Jennifer?" Allison asked as she grasped a tablespoon and began to sip the broth.

"In the bathroom."

"Performing unmentionable acts," she added, coldly without the suggestion of humor one would have expected with such an observation.

He sat down, picked the automatic channel changer off the night table and tossed it nervously in the air.

The door opened and Jennifer came in. "Hello again," she said as she walked across the room and stood at the foot of the bed. "I just spoke to the agency, told them no bookings and asked them to send out the checks they owe you."

"Thank you," replied Allison. "Of course you could have called from in here, but then you couldn't have said what you said."

"I don't understand."

"Forget it."

"You have regards from everyone."

Allison nibbled at the toast. "Thank them for me," she murmured indifferently. The last thing on her mind was her career and all those people who had clogged her life to the point of suffocation—or at least that's how it seemed to her now.

Michael and Jennifer exchanged worried glances. He placed the channel changer back on the table.

Allison continued to sip the chicken broth. "Can I have some water?" she asked.

Michael poured a glass. "Take two of these with it," he said while removing two cylindrical pills from one of the vials.

Allison extended an unsteady hand, grasped the glass, removed her right hand from the crucifix and took the pills, which she tossed into her mouth with distaste. More pills. It seemed that she had eaten every pill on the face of the earth in the last week. But they kept on coming. She frowned as these two slid down her throat.

She grabbed the crucifix again.

"I think you're getting some of your color back," said Jennifer.

"You do?"

"Yes."

"I appreciate the sentiment, but you do know what the word bullshit means."

Jennifer glanced at Michael. "A day or two rest and you'll be as good as new."

"Sure. No doubt about it." Her statement was re-assuring; the tone and underlying conviction were not.

Michael stood. "Take my seat."

"No," said Jennifer. "I have to get home."

He leaned back against the dresser, observing the tense silence that began to oppress the room. "We can all go up to the mountains," he finally said, "this weekend."

"That would be nice," said Allison coldly.

Michael rubbed his chin, thinking. "Bear Mountain. We'll get a cabin for the day, cook something special and mix a batch of rum grog." He smiled expectantly. Allison stared blankly.

Jennifer stammered, "I'll be back in the morning. Would you like me to bring you something?"

"No."

"You're sure now?"

"Yes."

Jennifer smiled uncertainly and turned to Michael. "Where'd you put my coat?"

"In the hall closet."

"And the books?"

"In the closet too."

She looked at Allison once more. "Get some rest and don't sit up worrying. Everything will be fine."

Allison smiled meekly.

"I'll walk you out, Jennifer," volunteered Michael. He followed her toward the living room. As he reached the foyer he looked back at the bedroom door, which he had just closed. His expression hardened and he grabbed Jennifer by the arm. "She might break down completely," he said.

"Are you sure?"

He reached into the foyer closet, removed Jennifer's coat and art books and laid them in her outstretched hands. "The doctors have raised that as a possibility."

"She's very hostile."

"Depressed is the better word. And frightened." He paused, then added, "The combination is debilitating."

"What can we do?"

"I don't know."

"If you need me—"

"I know where to find you." He leaned forward and kissed her on the cheek. They exchanged smiles. "Thanks," he said.

He closed the door softly behind her and glanced quickly back to the bedroom. It was quiet; the entire apartment lay still. He dug nervously in his shirt pocket and removed a small black telephone book. He opened the pages, surreptitiously walked to the wall phone near the table—the phone that had no extension in the bedroom—and quietly dialed. He listened attentively to the ringing of the distant phone. It rang twelve times. The automatic service answered. No one was there. He hung up disgustedly and returned to the bedroom.

The dinner tray lay on the carpet next to the bed. The stereo continued to play softly; the effect was soothing and sleep-inducing, precisely the mood with which he wanted to surround her. The quieter she was and the more sleep she got the better.

He lifted the tray from the rug and laid it on top of the dresser directly behind him. Then he sat down in the leather armchair. Leaning back, he stared sympathetically at her closed eyes and noted, after watching the steady rise and fall of her chest, that she was breathing more easily than she had in the past three days, when it seemed at times that her lungs would explode like overstretched balloons.

She opened her eyes.

They studied each other judiciously.

"You think I'm going crazy," she said after a long silence.

"I haven't said that!"

"You haven't had to!"

Again there was silence.

"At times, for all of your painstaking reserve and neutrality, you're very easy to read," she said.

"Am I?"

She nodded.

He sat back in the armchair, massaging his temples, his eyes racing over the walls from picture to picture. Abstracts. Crashing lines and forms. Colors. Jumbled. "Allison," he said. He stopped to think out the rest of his statement.

"Yes," she prompted.

"All right, I'll admit that I think the pressure of your father's death has caused you to conjure up an incredible fantasy."

"That means you think I'm crazy."

"No it doesn't."

"Then what does it mean?"

He stammered. "It means exactly what I said."

"I see." She didn't.

"Do you want to talk about it?"

"Yes."

"You're sure?"

"Positive."

Breathing sharply, he stood up and paced across the room, shut off the stereo, turned and began: "Let's look at what we know about that night. You were tense and disturbed, having had another of your recurrent nightmares. You had fainted the day before and had just found out that no one was living in the building."

"But—"

"Let me finish! You got all kinds of brave and decided to go upstairs and find out who was making the noise. You grabbed a knife. You were scared shitless. Then you stepped on a cat."

"Jezebel."

"A cat! You walked into a room in a situation that would have frightened anyone to death and then you confronted your—" He stopped and shook his head. This entire thing was ridiculous. Her father!

"Go on."

"Okay. Your father was in bed with two women. Naked." He walked to the window and looked out at the rooftops.

"Well?"

"It's getting dark earlier."

"That happens during the winter."

He looked down at the cars crawling along the street, their braking lights erupting in spasms of red. He listened. The clamor of the street was trapped below, except for an occasional honk that pierced the room.

He spun toward Allison. "Let me ask you a question."

"All right."

"What made you frigid?"

Angered, she challenged, "What has that to do with anything?"

He interrupted. "Why did you leave home?"

She held the crucifix tighter.

"Why did you see your father and two naked women in the brownstone?"

She winced.

"Why did you try to kill yourself after Karen's death?" He paused, then asked, "Do you want me to tell you?"

She remained silent.

"I can because I know," said Michael.

"I wanted to become a model."

"That made you frigid?"

"Perhaps."

"Let's cut the bullshit. This is me you're talking to, Allison."

"I know, Michael. How could I possibly mistake you for anyone else?"

"Supposedly, you love me."

"I do."

"Then you should have told me a long time ago. There was no reason not to, since you told me everything else."

She lowered her eyes. "You've tried this ploy before."

"But this time I know."

"How?"

"That's my business. There are ways to find out anything if you want to badly enough and are willing to pay the price."

The room fell silent, he leaning against the window, she lying against the pillows, her arms draped over the bed.

"What do you know?" she asked, resigned to the fact that he did.

"Everything," he said softly. He opened the top dresser drawer and removed a manila portfolio from

which he pulled several documents. "Psychiatrists'
reports and police transcripts. Several other papers.
All very enlightening." He held one up to the light.
"This for example. Just the pertinent information.
Psychiatrist's transcript dated March 12, 1966. Dr.
Risenstadt:

"Father gave me the crucifix on my tenth birthday. At dinner. It was beautiful. I put it on
at the table. I never took it off.

"Another dated April 9, 1966:

"I had always thought Mother and Father were
happy. I was wrong. They became very cold
toward one another. And the arguments were
incessant. He would come home drunk and beat
her up. She'd claim he was with other women.
He'd scream like a madman, calling her a
puritanical Catholic. I would run down the back
staircase and hide in an alcove. One day he
found me and beat me up also. I had blood
all over. . . . I was very religious. He wasn't.
Yet he insisted on my constant devotion to the
church. It didn't make much sense. I was confused.

"Another dated October 16, 1966:

"I hated him. I was terrified whenever he came
near me. My own father. He killed my puppy.
He kicked him in the stomach and Bugle died.

"Should I continue?" he asked.
She nodded indifferently.
"Police transcript, 1966. No specific date. You
know what this is?"
She nodded again.
He read:

"Mother and I had gone for the weekend to a lakeside resort about thirty miles from town. We were to stay over and return Monday, but I suffered a bad sunburn and decided to come home a day early. I took the bus from Lake Junction to the post office and walked the rest of the way up the hill. It was ten in the evening. I entered the house, climbed the stairs to the second floor, turned to walk toward my room, then stopped. Laughter was coming from my parents' bedroom. No one should have been in the house. Father was out of town on business. I walked to the partially opened door, swung it back and looked inside. Father lay naked in the bed with two naked women. They were all drunk. The larger of the two was sucking his testicles, while the other woman fondled the larger's breasts. I vomited. Father spun off the bed—frightened and hysterical—and began to beat me about the head. I lifted my hands to defend myself, but he wrapped his hands around my throat, then grasped the chain of the crucifix, wound it tightly around my neck and squeezed. I gasped for air. He jerked me down to the floor and pulled the chain tighter and tighter, causing my skin to bleed. I have a scar there. I kicked him in the groin. He stopped. I tried to catch my breath, but I vomited again. Then I looked at the broken chain in my hand and the crucifix dangling from one end; I watched him panting wildly, clutching himself. I was crying. I threw the chain and hit him on the chin. The chain and cross fell to the floor. I never wore it again. I never stepped inside a church or attended a service again. Mother sealed the bedroom. I left home. For New York.

"Sound familiar?"

"Yes." She closed her eyes. Finally, she thought to herself, disgusted that she hadn't the nerve to tell him herself—or was it a far more complex psychological inhibition?

He held up another document. "Police transcript. Also 1966. Describing a suicide attempt, soon after the confrontation with your father. You tried to slit your wrists. A failure. You never told me about this one."

"I would have told you everything eventually."

"But not before he died."

"No."

"You should have told me last week. He was already dead."

"Yes, I know."

Michael walked over, lifted a piece of toast from her tray, then sat down on the edge of the bed.

"You tried to kill yourself seven years ago because of guilt, depression, hatred, loneliness. Then you tried again after Karen died because of guilt over your own involvement in an adulterous relationship."

She did not respond, just lowered her head.

"What about the nightmares?" he asked.

"Nightmares?"

He held up another document and read: " 'I had terrible nightmares.' " He looked at her for an admission. She bowed her head again and said, "Yes."

"You admit that you had nightmares about that night?"

"Yes."

"Often?"

"Yes."

"And might have some again?"

"Perhaps."

"And had one last week on a rainy night."

"No! No! No!"

"You can't admit that as a possibility?"

"No."

"You're not thinking."

"I don't have to. I was there. I know a dream from reality."

"But—"

"No!"

He raised his hand in defense. "All right. Let me go on. You ran from him and he caught you—like years ago—and then you stabbed him to death with the knife you were carrying."

"Right."

"There's no blood, no body, and it's hard to stab a man who's been dead and buried for three weeks!"

"It may be hard, but I did it!"

He paused, thought over her last remark and countered. "The police checked the apartment—in fact the entire building—and found nothing that would indicate any struggle."

"Gatz checked the building!"

"There were other police there also. Gatz wouldn't make this all up."

"He wouldn't?"

"The last thing he would do is hide evidence or a murder or killing where I'm involved!"

"He's unpredictable and capable of anything."

"Only to a point."

She coughed spasmodically and covered her mouth with her left hand, while keeping her right hand on the crucifix. It was her sustenance, the giver of strength.

"Let me ask you a question," she said.

"Okay," he replied guardedly.

"It's now a matter of official record that no one besides the old priest and I live in that building. Right?"

"Yes."

"Then who is Charles Chazen and where did he come from?"

"I don't know. I didn't see him. No one has."

"And the others?"

"The same goes for them. Maybe you think you saw lesbians because the two women in the bed were engaged in lesbian activity."

"Nonsense," she said.

"I—"

"You saw the cat on the steps, just like I described her."

"I saw *a* cat, not necessarily his cat."

"But the picture, Michael! The picture! You saw that! You saw Chazen in the little gold frame."

He bit his nails and repeated softly, "That's the one thing I can't quite figure out."

"The one thing that makes you question your conclusion that I'm cracking up?"

"Perhaps. But that picture might have been in the apartment before and, under all the tension, you dreamed an extension of the character."

"Look who's creating vague suppositions and explaining away coincidence." The last thing she would allow him to do would be to hypothesize her into capitulation. It was one of his favorite gimmicks, and a successful one at that. Especially with people who had a weak sense of conviction. But if it took every ounce of her remaining energy, she would stand up for what she knew had happened. Chazen, Clark, the Klotkins and the others had been there, she had seen them, and what had occurred the night of the killing had occurred with her "father" present. The thought made her shudder and pray silently to herself.

"I don't think we're getting anywhere," said Michael.

"We might if we addressed ourselves to two questions."

"And they are?"

"Chazen and the others exist. Where are they? Did they have anything to do with what happened that night, and, if not, who did?"

"I don't know, I just don't know about any of this. But I'm worried about you." He leaned forward and took her in his arms. "I don't care about Gatz, Chazen, your father or anybody else. Just you and your health."

She lifted her arms and put them around his neck. Across his shoulder lay the crucifix. She looked at the body of Christ and closed her eyes tightly.

"You're not going back in that house again," he said. "It's all over."

"Is it, Michael?" She pushed away and stared at him blankly.

"Yes."

"You're sure?"

"Yes."

She laughed.

"What's the matter?" he asked.

"Sometimes you're very naïve," she said and laughed again.

"Why?"

"Because it isn't over."

"How do you know?"

"I just do. Things like this are never over."

She had been alone for the last hour. Fortunately, Michael had returned to his office to complete an appellate brief; she could not have stood more questions, probes or rationalizations. Yet, instead of making herself think of other things, she continued to explore her life and the events of the last two weeks, reading the psychiatrists' and police reports, remembering. She began to formulate her own rationalizations and construct some haunting parallels.

And finally, near exhaustion, she burrowed through the file cabinet in the hall closet and removed an old newspaper article, taking it to the living room desk.

She adjusted the lamp and laid the rumpled clipping on the blotter. She read:

DEAD GIRL'S HUSBAND
PRIME MURDER SUSPECT

Chief of Detectives Morris Lazerman revealed today that police have developed an alternate theory in the Karen Farmer case. Prior to the new pronouncement, it had been presumed that the death of the twenty-six-year-old former socialite was a suicide. However, according to the Chief of Detectives, Karen Farmer might not have taken her own life on the night of March 22, but might have been the victim of a carefully executed, premeditated murder.

"Although initially we presumed that the death was an apparent suicide," said Lazerman, "recent facts and conflicting evidence have forced us to modify our opinion and entertain the possibility that the woman might have been murdered."

Detective Captain Thomas Gatz, who has been directly in charge of the investigation, seconded the statement of his superior but would not clarify his later statement that "the husband, attorney Michael Farmer, is a prime suspect." Curiously, Lazerman in his earlier statement had ruled out the possibility that the husband might have been involved in the death. The ensuing investigation revealed that the victim's husband had been involved with another woman, a fashion model named Allison Parker, and that Miss Parker apparently had had no prior knowledge of the wife's existence.

It was later learned that, two weeks before the alleged suicide, Mr. Farmer asked his wife for a divorce. Subsequent accounts by mutual friends of the couple revealed that Mrs. Farmer had laughed at her husband's request and had declared that "she would never give him an uncontested divorce and that he would have to kill her to get rid of her."

Mr. Farmer has previously been credited with an airtight alibi, but obviously some cracks are beginning to appear, or so think the police, or more precisely Detective Gatz. He has been quoted as saying that the mistress, Allison Parker, who has been in seclusion, has been totally freed from any suspicion in regard to the case.

Mr. Farmer, who so far has not been officially charged with anything, is an attorney. He had been a respected member of the Manhattan District Attorney's Office for several years prior to his entrance into private practice. An interesting element of the case is the relationship between Detective Gatz and Mr. Farmer. Farmer has charged that animosity exists between the two of them dating back to his days in the District Attorney's Office and that the detective is waging a vendetta against him. As of yet, none of these charges have been substantiated.

Both Chief of Detectives Lazerman and Detective Captain Gatz predicted that new announcements would be made concerning the case within the next few days. But the nature of the announcements, at this point, seems quite vague in view of the conflicting positions taken by the two police officers.

Fascinated with what had been a dead memory, she read the article once more, then folded it in half and replaced it in the file.

15

The office was tiny, the windows barred. A bulletin board dotted with circulars and notices was attached to the wall. The desk that stood nearby was ancient and worn; the original brown varnish had been worn down to streaks of bare wood. Besides the phone that sat precariously on the edge of the desk, the old broken chair behind it and the coat rack just inside the entrance, there was little else in the room worthy of note.

"Next," demanded Gatz. He was seated behind the desk, concentrating on a projection screen. The omnipresent cigar hung loosely from his mouth.

"Next."

In his hands he held a long wire hook which he had fashioned from a coat hanger. He edged the hook closer to a cocked mousetrap on his desk, then lashed out and snatched a small clump of cheese from the jaws of the closing trap without catching the wire. He pulled the cheese from the hook, placed it back on its platform and reset the trap for another attempt.

"Go back to the picture of the living room!" he snapped.

The projectionist clicked another slide onto the screen.

"No, before that. That's it." Gatz picked up a series of transcripts and read them silently. "And the one before that," he said as he flipped the pages.

The slides changed.

"Does it look to you like anyone's been living in those rooms?"

The projectionist turned. "No," he declared.

"Interesting," mumbled Gatz. "The place is a mess. Dilapidated. But there's something." He checked his notes. "Magnify that picture."

The projectionist changed lenses, increasing the size.

The closer view provided no new insight. Gatz sat back thinking, twirling the wire hook between the fingers of his right hand. Then he opened a folder on his desk and removed a police transcript. He studied it briefly, having examined it in detail before. He glanced at the projectionist, who sat quietly waiting for another command. "What's your name?" he asked.

"Hogan," the man replied.

"How long you been on the force?"

"A year."

Gatz studied him carefully. "When I joined they didn't allow long hair and mustaches."

The projectionist nervously fingered the well-barbered growth beneath his nose.

Gatz bit deeply into the cigar. "Last week a woman was brought in claiming she killed her father with a knife. She says she stabbed him in a room in her brownstone after she found him in bed with two naked women and he tried to strangle her. There are no signs of struggle. No body. And we know the father had been dead for three weeks at the time of the alleged homicide. We also know that the woman has a suicidal tendency, having tried to kill herself twice before." He picked up the police transcript and held it out. "And we've just discovered that seven years ago the woman walked in on her father and two women in her parents' bedroom—an almost identical situation—and he tried to strangle her then."

The projectionist stared.

"The question is what happened last week." Gatz raised his brow, prompting a reply.

"She might have been dreaming or hallucinating," said the projectionist.

Gatz nodded.

"Or she stabbed someone who she thought was her father. A setup perhaps."

"Perhaps."

The projectionist rubbed his forehead, thinking.

Gatz smiled. "Or she made up the whole story for some unknown reason."

"Yes."

"Maybe," Gatz said solemnly, shaking his head.

The room fell silent for several minutes as Gatz re-examined his notes and transcripts, occasionally glancing at the magnified view of the living room of 4 A that hung on the wall. "Damn," he finally announced, throwing the documents on the desk. "That's enough. I'll call you if I need you."

"Should I leave the machine?"

"Yes."

The projectionist nodded and left.

Gatz leaned back and cocked his head thoughtfully while relighting his cigar.

Someone knocked.

"Who is it?" he asked coldly.

"Rizzo," answered a deep baritone voice.

"Come in."

The door opened; a detective entered with several sheets of paper and a picture in his hand. He released the door and stood quietly at attention.

"What?" Gatz asked.

Rizzo stepped forward, his pot belly protruding slightly between the buttons of his white shirt. He handed Gatz the papers and picture. Then he stepped back and ran his hands nervously through his thinning black hair.

"Absolutely nothing on Chazen?" Gatz asked after looking at the papers.

"Not a thing."

Gatz handed the papers back to Rizzo but held the picture.

"Did you run this through the mug files?"

"Yes. There was nothing there either. I even had the paper analyzed and tested, hoping we could get a lead on where it was taken, but the lab came up with nothing worthwhile."

"Shit! What about the others?"

"The same. Nothing." He paused, then continued. "We had the father's body exhumed."

"And?"

"Rotting like a worm."

"Did you question the renting agent?"

"We're trying to locate her."

"Try harder!" Gatz shrugged disgustedly. "What did the landlord have to say?"

"He still maintains that no one other than the priest and Miss Parker has lived there in three years. The more I look into this, the more I think the girl is crazy as a loon. There's been no one in that building. And there was probably no one stabbed there either."

"I'm not so sure."

"Why not?"

Gatz shook his head and looked at his associate. He lifted the piece of cheese from the uncocked trap, held it up to his nose and took a deep breath.

"Why not?" he repeated. "Because something smells. Everything says that the girl is bats and that's what I don't like. Especially since Farmer's involved. There's something more here, probably buried way under the dung heap, but my nose tells me it's there, and like I told you a thousand times, my nose has never been wrong."

"But what's the crime, even if what she says really happened?"

"I don't know, Rizzo. But first we'll play detective and find the facts. Then maybe we'll be able to come up with a crime. Don't you think?"

Rizzo nodded nervously.

"You're too impatient," said Gatz, "Too quick to dismiss. You need some patience."

"Yes, sir."

"I've been waiting two and a half years to get Farmer. Two and a half years. Eating my guts out. That's patience. Without it, you'll remain a detective, third grade, forever."

Rizzo squirmed as he digested the lecture.

Gatz held up the picture of Chazen and examined it closely. "Stupid-looking old coot, isn't he?"

"Yes, sir," agreed Rizzo.

"Kinda looks like a stewed prune."

Rizzo nodded. He shuffled the papers in his hand, withdrew another from his pocket and held it up for Gatz's inspection. "Here's the list of names Jennifer Learson gave us."

Gatz took it, glanced over it quickly and returned it to Rizzo. "Anything?"

"No. No records. No one who has reason to have anything against the girl or Farmer."

"Hold on to the list. It may come in handy."

"Sir?"

"Yes?"

"Maybe we should bring in Parker and Farmer again for questioning? Perhaps under pressure we could find an inconsistency."

"No. That would be a waste of time. Unless we come up with a body, we've got nothing. I want that entire brownstone checked from top to bottom again. And all the neighbors in the other buildings who were questioned, have them questioned again."

"Yes, sir."

"I want you to be there with the other officers. Understand?"

"Yes, sir."

"And I want you to be patient."

"Yes, sir."

"And get me facts."

Rizzo shuffled nervously out the door, closing it quietly. Gatz snorted, satisfied with the effect of his authority. He lifted the phone and dialed another extension.

"Richardson, bring in the file on the Karen Farmer

case and also the notes from the last session with Michael Farmer. I think that was two days ago."

He set the receiver back in its cradle. He picked up the wire and whipped the cheese once again from under the snapping bar.

He held the cheese up to the light and thought about his major problem: No body, no case.

16

The staircase was familiar. Steeply angled, warped and eroded. But for no apparent reason it seemed even more precarious than the day she had first climbed it to the rental office. Undoubtedly her own apprehension had much to do with it. She was tense, irritable, strangely terrorized by the expectation of a confrontation with Miss Logan. Earlier in the day she had decided that the time had come for the agent to answer some additional questions, and since the agent had refused to answer the office phone, and since no home listing in any borough or suburb for a J. Logan could be found, a trip to the office became the only realistic alternative.

Staring upward for several minutes, she ran her hands over the heavy makeup she had applied to cover her pallid complexion, then climbed the staircase and tried the office door. It was unlocked; she entered. The room was precisely the way she remembered it, but empty of Miss Logan or anyone else. The dust on the desk chair indicated that no one had been

there in several days. Strange. Miss Logan wasn't
the type to have left her door unlocked or office untidy.
And what had happened to the famous associate—if
there was such a person. Allison was no longer sure
of the associate's existence, even though the agent
had referred to it, because she now had serious doubts
as to certain other representations made by the
spinster. But it wasn't just the presence of dust that
suggested the place had been abandoned. The calendar
date was ten days old and the last dated application
was the same. And she couldn't ignore the coincidence.
It had been ten days since her merry jaunt into apartment 4 A in the middle of the night.

She shuffled through the desk papers, as that seemed
the obvious thing to do, and found nothing startling
—except for a phone number with the name "Joan
Logan" written next to it. She dialed the digits, but
a voice answered and declared, "This is not a working
number. Please consult your directory for the appropriate listing." She had already. She slammed
down the phone and rubbed her eyes, which ached
constantly, looked around the office once more, then
hesitantly made her way down the staircase to the
street.

She looked down the block. Several feet away was
the entrance to a flower shop. She walked over and
stared in the window. An old woman in a dotted
dress walked around the wrapping table, glanced in
her direction and smiled. She entered.

"Can I help you?" the woman asked, brushing
away discarded stalks.

Allison glanced at the refrigerated display case
in the rear of the store. "I'd like a rose."

"Red?"

"Yes."

"I have some beautiful new arrivals," the woman
said proudly. She turned, opened the cabinet and removed a long-stemmed Tropicana. "It will take just a
minute."

Allison leaned against the wall, watching the woman

gather some greens to add to her package. "Would you know the rental agent next door?" she asked matter-of-factly.

The woman looked up. "Miss Logan?"

Allison nodded.

"Not well. She comes in every so often to buy some flowers for her office." The woman narrowed her eyes suspiciously. "Why?"

"Just curious. I'm one of her tenants. I've been trying to find her, but she seems to have left town."

"Wouldn't know," said the woman, "but come to think of it, I haven't see her in about a week—or maybe more." She pulled a sheaf of green wrapping paper from a spool.

"Her associate doesn't seem to be around either."

"Associate? I didn't know she had one."

Allison raised her brow. "I'm sure she mentioned an associate to me."

The woman shrugged. "Maybe she did. But since I've been here—and that's two years—I've never seen Miss Logan with anyone else."

"Do you know where she lives?"

The woman shook her head as she wrapped the rose in the paper. "There now," she said, holding up the order.

"How much?"

"Fifty cents."

Allison laid the money on the table and grabbed the rose. The woman held out a carnation. Allison stared.

"For your lapel," said the woman. "I see you haven't been well. This will help."

Allison touched her cheeks, then looked at her fingers. Rouge dotted the tips. She smiled wanly, grabbed the carnation and turned. "Thank you," she said. She stepped out the door, glanced quickly at the agent's brownstone, then hailed a cab to go downtown.

Michael protested. "There's nothing wrong with the food." He sat down, folded his legs and laid two aspirin on the table next to the decanter of sake, which now held the long-stemmed rose and the white carnation.

The protest. She had expected it in one form or another, though strangely he hadn't said anything negative since she had met him in the lobby of the restaurant. That did not mean that she was unaware of his conscious effort to remain positive and optimistic; rather, she had expected that too, though she knew sooner or later he would slip and provoke a confrontation. That had been the modus operandi since his return from Albany—that was the place, wasn't it? And she'd had no indication that the tension between them had subsided; in fact, if anything, it had intensified since her release from the hospital.

"The food was tasteless!" she repeated caustically, determined not to be bullied into a defensive position. She had been aggressively positive about everything since stating, upon arriving at the restaurant, that something had happened to the renting agent. And even his silence, which could have been considered an initial protest, had not changed her posture.

No taste? He wasn't surprised. One more symptom added to the growing list of malfunctions. He quickly catalogued them: Headache. Nausea. Dizziness. Loss of balance. Pain around the eyes. Blurred vision. Impaired hearing (she had complained about that earlier in the day). The fainting spell. And now the inability to register taste. The list seemed endless. He had accepted her increased mental instability. That was to be expected in the context of a breakdown and, in fact, he had expected a moderate physical decline as well. So did her doctor and the specialists. But as to the rest—very strange. They had found nothing to indicate any malfunction in her nervous system and they had run through an exhaustive series of neurological tests. But the doctors were stumped, at least as of this afternoon, when he had stopped by her physician's office to review her condition. The diagnosis: psychosomatic illness!

He couldn't argue with them; he didn't want to. But then again . . .

She leaned forward, picked up the aspirin and downed them with uncharacteristic courage. One gulp. No water. She grimaced at the taste, then looked back at him. "Satisfied?" she asked, referring to the aspirin.

"Yes," he answered. And he was. Both about the aspirin and the expected results of their dinner together. He had suggested the latter that afternoon when he had called to ask her several questions about her father's financial interests. He had just received the will and certain other administrative papers, and since he was going to represent the estate—unless he was challenged by one of the interested parties—he had felt a few preliminary questions were in order. Yet, in retrospect, he should have waited. Expectedly, she became upset at the mere mention of the documents, and he had to postpone any further questioning. But the primary purpose of the call had been to get her out of the apartment. Dinner and a walk couldn't hurt; they might even help, he had reasoned, certainly as much as the myriad of pills she had been taking without any visible improvement. If anything, the night out might alleviate the depression that had become as real a problem as her physical disability. She was wallowing in self-pity to the point where it was making him angry. When he had asked her what the doctor had said that morning about her eyes, she had replied, "He called them desiccated. Then he made some tests, but he made no aspersions as to my psychiatric condition."

"What do you mean by that?" he had asked.

"It's self-evident," she had answered, and then after he had said he would worry about her mental health after she was physically better, she had declared, "If ever."

He had challenged. "That attitude won't help you get better."

"That attitude will help me accept worse," she had concluded.

He had to end her depression, especially if the diagnosis of "psychosomatic illness" was correct, and he had no reason to doubt it.

The relaxed environment of a restaurant was a good place to begin.

"It's all nonsense!" he declared in his usual definitive way.

"What is?"

"Your strange maladies!" The word "malady" seemed more appropriate than "disease," referring to something mysterious and evasive.

"Are they?" she asked, disgruntled.

"Yes!"

"Why?"

"Because they're illusory. You're far too intelligent and aware to be doing this to yourself. You're taking strong tranquilizers and painkillers that could have any number of side effects and on top of that you're physically weak, which can only worsen any side effects that already exist. You've been running low grade temperatures and you have an overworked and overimaginative mind. Need I say more?" Logical and interesting, but for some reason he didn't quite believe it himself.

"Psychosomatic illusions are not my brand of hang-up!"

"Allison!" he warned angrily. "If you don't fight this collapse, you're going to continue having headaches and being nauseated and you'll wind up in an institution or dead."

"Amen."

He lashed out and grabbed her tightly clenched fist. "Can't you leave the damn crucifix alone for five minutes?" He pulled; she refused to let go. "Allison!" he said angrily. Her fingers dropped from the cross; he grabbed it and placed it under her shirt.

She sat back, mouth closed, eyes wide open, rigid. His frustrations were beginning to show; she was convinced he was wrestling with one essential reality, no matter how logical he wished to seem. It had been ten days since the events in the brownstone, events he had been unable to explain or understand, and no matter how hard he tried to help her relax, which he was obviously trying to do, that one simple reality would remain. Yet, she was more secure in the knowledge of his thought processes than in her own. She was uncomfortable. But she couldn't pinpoint the reason. True, the shock had much to do with it; she had trouble relaxing anywhere. But it was more than that. There was a feeling of revulsion. Maybe it was the presence of Gatz that brought the memory of the past into focus and with that memory the image of Karen Farmer. But then again, maybe not.

"We'll go for a walk," he said, breaking the silence. "It'll do you good."

She yawned, waited silently until the bill had been paid, then followed him out. "The food was delicious," she remembered to say, as though forgetting her earlier comment. He found that amusing, but he didn't laugh.

The night was clear and cold, the streets were dry. They walked the block to Broadway and Fifty-first, turned downtown and within minutes reached Times Square. Though her headache persisted, she resolved to put up with his attempt to distract her, and she followed him through a succession of parlors and shops. Eventually, they left the arcades and walked aimlessly on the side streets, stopping intermittently to examine the billboards and glossies on the walls of the darkened theaters.

Minutes short of midnight, he stopped in front of a wax museum and spoke to the dwarf who occupied the admissions booth.

"Let's go in," he said.

Allison frowned and looked away, disgusted.

"Come on," he prompted.

"Don't be ridiculous," she said.

"It'll be fun."

She looked at her watch and held it up for his inspection. "It's almost midnight. And I'm tired."

Michael glanced at the admissions booth, his expression inviting help.

"Half price for the lady," said the dwarf, the bells at the end of his pointed cap jingling in the night. He stood up on his chair and signaled Allison with his stubby hands.

She stared. The dwarf invoked images. Distasteful ones that should best have remained in the past. Tsk, tsk, tsk, she imagined him saying. The birthday party. Jezebel. Chazen. The Klotkins. The others. He would have fit perfectly. She questioned herself. Was the world evolving into a series of transitory images of that night? Had even the most familiar everyday occurrence become part and an extension of the ingenious plot against her sanity? She looked at Michael. He stared at her with the irrepressible stubbornness of Charles Chazen. His eyes said he would not relent; they would go into the museum together. She shuddered.

"What's the problem?" he asked.

"Must I be obvious?" she replied.

He smiled. "If you wish."

"Ten days ago I lived through a nightmare. I haven't been well since. I am not well now. I have no intention of becoming worse if I can help it. And the last thing I can think of to aid my state of mind is a stroll through an exhibition of depravity."

"It will be therapeutic."

She looked at him directly, angrily. "Oh, really!"

"Yes. Really."

"Michael, you can't possibly think—"

He interrupted, coaxing gently. "Are you going to run from the darkness for the rest of your life? Or live in fear of nightmares behind every wall?" He paused, his mouth twisted with concern. "I'm not going to let you do it to yourself. I'm going to make you return to normal. I told you that in the restaurant and I mean it!"

"Yes, he does," screeched the dwarf.

She looked at Michael and nodded her head. He placed money into the dwarf's outstretched hand, received two tickets, clasped her arm and pulled her through the door and down a carpeted staircase.

A red light illuminated the museum entrance. Beneath it a poster indicated the direction of each exhibit. Beyond was the darkness.

They entered.

The museum was a complex of corridors, cubicles and turns, each dedicated to a different theme. The halls were poorly lit; the exhibits highlighted by indirect lighting. The effect was startling, so much so that many of the wax forms seemed to possess a vitality approaching life.

Had she been in the museum before? She seemed to remember the layout. But it would have been a long time ago. Perhaps just after her arrival in New York. That might account for the feeling of familiarity, the sensation that she was walking through a recurring dream.

She listened to their isolated footsteps and the otherwise infinite silence. She watched their bodies move in and out of the artificial shadows. Intruders in a world of imagery. Walking slowly.

At each exhibit Michael paused to editorialize. She remained silent, unreceptive to his words.

Then she heard him laugh.

"Reminds me of Gatz," he declared.

She looked up. A deformed Caucasian stood over her, smiling insanely. "That's such a pleasant thought," she said. "I'm always amazed at how topical you are. If we were in a bakery, I'm sure you'd discuss the liberation of Auschwitz."

"Forget the cerebral exercises," he said and began to walk past the remaining statues in the exhibit, pausing to read the inscriptions. Reaching the terminus of the corridor, they cut back to the center, down another short hall and into the section devoted to torture devices. "Some pleasant toys," he commented as they began to slowly pass the glass enclosures.

"It's sick."

"It's history."

"I don't want to look at this stuff."

"Allison—"

She interrupted. "Forget the semantics and rhetoric, Michael. I want to go."

He shrugged and led her in the direction of the exit, through a dark doorway and into the main passageway, then down another side corridor.

She looked up. The sign read "Famous Murderers and Victims." Angered, she said, "What do you want from me, Michael? Blood?"

He stood motionless, silent.

There was a lot she wanted to say, but it was hopeless. The best she could do, rather than have another argument, was to close her eyes, follow him and let him get his charge. She had been stupid enough to let him take her in to the museum in the first place. She should have gotten in a cab, gone home and climbed into bed. That's where she belonged. Not here in the darkness.

The collection was typical: Jack the Ripper, Lizzy Borden, the Boston Strangler and other lesser mass murderers.

He walked slowly; she followed, keeping her head bowed, glancing obliquely at the exhibits. She was uneasy, the darkness invoking an image of the staircase in the brownstone. At any moment she expected to hear the high shrill screech of Jezebel and feel the round hairy body compress under her foot. With each step she looked out of the corners of her eyes for her father or Chazen or some other creature of her nightmare. Foolish apprehension? Perhaps. But as she turned the corner she saw it looming above her—a figure—a woman.

She screamed. He looked up at the hovering figure. He shook his head. Another murderess, so what?

She didn't even look frightening. Just an old woman with an ax.

"What's the matter?" he pleaded, grabbing her by the shoulders.

She stood paralyzed, shaking violently and staring at the figure. The inscription below the display read:

MRS. ANNA CLARK, CONVICTED MUR-
DERESS, SENT TO THE ELECTRIC CHAIR
AT SING SING, OSSINING, NEW YORK, ON
MARCH 27, 1948, FOR THE HATCHET
MURDER OF HER LOVER AND HIS WIFE.
REPUTEDLY, HER LOVER, STANTON
RIDGER, HAD FINALLY REFUSED TO
LEAVE HIS WIFE OF TEN YEARS' MAR-
RIAGE. THE MURDER WAS MRS. CLARK'S
GOODBYE. POLICE DESCRIBED THE KILL-
ING AS THE MOST GRISLY AND DIA-
BOLICAL IN THE STATE'S HISTORY. THE
MARRIED COUPLE WERE SLAUGHTERED
IN THEIR BED DURING THE ACT OF IN-
TERCOURSE.

Mrs. Clark, a friend of Charles Chazen, a tenant in her building, a missing person who had vanished into thin air several days before—dead twenty-five years, a murderess!

Allison lurched from Michael's grasp and ran into the darkness, once again unaware of her surroundings, fighting to escape, stumbling back and forth in the passageway, screaming hysterically.

As she reached the main hallway, he caught her. "Allison!" he cried. Her eyes rolled up into her head. "What's the matter?"

She choked and threw up. He stood helpless, holding her by the shoulders. Her lips were blue; a cold sweat adhered to her face. He pulled out a handkerchief and began to wipe the vomit off.

"Take your hands off me!" she screamed.

He blanched from the stench. "But," he stammered.

"Get away!" she cried again as she fought desperately to break from his grasp.

In desperation he slapped her. Then again.

A small door opened in the darkness and out popped a squat little man in overalls carrying a flashlight. The attendant. "What's going on here?" he asked. He walked across the room. "My God," he cried on seeing the vomit.

"Nothing serious," said Michael. "My friend saw something that upset her."

"Let's take her into the office."

"Right." He moved to turn her around.

"No," she said unexpectedly. "I'll be all right." She activated her hands and began to straighten her clothes.

The attendant stammered, "You're sure now?"

"Yes, I'll be fine. Could you get me a wet rag so I can wipe myself off?"

The little man scurried nervously back to the door and disappeared into the little room. Moments later he returned with a wet washcloth.

"Are you sure you're okay? You could come sit down in my office and I could call the doctor."

She braced herself against a pillar to prevent her shaking legs from giving way. "That won't be necessary," she said as she wiped her face with the cloth.

Michael stood several feet away, perplexed, unsure of what to say or do. "Let's get out of here," he suggested finally.

She nodded, then followed him up the staircase, out of the museum and down the block. Before they had reached the corner, he took her by the shoulders and turned her around.

"What happened in there?" he asked.

She did not respond.

He put his hand under her chin; she pulled away and leaned against a brick wall.

"Allison, you must tell me what happened in there!"

She turned on him viciously. "You know darn well—" She stopped. No, now was not the time for accusations. even though she knew he was aware of what she was thinking. That could come later. "It was the wax statue of the old woman," she stated. "She was one of the women at Jezebel's birthday party." She knew she had seen "Mrs. Clark" before.

"I should have realized," he said. "We're back to the house again."

How could he? she kept asking herself. Could she have been so wrong? About everything? She looked up at him. She clutched at the crucifix and declared angrily, "God damn it, what should I do? What do you want me to say? That it didn't happen or that I didn't see that woman in the house. All right, I'll say it: *It all didn't happen and I didn't see that woman in the house.* But I'm lying. I said it and I'm lying."

"That woman was executed twenty-five years ago. You know darn well she wasn't in the brownstone." He paused. "Maybe someone who looked like her, but—"

"She was introduced to me as Mrs. Anna Clark."

"There could be more than one."

"Stop," she screamed.

He exhaled deeply.

"Michael," she said, "I want to be alone."

"Why?"

"I just do. Please."

"I'll take you home and leave for a while."

"No, I want to be alone now."

"Allison, I can't let you, not after what just happened."

"I don't think you have a choice."

He was nonplused. "Allison," he said.

"No, I'm asking you again. I want to be alone. Go home. I'm going to take a cab and ride around. I'll be at your apartment in an hour. I just want to be alone to think."

He started to protest. She walked to the curb and waited, disregarding his objections. She hailed a taxi and crawled into the back seat. He started to follow. She slammed the door and locked it.

Angrily, he stepped back; the cab lurched forward. "God damn it!" he cried. Then he walked off as the taxi turned the corner and disappeared.

17

"Are you all right?" The driver turned and peered through the plastic partition. "Miss?"

The cab swerved into uptown traffic. The driver refocused his attention on the street. "I can take you to a hospital," he offered.

"Just keep driving," she said meekly.

"It's your money," he concluded. He looked through the side windows. "We've passed this spot five times already."

"Just keep going," she cried angrily.

"Yes, ma'am," he said. He pressed the brake, looked up at the bright red light that glowed overhead in the darkness and then looked in the rearview mirror at the passenger who lay sprawled on the back seat. He shook his head and shuddered. The woman looked near death, her swollen eyes reflecting a non-presence that infused the entire cab with a sensation of crawling terror. "Just drive on the West Side between Forty-second Street and One Hundredth Street," she had said, and for the last hour that was exactly what he had been doing. The girl was sick and needed a doctor. There was no doubt about it. If she suddenly croaked on the back seat it wouldn't have surprised him.

The light turned green; the taxi moved forward.

The last hour had been horrible. She had lain immobile, sprawled across the back seat, sweating like a pig, frightened, and unable to look out the windows or do anything other than choke. Her eyes seemed to be on fire; her head pounded. Relentlessly, she rubbed her scalp, gasping, her mind flashing to Michael. What was he up to? He knew the statue of the old woman was there. He had to or he wouldn't have been so insistent that they go into the museum. And if he knew that, he would know what had happened to Chazen, the lesbians and the others. And what had happened that night in the brownstone. But why? The more she thought, the more confused she became and the more nauseated.

She pulled herself up and leaned against the window. The rows of buildings and houses shot by in darkness. The cab was moving quickly, too quickly to allow her to comprehend the passing view.

"Pull over," she screamed suddenly.

"What?" he asked.

"Pull over. This is where I want to get off."

"Here?"

"Yes, stop the cab."

The tires screeched; the cab stopped.

The driver looked around the dark street and turned toward the back. "This is a bad place to get out, miss. A rough Puerto Rican neighborhood. I don't think—"

"How much?" she interrupted.

The driver shook his head and checked the meter. "Nineteen dollars and ten cents."

She dug into her pocket, removed a twenty and laid it on the protruding dish. "Keep the change," she declared.

She kicked open the door, stepped onto the curb

and looked up at an old and beaten two-story building.

The cab driver leaned partway through the open door. "Miss, you really don't look too well," he cautioned hesitantly. "Why don't you get back in the cab and I'll take you to a doctor or a hospital." He paused. "Can you hear me?"

He listened but received no reply. His patience ended, he slammed the door and sped off down the block.

She watched the cab recede into the darkness, then glanced at her hands; they were shaking, bloodless. Blinking nervously, she turned toward the curb. A brown paper bag blew across the concrete in front of her, tossed aimlessly by the swirling wind blowing off the Hudson. She looked about. A crusty mongrel romped in a pile of garbage cans nearby; the remainder of the block was empty and silent. Most of the buildings were boarded, marked for demolition. The street was gouged by potholes. Broken furniture lay on the sidewalks, decorated with graffiti written in English and Spanish.

She coughed and held her spinning head. The street seemed to fade in and out of reality. She squinted, tensing, fighting for balance. Then she turned toward an old building and looked at the inscription over the doorway: "CHURCH OF THE IMMACULATE CONCEPTION." The letters were large, cut in stone and eroded, the once sharp incisions now rounded and dull. She had seen the legend out of the corner of her eye when she had pulled herself up in the seat. It had startled her. Yet, now, standing in front of the building, it seemed as if some unexplainable force was impelling her to do something she had not done in so many years. A strange coercion, but not unprecedented in its similarity to the impulse that had eased her into her father's bedroom to retrieve the crucifix.

To enter a church! Unexpectedly, the thought was anything but repulsive. She climbed the cracked and displaced front steps and walked into the outer vestibule of the chapel. To the right was a marble bowl sparingly filled with holy water; above was a statue of the Virgin Mary.

"Hail Mary, full of grace," she murmured, staring at the Holy Mother. The words were strange, yet rapturous. "The Lord is with thee. Blessed art thou amongst women, and blessed is the fruit of thy womb, Jesus." She was surprised that she remembered the words after such long disuse. "Holy Mary, Mother of God, pray for us sinners. Now and at the hour of our death. Amen."

Trembling, she dipped her hand into the holy water, crossed herself, and walked through the chapel door.

Michael hurried down the sterile corridor and located the editor's office.

"Could you help me?" he asked as he closed the scalloped glass door behind him.

"Perhaps," the editor said. He reached over his cluttered desk and adjusted the desk lamp.

Michael sat. Glad to be off his feet. He was tired. He had been walking the streets for the last hour, thinking. "I need some information," he declared. He removed a ten-dollar bill from his pocket and dropped it on the desk.

The editor put on his glasses and regarded the ten hot appreciatively. "About what?" he asked curiously.

"An apartment ad that appeared in your Sunday section three weeks ago. I want to know who placed it. How long it ran. And any information you might have on a J. Logan, a renting agent."

The man tossed Michael a pad. "I'll need the address."

Michael smiled, pleased with the expectation of additional information. He scrawled the address and tossed the pad back on the desk.

The editor glanced at the paper, paused to shift

his glasses to his forehead, then lifted the desk phone and asked for Real Estate.

The chapel was empty. The silence unbroken. The darkness absolute, except for the light expelled by the myriad tiny candles that burned on the small altars on either side of the room.

Allison walked down the aisle, genuflected, crossed herself and moved to a kneeling position in a pew. The crucifix that hung from her neck lay securely in her hand. She looked around. Now what? What should she do? And why was she here? This place was alien. A world she had deserted. She clasped her hands together and bowed her head. Could she remember the words? "Our Father who art in heaven, Hallowed be thy name." That was it. She had said them a million times as a child. "Thy kingdom come. Thy will be done . . ." The darkness. The headache. The nausea. But the words felt so good. "On earth, as it is in heaven." Michael or no Michael, she was going to pray. She had come back. First the room. Then the crucifix. Now this. "Give us this day our daily bread." It had taken so long. "And forgive us our trespasses, as we forgive those who trespass against us." It was almost as if nothing bad had ever happened. "Lead us not into temptation, but deliver us from evil. Amen." She said the prayer three times.

Grasping the crucifix in a damp hand, she pulled herself to her feet and stepped from the pew. The soft light of the wicks illuminated her presence. She fumbled in her pocket and removed a dime. It was cold; the silver had retained the chill of the frigid night air. She dropped the money in a box, pulled a taper from a container and, crying, lit a candle for her father. Yet she could not pray for him. Instead, she stood immobilized, staring at the flickering lights.

A cold chill ran down her back as if a draft had blown through the church from a hastily opened window. She looked at the candles. They burned erect; the air was still. But she had sensed something, perhaps a manifestation of the subconscious dread of the coming self-revelation. Her skin tingled as her perception of the circumscribing darkness intensified; she could feel it pressing against her. If this had been any place other than a church, she would have cracked under the horror of the absolute emptiness. Yet it was precisely this feeling of isolation that pushed her toward the confessional.

She carefully measured her steps. "Hello," she cried. "Father." Her voice reverberated among the walls. "Hello, Father, Father."

But there was no reply.

Another step. She listened to the echo of the footsteps, mixed with the lingering vibrations of her calls.

Another step. The chill again. She had to take confession.

"Father." No answer. "Father . . . Father . . . Father . . ."

She stood silently before the booth. Pulling the drape aside, she stared at the bleak interior, the worn oak paneling and the small velvet stool. She eased into a kneeling position, bowed her head, folded her hands and whispered dolefully, "Bless me, Father, for I have sinned."

"When's the last time you were to confession, my child?"

She gasped.

"When was the last time you were to confession?" The voice was deep and authoritative.

Her heart pounded from the sudden, unexpected intrusion. The voice came from the other side of the tiny grating, the side where the priest should have been during the time for confession—or when summoned—but not at this late hour in a darkened church with no sign of life anywhere.

And he hadn't answered her calls.

She panicked, gripping the grating and moving closer.

"Are you all right, my child?"

She stammered, "Father?"

"Yes, my child, go on."

She grabbed the curtain and held it aside, ready to spring from the booth. "Father, you are a priest?"

"Of course, my child," he said benignly. "Go on."

"I . . . uh . . . how . . ."

"I'm here to listen to you."

"But you didn't answer my calls!"

"I'm here to listen to you. Don't be frightened."

"I am, Father. Very!"

"That's why I'm here—because you are frightened. I am here to rid you of your terror by hearing your confession."

She leaned her head against the wall over the grating. Was he a priest? Could she trust him? She had to. She had to reveal herself, accept penance and receive his absolution.

But why hadn't he answered when she had called?

"It's been eight years since I've been to confession, Father!" She stopped.

"Yes?" he prodded.

"I can't believe it's been so long." There was a nervous pause. "Why am I here?" she gasped.

"You are here to be heard!" replied the voice. "I am here to listen."

She whimpered, then quickly caught her breath. "I have committed the following sins: I have not been in church in eight years! I've rejected everything. But most of all Jesus Christ. I want to come back to the church and to him." She stammered unsurely. "I need to tell all that's been kept inside me for so long!"

She fell silent and wept.

"Why did you desert the church, my child?"

"Why?" she mumbled as if the question had been incomprehensible. There was another long silence, after which, fighting back tears, she began to tell him of her adolescence, her early devotion to Jesus and the beginnings of her doubts and denials. She told him of the degeneration of her father. The adultery.

The drunkenness. The beatings. The virtual destruction of her family. And she told him of that night!

Then she laid her head in her hands and coughed spasmodically.

"Is that all, my child?" he asked in a hollow-toned voice.

"No," she rasped through the grating.

"Tell me."

"Father, I have committed adultery! I didn't know he was married when I met him—"

"Yes?" he prompted.

"I began to suspect, but I didn't want to know that I loved a man who was doing to another woman what my father had done to my mother." She swallowed arduously, her saliva creeping down her throat like molten lava. "His wife committed suicide!"

"Did she?" asked the priest suddenly. "Is that what happened?"

"Yes," stammered Allison. Why should he question her admission? Did he doubt her word? Or did he know something to the contrary? No! That was impossible. "After the suicide I knew of Karen Farmer's existence." She stopped again and waited silently.

"Is there anything else, my child?"

"Else?"

"Yes, my child."

"No."

"There is! Tell me!" He was probing as if he were searching for something specific.

She held her breath. "I have tried to kill myself," she declared agonizingly, rushing her words quickly through her lips, as if hoping that they would not be heard. "Twice. Once after I found my father and the two women in bed, the second time after the death of the wife. I felt so guilty, so evil."

"Other than that?" he cried, his voice rising. "There is more! Tell me!"

Other than that? Wouldn't he want to hear more of the suicides? Or did he know everything already? Impossible!

"Tell me what else!" he commanded sternly.

"I'm frightened, scared and alone. I can't take the pain any more." She was stuttering. "Someone is trying to hurt me."

"Who is trying to hurt you, my child?"

"I'm not sure, Father. But it may be the person I thought loved me, Michael." She waited for his response; he said nothing. She continued. "I met these people in my home. I found that they didn't exist, and then one night I—"

She stopped. No, that she couldn't reveal, even though she needed his counsel.

"What happened that night?"

"I was frightened by footsteps and I ran from the house."

"And?"

"I got sick." The image of the hospital momentarily emerged, then dissolved. "Today Michael took me to a museum. There was a statue of a person whom I'd met in the brownstone and who was dead—yes, she was dead. He must have known it was there! I just can't comprehend!" She hesitated, ran her tongue over her dry lips and said, "Then I came here."

"Is that all?"

"Yes."

"There is more!" he cried angrily. "Tell me!"

She could see the wisps of his breath through the grating.

"What else happened that night you ran from the brownstone? Tell me!"

The confessional shook from the pounding of his voice.

"Tell me," he repeated loudly.

"No," she pleaded as the sweat dripped from her face.

"Speak, my child. Tell me what you must!"

"I saw my father," she blurted.

"Yes," he prompted. "Yes!" His voice was almost exhilarated.

"I stabbed him! But he was dead already!"

Silence that seemed to creep over the darkened walls like a stalking spider. Then the sound of sobbing.

She wiped her wet cheeks and leaned her head against the screen. She was exhausted, having extirpated the filth and torment. She had felt like a balloon releasing air. Yet, unlike the balloon, she hadn't shriveled.

"Is that all, my child?"

"Yes, Father."

There was nothing. For what seemed an eternity.

"You feel lost, my child," he finally said. "Since you abandoned the church and Jesus Christ, you've been lost and without guidance. And now you must come back for that guidance as you have done tonight. Sin is a dangerous thing, my child. It spawns guilt and that is as it should be. But if the sin is not recognized and absolved and the guilt is allowed to remain, it can breed suspicions and deceptions. It can materialize evils and threats that don't exist, except in the recesses of the mind. And that is why you have conjured these horrors. Because you have lived in sin, continue to do so and have not absolved yourself. You must do penance. Once that is done and you have re-embraced Jesus Christ, the suspicions will fade, the evils will disappear and the pain you talk of will haunt you no more. You must come back to Jesus Christ and believe in him. For he is good and by rejecting him you have embraced evil. You must reclaim your faith in the Holy Father. Open your heart to him. Reject suspicion and self-deception. Receive openly the love of your loved ones, and do not fashion that love into other than it is. Believe. And live your life with Christ.

"You say you were impelled to come here. The Lord works in mysterious ways, and it is difficult to understand. We cannot, and that is why we must have faith and believe that God will guide us on the path to righteousness. Only when you root out the sin, embrace Christ, believe in him and trust again will the fears, horrors and doubts disappear. Forget

the past and believe. And he will give you the inner
strength to fight the evils around you.

"To start you on your way, I want you, for penance,
to say a rosary every day and to start practicing your
religion by coming to church again, having commu-
nion, and believing in God. If at any time you have
doubts or fears, do not hesitate to come back to me
for guidance.

"Now say the Act of Contrition and I will absolve
and forgive you."

She bowed her head and started to chant.

The priest began his absolution, his back against
the wall of the booth. His bushy gray hair and long
gray eyebrows stood out in the darkness. He too was
sweating. He wiped his forehead with freckled hands
that were covered by little tufts of white hair.

"That's impossible!" Michael cried.

The editor sat back, adjusted his spectacles and
wiped his brow. "Impossible or not," he began, "no
notice was ever ordered. And no payment was ever
made." He handed Michael a newspaper section.
"And as you will see, no notice appeared."

Allison stepped through the front door of the old
church, looked up at the inscription over the doorway,
then turned away and started into the darkness.

Twenty minutes later she opened the door to
Michael's apartment, removed her coat, hung it in
the closet, then walked into the living room and glanced
coldly toward the picture window.

Michael was sitting behind his desk, hands clasped
in front of him, head bowed. His face was drawn
and pale.

She coughed, placed her bag on the coffee table
and sat down on the couch.

The room was quiet. He deep in thought, she
discreetly observant.

He raised his head and blinked. "Hello," he said

unemotionally. He seemed almost petrified, motionless.

"Yes, hello," she replied.

He looked at his watch. "It's been two hours."

"Has it?"

He nodded.

"I'm sorry."

He rested his head in his cupped hands. "I've been
worried," he said tensely.

"Yes, I can see."

"Can you?"

"I'm not blind, Michael—or crazy."

"I never said you were."

"That might be subject to argument."

He looked away, eyed the moonlight that invaded
the living room through the uncovered window and
asked, "How do you feel?"

"Better."

"The headache?"

"Gone."

"And the nausea?"

"Gone also."

"Good."

Their voices parried tonelessly, as if each were
waiting for the other to open up and submit.

"You shouldn't have run away like that. In the
condition you were in anything could have happened."

"It seems that's been my fate, no matter what my
condition."

"You were irrational."

"I made it back, didn't I?"

He mumbled a drawn-out "Yes."

She took off her shoes and threw them in the corner.
"Can I have some water?"

"You don't have to ask."

She stood, walked to the kitchen and returned
quickly, glass in hand.

"Where'd you go?"

"For a ride in a cab."

"For two hours?"

"No, I went into a church."

He frowned. "Why on earth would—"

"To pray. If there ever was a time in my life for prayer, it's now."

"Are you sure?"

"Yes. I took confession and the priest absolved me. My headache and nausea subsided. First my father's room, then the crucifix and now this. I feel like I've come back to myself. Like it hasn't been me all these years, but someone alien."

"Nonsense."

" 'Nonsense' is a catch-all for 'I don't understand.' "

"Who fell in love with me? Mother Hubbard?"

"Maybe."

"Allison!" His tone was harsh, as if he were about to attack her, but he stopped, reflected and slumped down in the chair. He sat quietly, then whispered, "You know how important you are to me."

She nodded and turned away.

"While you were gone I was thinking," he said.

"So was I."

"About the brownstone?"

"No, about you."

"Anything interesting?" Michael asked.

"Yes," she said.

He leaned over the desk. "I've had some interesting thoughts also. Maybe there's more to this than I thought. Maybe you weren't imagining everything that happened."

She turned back to him, surprised that he had finally admitted the possibility, but then again he was still under suspicion—the wax statue of the woman. Yet she kept hearing the words of the priest: Trust, believe, especially in those who love you.

"I just don't know," said Michael. "I keep going over this entire thing and something keeps kicking me in the gut. I think it's time I took a careful look at that house!"

"Now?"

"No."

"When?"

"Tomorrow. In the morning. If I have to, I'll tear the place apart."

She stared hard at him. "I want to go with you."

"No."

"Michael."

"No. That place is off limits for you."

"I said I want to come." Her voice was unnaturally stern. "And you can't stop me."

He rose, walked to the window and stared at the bright lights that shone in the silhouetted skyline. "I'll think about it tonight. More than that I won't say. But if I decide you're not coming with me, then you're not coming. And that's final." He walked across to her. "Finished?" he asked.

"Yes," she replied as she stood up and handed him the glass.

They were face to face; not more than six inches apart. Her expression was less contorted. He could sense the absence of pain. That for the first time in days she was feeling some kind of peace, both physical and mental. Yet there was still something wrong. It was her eyes. He lifted his hand and touched one of the lids with the tip of his finger. It rasped like sandpaper. But he had known that. The doctor had seen it earlier that day. It was just getting worse. He would have to call the doctor in the morning.

"I'm going out to get the paper and something to eat. Do you want to come?"

"No. I'm tired." She yawned.

He walked solemnly past her, then turned. "After you ran off, I didn't come back here right away." He stopped and thought for a moment. She looked up. "I walked over to *The New York Times* and went through the edition you used to find the apartment. There was no advertisement in the real estate section or any section for the brownstone. Nothing."

She grimaced.

"There was never a placement! But we know you saw something. Another hallucination? A big fat irrelevant coincidence? A fraud? I don't know. But I'm going to find out."

"I showed the ad to Miss Logan. She saw it!"

"Did she?" He paused. "Or did she pretend to see it?"

"I don't know," Allison said thoughtfully.

"After I examine the brownstone, I'm going to speak to her."

"If you can find her," added Allison softly.

"Yes," he stated, "if I can find her."

"Miss Logan told me the landlord placed the notice."

"His name is Caruso. Do you have the lease? His address would be in it."

"I never received a copy."

He bit his lip, reflected briefly. "I'll find him tomorrow. He may know something." Shaking his head incredulously, he turned and left the apartment.

18

Detective Gatz eased into the squad car and shut the door. "Damn car's freezing," he said.

"It'll warm up," said Rizzo.

Gatz beat his arms with his hands to speed the circulation. "Where's the lot?" he asked, stiff-jawed.

"Near Amsterdam," said Detective Richardson, seated next to Rizzo.

Rizzo started the car and raced it out of the precinct garage.

Gatz pulled a cellophane bag from his raincoat pocket. He laid it on his lap, opened the top and took out a ham and cheese sandwich, heavily bathed in mustard. "Anyone want part of this?"

Neither officer replied.

"It's not poisoned."

"We ate," confessed Rizzo.

Gatz scowled and sat back, quietly chewing, watching the car slide along the streets on the upper West Side, past the broken tenements and small shops that had resisted the onslaught of high-rise apartments, supermarkets and chain stores. The sidewalks were dirty. Broken. Choked with the odor of decay. He hated the neighborhood; he had been there too long.

"What do you think?" asked Rizzo.

"Don't know. Let's wait till we get a look. Did you get a list from missing persons?"

"I have it with me," said Richardson, indicating the bulge in his breast pocket.

"Good." Gatz turned to Rizzo. "Who's there now?"

"Jake Burstein."

Gatz smiled; Burstein was a good cop.

Rizzo pulled the car to a stop behind another police car, parked mid-block in front of a pizza parlor, where a group of spectators had gathered behind a blockade. Next to the parlor was a small lot, bordered by a gray tenement on the other side and covered with the rubble of the building that had been razed some time ago.

They got out of the car and walked over the bricks and shattered wood.

In the rear was a larger area, ringed by aging brownstones and strewn with garbage and discarded kitchen appliances. To the far right was a pile of auto bodies, encrusted with rust. A spotlight had been set up nearby, the beam focused on the cars. A swarm of police officers crawled over the refuse. Seated on a bench behind the pizza shop was a group of boys in their early teens.

Gatz approached a plain clothesman standing in the center of the debris.

"Tom," the tall man said, seeing Gatz.

"Jake," Gatz acknowledged.

"Want a look?"

"Yes," said Gatz.

"It's messy."

"Aren't they all?"

Gatz followed the officer to the autos and into the frame of the beam, which reflected brilliantly off the mangled chrome. The trunk of one of the cars was open, revealing a mutilated arm. Inside was a blood-soaked body.

"A bad way to die," said Jake, shaking his head.

"No worse than most," announced Gatz disdainfully, leaning closer to get a better look. "Any identification yet?"

"No."

"Nothing on the body? Cards? Notes?"

"No," said Jake. "But the print boys just took an impression."

Gatz toyed with the trunk lid; it rasped loudly as it moved slowly open. He bent down and examined the victim's clothes. The raincoat was badly torn as was the gray suit beneath. The black sport shirt was encrusted with blood and it too was badly mangled. He pulled out a flashlight and turned it on the wounds. They were deep and irregular, discolored and heavily scabbed. Most were on the chest and face. "How many wounds?"

"It's hard to tell."

"A guess?"

"Fifteen. Twenty. It doesn't matter much."

"Perhaps."

Jake leaned against the fender of the car. "He's been here awhile."

"How long?"

"At least a week. Could be longer. He's pretty decomposed."

Gatz ran his thumb along the victim's forehead, then rubbed his fingers together, examining them with the flashlight.

"Any trace of makeup on the body?"

Jake looked at Gatz quizzically.

"Makeup," Gatz repeated irritably. "You want a definition?"

"No. No makeup."

Gatz shrugged. "Who found him?"

Jake pointed to the tallest boy on the bench. "They were playing hide and seek. He tried to get into the trunk. It was locked. He wedged it open and out popped the arm."

"Like opening a box of Cracker Jack."

"Almost." Jake smiled. "There are blood tracks leading to the street. Want to see?"

"Later."

They stood aside as a police photographer approached and began to snap pictures of the corpse.

Jake glanced at the searchers. "A waste of time," he said. "There's so much junk in the yard it'll be impossible to tell if something was dropped by the murderer."

Gatz looked about. "Were you able to question any of the storekeepers?"

Jake shook his head. "They were all gone. We'll pick up in the morning."

Gatz motioned to Rizzo, then turned to Jake. "When can we get a blood type?"

"Very soon, they've already taken some samples."

Rizzo arrived; Gatz looked at him levelly. "Compile all the information you can on this by the morning and have it on my desk."

Rizzo nodded and hurried away.

Jake bit his lip. "Doesn't look like a robbery or gangland."

"No," said Gatz, agreeing.

"Could have been killed by a nut."

"That's the best bet."

"Any psychos on the loose?"

"Officially?" asked Gatz. "No. Unofficially the city is filled with them." He looked over the area. "No knives around?"

"None."

"And the weapon definitely was a knife?"

"Yes. A big one."

"Two-edged?"

"One."

Gatz turned and began to walk about the enclosure, thinking. Another murder. So what? Homicide was averaging about five a week. Yet he felt a peculiar twinge in his stomach, telling him that there was something special about this one. He bent down and picked up a broken doll that was losing its stuffing. He held it up, put the material back inside and shook it; the head fell off. He tried to put the head back on its post, but could not. He threw the dismembered body back and walked over the piles of beer cans, sifting vainly for a clue. Failing to find anything, he unwrapped a new cigar, shoved it into his mouth and squinted at the spotlight.

Rizzo walked over, the missing persons list in his hand. "There are a few MP's that fit the description."

Gatz nodded. "Run them down. Get pictures." He paused. "But for some reason I don't think this cat has been reported." He stood up, walked to the bench and sat next to the tall boy who had discovered the corpse. He pulled a picture of Michael Farmer from his pocket. "Son," he said, "do you play here often?"

"Yes, sir," answered the boy tensely. "At least several times a week."

"At what time?"

"Sometimes early. Sometimes late. Tonight we snuck out around eleven."

"Ever see people back here? Not the storekeepers. Or kids. You know. People?"

"Yes, sir. They bring junk."

Gatz held up Michael Farmer's picture. "Ever see this man around?"

The boy looked closely, then shook his head.

"You sure?"

"Yes."

Gatz handed the picture to the other boys; none of them had ever seen the man before either.

Gatz smiled and stood. "Stay out of old cars," he advised. "They're dangerous." He walked away and rejoined Jake and Detective Rizzo. "What time do you have?"

Rizzo looked at his watch. "Two twelve."

"I'm hungry. A ham and cheese can only hold me for so long." He puffed heavily on his cigar. "Rizzo, you stay with Jake."

Rizzo nodded. "Yes, sir," he said.

"Jake," called Gatz. "We'll speak in the morning."

"Want a quick look at the blood stains?" asked Jake.

Gatz nodded and they walked into the alley entrance.

Jake pointed to several markers that identified traces of brownish-red scratch marks. They extended halfway to the street.

"There are eight," said Jake. "Probably all from our friend in the trunk. We're checking to make certain." He looked at the trail of markers, shaking his head. "It's hard to believe that the victim was still alive when he was brought here."

Jake smiled as he tugged at his gloves. "You look as if you have some ideas."

Gatz smiled back. "Just one, and a wild one at that. I'll tell you in the morning if the additional information we get supports it."

Gatz turned and waved for Richardson. Reaching the car, he turned to the cop. "Did you get a look at the stiff's face."

"From a distance."

"He was terrified when he died. A big tough-looking guy, but he died horror-struck."

Richardson lifted his shoulders, unable to form an opinion.

Gatz started to open the door, then looked back toward the lot one last time. "Not just frightened, but horror-struck," he repeated.

They slid into the car and drove off.

Gatz slept in his office and woke at 8:00, sore and stiff-backed. But it had been better than the alternative: a quick trip home, a short nap, and a faster trip back to the precinct.

He put on his shoes and stumbled into the locker room to wash and shave. That accomplished, he grabbed a cup of black coffee and walked back to his office to wait for Rizzo.

He had barely finished half the cup when Rizzo arrived with a list of the lab results and other particulars on the corpse. He read them carefully, fascinated. He couldn't have asked for more interesting information; it was almost too good to be true.

"You familiar with this guy?" he asked.

"No," Rizzo replied blankly.

"I am," said Gatz. "And the killer couldn't have found a more deserving victim."

Rizzo backed off. "Do you think—"

Gatz interrupted. "Think? I know, but I need facts. I want everything that you can dig up on this character. And everything he has done for the last five years. Use informers if you need to, but get it."

"Yes, sir," Rizzo said and left.

Gatz smashed his fist on the desk; then he sat back and smiled.

19

"The man was standing like this with his back to you?"

"Right."

"And then what?" asked Michael.

"I approached him from the rear."

"Where were the women?"

"I guess in bed."

"Guess?"

"I didn't see them until I started to stumble out of the room."

"Okay, show me."

She extended both hands: one to simulate the presence of a knife, the other the flashlight. She studied her approach, recalled her exact movements and deliberately retraced her steps across the floor.

"As I tapped him on the shoulder," Allison said, "I jiggled the flashlight again and it went on. He turned, I saw who he was and I panicked. I fell backward trying to get away and I landed there in the corner."

He walked to where she had fallen among the cobwebs and dust. He ran his hand along the floor, leaving a trail of five fingers. "The police left so many footprints that any imprints made that night are indistinguishable," he said thoughtfully. "Look, I want you to trace your every move from this spot until you left the apartment."

"I'm not sure I remember."

"Try."

She nodded, unsure of her ability to re-enact the events. She walked to the corner where he was standing and sat on the floor.

"I guess I was sprawled somewhat like this." She extended one leg and tucked the other beneath her. "When I saw him move toward me, I pulled myself up and spun around. The flashlight was waving wildly and that's when I saw the women in bed, I think." She walked backward toward the hall. "When I finally straightened up, I ran as quickly as possible into the hall, colliding with the wall several times, and then I somehow made it into the living room."

He stopped halfway down the hall, turned, studied the walls and floor and joined her at the edge of the living room.

"Nothing here," he concluded. "Now what happened?"

"I knew he was behind me, because I heard his footsteps. I stumbled and hit that armchair and fell over backward onto the floor. The chair toppled over on me. I heard the door slam—I had left it partially open—and I saw him standing there." She pointed. "I pushed the chair off, jumped up and ran for the door, but collided with him in the middle of the room." She walked to the center of the rug and stopped. "Right here."

He stepped to the spot and assumed the position of the "father."

"He grabbed me by the hair and then by the crucifix, choking me. I didn't know what was going on or what I was doing. Everything was spinning." She paused, lowered her head, and then murmured incredulously, "I was fighting to save my life."

He nodded, biting his nails.

"I started stabbing him with the knife. I remember the blade going up and down and I remember the feeling of it going into something. And then there were the screams. I felt myself falling, but that's it.

Nothing else. The next thing I remember was the hospital."

He kneeled down over the point of contact and examined the floor with his hand. "If there had been the slightest trace of blood here the police technicians would have found it."

"Could it have been washed away?"

"No. The chemical analyses would probably have detected even the residue."

He jumped to his feet, walked to the armchair and sat down. Calculating the dimensions of the room, he attempted to find a missing key, if there was one. Then he rose again, went to the bedroom hallway, turned and walked slowly from there to the apartment door, carefully counting his steps. He returned to the hall entrance and performed a similar maneuver, from there to the chair, where he sat down again.

"One thing puzzles me. You say that he started moving toward you very slowly and that he had difficulty walking."

"Yes."

"His leg was partially paralyzed?"

"Yes."

"Show me how he walked."

She stiffened, hesitated, then took three or four painful steps with her right leg dragging behind. "Very slow and awkward."

"Are you trying to tell me that by the time you had fallen over the armchair he had limped into the room, crossed the entire floor—approximately twenty paces—and shut the door?"

"I guess so."

"No, it doesn't make any sense. First of all, why close the door in a deserted house, and secondly, he couldn't have possibly gotten to the door that quickly, according to what you've told me. I would have trouble and I'm not only pretty agile, but I'm not dead."

"That's very funny, Michael. Hilarious."

"I don't mean to be funny. Assuming you did kill

someone, I think he came into the apartment during the melee. But remember, I said 'assuming.' There's no body and no blood. And if someone was in the other room, and again I say 'if,' he wasn't the person you stabbed."

She reflected, then nodded, accepting the possibility.

"That still doesn't solve anything," she said, sitting down on the dusty sofa.

"If that's the way it happened, it might."

"How?"

He bit his lip. "I don't know yet."

"If I did stab someone who came in, what about the figure in the bedroom and the women?"

He shrugged, yet his expression indicated he was exploring a possible answer to the question.

He stood up and began to pace the room. Then he walked to the mantel and ran his hand along the top. The grime was thick, evenly layered and laced with spider webs. He looked at his palm, blew off most of the dust and then finished the job by rubbing his hand against his pants.

"What are you thinking about?" she asked.

"The facts! There's no body, no blood, no evidence of struggle, no evidence of people in the room, no sign of the lesbians or Chazen. Yet we have an assumption: You stabbed someone who came to the door. Then where is the body? Reasoning logically? Someone removed it, cleaned up the blood by some meticulous means unknown to me and covered all footprints with dust." He glanced at Allison and smiled. She remained impassive. "Who removed the body? The imaginary people in the bedroom?"

"They were real," she declared.

"Or the real people in the bedroom?"

Allison sat forward on the couch.

"If they were real, where did they go?"

Allison stood and stared at him blankly.

"Let's see if we can get into Chazen's apartment."

They walked to the door, which he opened; it creaked from years of disuse.

They climbed the staircase to apartment 5 B and tried the door. It was locked. He withdrew a set of keys from his pocket, inserted the skeleton and opened the lock.

"Opulent," he declared with a note of humor in his voice. It was more a statement of frustration than anything else. He kicked at the dust, walked to the middle of the room, lifted the solitary chair, sat and looked around him. "I wouldn't call this a well-planned library. Plenty of books, one seat."

"The furniture is here somewhere," she said as she moved by him, looked out the window and peeked into the kitchen. "Maybe even the people. The table was there." She pointed. "The Gramophone was there. Plants everywhere. The bookcase—" Her eyes constricted. "The bookcase was here." This time she remembered. "There were plants all over it, but it was here."

She walked to the shelves and blew the dust off the third row of titles, dust that had resettled since she and Miss Logan had inspected the room. She reached up and removed a blue-covered book. *The Charterhouse of Parma* by Stendhal. An extremely old version published in 1839, an original edition, the book nearly in shreds. She weighed it gently in her hand, then she threw it on the floor next to Michael. "Enjoy." Unmindful of their condition, she pulled the books off the shelves, inspected them briefly, then tossed them to the floor. Several fell by themselves.

"Here's the winner. *The Techniques of Torture* by Alard."

He extended his hands; she tossed the book. He caught it and thumbed through the pages.

She removed another volume, examined the cover and then, holding the binding securely to prevent the loose and detached pages from falling, opened the book. She sifted the pages quickly. "You'll like this one for variety."

"Let me see."

She tossed the book.

He examined the cover and then turned to the inside. "What do you mean by variety?" he asked.

"All the pages are the same," she replied.

He looked again. The book seemed perfectly normal, normal to the extent that the pages were numbered consecutively and each page contained different words and sentences.

"Well?" she asked.

He looked at her puzzled. "There's nothing strange about this book."

She lashed out and grabbed it. "What do you mean?"

"Just what I said."

She re-examined the pages; they were still identical. "They are all the same!" she cried, handing it back.

He reviewed the volume, then closed the cover and placed it in his lap. "Very interesting," he said, glancing at the crumbling shelves. "Obviously, one of us is seeing something that isn't there, or just lying."

She felt the blood rush to her head. It would be just like him to admit what he was doing at the same time he was denying it. Perhaps her suspicions were justified. As of yet, he still had not exonerated himself, though she had to admit that so far he had been incriminated by what could be mere circumstance.

"Still, this isn't that surprising," he said cautiously. "You saw the apartment advertisement when there was nothing in the paper. Perhaps what you see here is a different manifestation of the same phenomenon."

"I don't like the word 'phenomenon,'" she said. "It implies a natural occurrence."

"Call it what you will." He took a pen from his shirt and ripped the front page from one of the discarded books. He handed both to her.

"I want you to write down exactly what you see—word for word."

She continued to stare blankly, then crossed to the lone chair and sat. She looked over the first page, compared it to the following and carefully began to transcribe each letter on the paper.

Michael knocked.

He waited and knocked again. There was no answer. The dark brown door bearing the lettering 5 A remained closed.

"I still have a feeling there might be a connection between the priest, our disappearing friends and your 'hallucinations.'" He raised his fist once again, hesitated and let it fall meekly against the door. Allison listened to the faint tap, bowed her head and leaned against the banister, certain that this final perfunctory summons would go unanswered.

"Maybe he knows someone's here but can't answer the door," she suggested.

"Maybe," he said. "But I think he just prefers to remain undisturbed." He took the skeleton key out of his pocket.

"Michael," whispered Allison nervously, indicating her disapproval.

"Quiet," he commanded.

He slipped the key into the lock and twisted, but nothing happened. Shaking his head, he pulled out the key and returned it to his pocket.

"Does anyone ever come to take care of him?" he asked.

"No one," she replied. "All I know is that the rent is paid by the Archdiocese of New York."

Nodding, he turned her around and led her to the staircase, which they descended slowly, acutely aware of the old paneled walls, the sturdy banister that guarded the worn and perilous staircase, and the empty, silent apartments on every floor that perhaps concealed a terrible truth. They walked hand in hand, eyes riveted on the steps before them and ears listening for any sound that might indicate an intrusion into the deafening silence in which they moved.

Allison performed the various rituals she had instituted in the weeks past. She stopped in front of the door to apartment 4 A, stared nervously, then quickly scurried for the safety of the staircase to the third floor. Apartment 2 A. She hesitated before going farther, repelled by the fear that the lesbians might appear at any moment. But Michael was there. Whether or not he had been involved in the events, nothing would happen now. So the hesitation was momentary and she continued walking behind him down the main staircase where she stopped, as usual, and tested the still sturdy banister before stepping onto the tiled lobby floor.

Outside Michael pulled a monogrammed white handkerchief from his pants pocket and blew his nose. "I want you to go back to my apartment and wait," he said. "I'm going to have this translated." He held the piece she had transcribed from the book. "Then I'm going to see if I can locate Miss Logan and the landlord."

"Can't I go with you?"

He shook his head. "Get some more rest. As soon as I'm done I'll come back to the apartment. It shouldn't take me more than an hour or two." He touched her cheek gently, supportively; she did not respond. "Let me get you a taxi."

They walked to the curb where they waited for several minutes and then hailed the first empty cab that turned down the street. He kissed her cheek as he opened the rear door. "Seventeen East Seventy-first Street." The driver nodded; the cab lurched forward.

She rolled down the rear window and watched Michael disappear into the distance. She blinked and turned her eyes to the windows on the fifth floor. Yes, there was something there. An outline. The old priest. Sitting as he had been for— She did not know how long. Father Matthew Halliran. He had to have had something to do with the events in the brownstone. What, she didn't know. But something. She continued to stare out the window as the sun angle changed. Something glistened—a metal object—but only momentarily. Then the cab turned the corner.

20

The drive to the Morningside campus of Columbia University was direct and short. Michael paid the driver and walked through the main gate onto the lower campus. He consulted a piece of paper and turned left, away from the Broadway side of the quadrangle toward a large building that bordered Amsterdam Avenue. He entered and read the glass-enclosed directory. Over a list of eminent names was the department title: "LITERATURE AND FOREIGN LANGUAGES." He consulted the paper again and searched the list of faculty members. "GREGOR RUZINSKY." The name was near the bottom. Probably Polish. An associate professor.

He walked up the staircase, located room 217, opened the old wooden door and entered a small unevenly lit office.

Behind a desk was a man in his early thirties. Ivy-Leaguish. Incurably unkempt. "Come in," Ruzinsky said belatedly.

"Thank you," Michael replied, turning to a chair.

"I assume you are the gentleman who phoned me before."

"Yes."

"Very interesting."

"What?"

"You. I have a hobby at which I have grown quite proficient."

91

"And that is?"

"Conceiving a predetermined image for an unknown voice. You are precisely as I pictured, most remarkably so, even your clothes. But—" He paused.

"But?"

"I detect an urgency in your expression that did not come through the phone. That is most peculiar."

"Are you sure there's an urgency?" Michael asked, fascinated by the man's intuitiveness.

"Yes," Ruzinsky said somberly.

"What else can you see?"

The man smiled. "Would you like some tea? It's almost ready." He turned about in his swivel chair and reached for a teapot that sat on a small portable burner.

"No, thank you," said Michael.

"You should try some. A very rare blend from southern China. Exquisite taste and aroma. Are you sure you wouldn't like to try it?"

"I've never been much of a tea drinker. Thank you anyway."

Ruzinsky motioned to the pot. "Then you wouldn't mind?"

"Of course not," said Michael, surprised that the man would ask for permission to drink tea in his own office. But then again, Europeans were very proper. He wondered what the man would have done if he had objected.

Ruzinsky carefully drained the tea through a strainer. "It's more difficult than using a samovar," he declared as he lifted the steaming cup. "Absolutely delicious. There's something in this tea that relaxes me and allows me to think more clearly." He placed the cup on the desk, picked up a pack of Pall Malls and offered them to Michael. "Smoke?"

"No, thank you. I don't smoke."

"No vices at all?"

"Not quite. Let's just say I don't smoke."

Ruzinsky regarded the red pack, half empty, and threw it to the side. He opened the desk drawer, removed a hand-carved pipe, filled it with tobacco, lit it and sat back in his chair. "Now what may I do for you? You mentioned something about a translation."

"And you said you could do it."

"I did, assuming that it is what you say it is. Might I see the material?"

Michael reached into his pocket and removed Allison's transcription. It was rumpled; he laid it on the desk, pressed out the wrinkles with the palm of his hand and passed it to the curious professor, who moved the lamp slightly and perused the document.

"Very interesting," Ruzinsky said. "A form of early Latin, used well before the reigns of the Caesars, maybe three or four hundred years before. You only find it in very old and selective writings."

Now how had Allison come up with something like this? "Can you translate it?"

Ruzinsky suffered the affront and replied indignantly, "Of course. It is simple compared to other extinct languages and idioms. In fact, if you have several minutes, I will work on it now. It shouldn't take too long."

"I have all the time in the world."

Ruzinsky removed a yellow legal-size pad from the desk drawer, sharpened his pencil and attacked the task with enthusiasm. His attention was absolute; he huddled over the desk like a nearsighted monk, eyes only six or seven inches above the paper and hands held ready for execution. There was a preciseness about his manner that assured Michael that the man would do his best to make the translation as accurate as possibe. Several times the scholar crossed out a word or phrase, studied the transcription and substituted a more appropriate English equivalent. Each time he would say, "No, no. That's not right," and then, after some study, would exult, "Ah, much better, much better."

It took him slightly under ten minutes to finish,

during which time Michael fidgeted nervously, looking at books he had never heard of, let alone read,
and doodling aimlessly on a piece of paper that
Ruzinsky had given him after he had caught him writing on his desk.

"Are you almost done?" Michael asked after some
time.

"Yes, just one more word, I think, right here
and—good! The remainder are repeats of the first segment."

Michael sat forward in his chair, expectant. Ruzinsky held out the translation and read:

"To thee thy course by Lot hath given
Charge and strict watch that to this happy Place
No evil thing approach or enter in."

"Is that all?" he asked.

"Yes," replied the scholar.

"But the page was—"

Ruzinsky interrupted. "The phrase was repeated
five times."

"I see," said Michael, nodding. " 'Happy Place,' "
he repeated thoughtfully.

Ruzinsky began to straighten the desk.

"What does it mean?" asked Michael.

"I don't know," said Ruzinsky, shrugging. He
paused. "Though I can't help but feel it is familiar."

"Yes."

"Maybe it's from some piece of literature, at least
that's what a little voice keeps telling me."

"What piece?"

"That I wouldn't know. I'm a linguist, not a historian
or literary expert."

"Ask the voice."

"Americans have such a piquant humor," he
replied, unmoved. "As it is, I read very little that
is not written in Latin, Greek, Hebrew or Chinese,
and that piece is not from anything I'm familiar
with."

"Who might know? Someone in the literature department?"

"Perhaps, but I'm sure most have left for the weekend. Let me see." He consulted his directory. "Mr. Scheffer or Mr. Paulson might know." Ruzinsky turned and picked up the phone. He dialed one extension, waited, redialed, waited again, then hung up concluding that the man was not in. He consulted the book again for the other number and then dialed once more. No one was there either.

Michael stood and began to pace about the room.

"Where did you find the passage?" asked the professor.

"Where? An old book."

"Can I see it?"

"I don't have it with me."

"That's unfortunate. It might have proven helpful. Why don't we do this? Leave the translation with me, and on Monday I will speak with someone who might be able to identify it, that is assuming it is from some piece of recorded literature. I will call you."

Michael nodded; he had no choice, even though he did not relish the prospect of waiting until Monday for his answer.

"Don't you know anyone else we could ask about the passage? It's important."

The professor shook his head. "I'm sorry."

Michael picked up the translation and copied it on another piece of paper. Then he folded it in thirds, added the original transcription and put both in his pocket. "Thank you for your help. Here's my number," he said, writing it down. "If you do find out anything on Monday, please call me."

Ruzinsky placed the paper in his pocket. As Michael turned to leave, the professor smiled and said, "It was my pleasure."

Stepping into the hall, Michael walked down the staircase and onto the campus, his thoughts weighing heavily. He drew the paper from his pocket and studied it. Interesting, but meaningless. What puzzled him more than the meaning was the source. Allison! If she was going to dream up something, why such gibberish. And in old Latin. It had no relation to anything that had happened or to anything she had said. But then again, if she had perceived it, it must have had some meaning. And there must have been a coincidental stimulus.

He studied the paper again. Who was charged? She? To watch what happy place? Certainly no place they had been around recently. The brownstone happy? Ridiculous. And what evil thing? He knew no answer; each question led to another puzzle.

He left the campus, found a telephone booth, pulled another piece of paper from his pocket and dialed the number that was written in red ink. He waited as the phone rang several times. Then there was a click and a recorded voice said, "This is William Brenner. I am not in at the moment, but should be returning soon. Please leave your . . ." He hung up and called Miss Logan's agency. There was no one there. He dialed information, and asked for the number and address of David Caruso, the landlord. The operator replied that both were unlisted. He dropped the phone and leaned against the glass and metal frame, thinking. He wanted to speak to Miss Logan, but she was obviously unavailable. He also wanted to talk to David Caruso. But to do that he needed the owner's address, which, unfortunately, according to Allison, was not posted in the hall of the brownstone. He could ask the police, but they probably would not tell him and even if they did, there would be questions. He stepped out of the booth, concluding that he would have to locate the owner by more circuitous means.

He crossed the Broadway uptown lane onto the central mall, entered the 116th street station of the IRT, took the subway to Foley Square and located the Bureau of Licenses, where he examined Joan Logan's license registration. Everything seemed in order; there was nothing to indicate anything clandestine, nor was there any indication of a registered associate. He also stopped at the Department of Taxation, where he culled David Caruso's address from the tax rolls. From there he went uptown to Miss Logan's office. Having verified Allison's observations, he then taxied back across the park to the west side to David Caruso's apartment, only to be told by the doorman that the landlord had left earlier in the day after the departure of a Detective Gatz.

The last hour had been hectic. He took a deep breath, concluding that he would try to get back later to speak to the landlord. The chance was slight, but the man might know something or at least admit something he would be reluctant to tell the police.

He began to walk up the street, but hesitated suddenly as a vivid image crossed his mind. He shook his head, but the thought persisted.

Father Matthew Halliran.

21

The cab had just exited the Park on Seventy-ninth Street when Michael ordered it to the curb. He sat for several minutes deep in thought while the meter ticked away and the cab driver fidgeted; then he canceled the order for 17 East Seventy-first Street and ordered the driver down to Fiftieth Street and Madison.

While crossing the park he had examined the possibilities. Sifting the facts and clues, he had laid them one on top of the other, and then shuffled them, hoping to arrive at a rational theory that might accommodate the past events. He had found nothing. Frustrated, he had questioned where to start. But all he could think about was the priest. If there was something sinister, the priest had to be involved. How and why he couldn't guess. But yes, he was involved!

The cab stopped on the corner of Fiftieth. He stepped out, slammed the cab door, then looked up at the massive old building that filled the entire block between Fiftieth and Fifty-first streets. Across the entrance in bright gold letters were the words "ARCHDIOCESE OF NEW YORK."

The chapel was small.

A priest kneeled in front of the altar, his hands clasped and his head bowed.

Save for the low hum of his liturgy, the room was quiet. The priest's attention to his prayers was absolute. Even the sound of the rear door opening and closing did not break his concentration.

Michael walked to the front pew and sat down.

The priest murmured the final words, crossed himself and got up.

"Monsignor Franchino?" Michael asked.

The priest nodded. "Can I help you, Mr. Farmer?"

"Yes, you can," Michael replied and after a pause added, "I hope I didn't interrupt."

"No," assured the priest. "I was informed of your arrival."

"You are a difficult man to find. I must have spoken to a dozen people before one led me to you."

"I am a very busy man. And a very personal one. I prefer to perform my services for God in an atmosphere of anonymity." The priest stepped to the pew and laid a gentle hand on Michael's arm. "Shall we go to my office?" he asked.

They left the chapel, climbed the stairs to the first floor and walked down a busy corridor. The activity was surprising—what one would expect in a brokerage house or large corporation rather than in the offices of the Archdiocese.

"The church supports many of its clergy who no longer live in rectories or convents," explained Franchino. "It is our obligation to sustain those who have given their lives to our Savior, Jesus Christ."

"I see," said Michael, his mind marveling at the maelstrom of organized movement.

The monsignor stopped in front of an office. Opening the door, he said, "Who is the particular individual in question?"

"A Father Matthew Halliran."

Franchino walked to his desk, turned, and reflected. His expression remained blank, suggesting his inability to place the name. "Father Matthew Halliran?"

"Yes, Halliran. H-A-L-L-I-R-A-N."

The priest pulled up his chair and sat down. He motioned with his hand toward the handsome seat which stood directly across from him.

Michael sat.

The office was large and lavishly furnished, befitting a man of the monsignor's position and stature. A beautifully carved crucifix hung on the wall. On one side was a picture of the pope, on the other the cardinal. The resemblance was remarkable, as if by some grand design God had chiseled the features of his disciples from the same pattern. Even Franchino's face was somewhat . . . Michael shook his head. His mind was wandering, perhaps prompted by the surroundings. But right now he had to keep his thoughts focused. He examined the rest of the room. It consisted of two more chairs, a coffee table, a series of file cabinets and one heavy lead cabinet immediately to the right side of the desk that seemed to be double locked.

"Halliran?" the priest repeated. "No, the name isn't familiar."

"The address is Sixty-eight West Eighty-ninth Street, and he lives on the fifth floor.

"Let me look in the files."

Monsignor Franchino stood up, stretched his long athletic body and walked to the filing cabinets, from which he removed a master folder marked "G–J." He returned to the desk and riffled through the contents until he located the specific manila folder in question. He removed it.

"Matthew Halliran," he stated, reading the information on a long statistic sheet. "Yes, I recall the man now. It's been years since I've dealt with any matter connected with him. You see, most of the accounts are not handled from this office. They are kept up to date and are systematized so that the work may proceed automatically. Now let me see ... Matthew Halliran. Lives at Sixty-eight West Eighty-ninth Street in Apartment 5 A. As I remember, a kindly gentleman."

"I wouldn't know," said Michael. "I've never seen him. Nor has the renting agent or the present landlord."

"Mr. Farmer, your clients should try to maintain some type of contact with their tenants."

"Only if the tenant is willing. The priest seems to prefer a constant view from the window."

"I see." Franchino looked back at the file. "A view from the window would be difficult for Father Halliran. These records indicate he is blind."

"I meant that he sits in the window all day and night."

The priest nodded, satisfied with the correction. He continued to review the file. "No living relatives. Was pastor at the Church of the Heavenly Angel in Flushing, Queens, for many years; retired in 1952 after the congregation was disbanded and the church torn down. It seems that his decision to leave the church was prompted by a slowly deteriorating mobility caused by a chronic case of palsy. Father Halliran has, obviously, led a very difficult life. It is understandable that he would become sedentary."

Franchino dug into his desk and removed a long computer print-out. He searched the list carefully and circled something in red. "I think you can see from the listing that your client must have been mistaken." He handed the list to Michael. "There are no errors in the rental payments."

Michael glanced at the sheet. "Could there possibly be a mistake?"

Franchino shook his head. "I doubt it. In fact, I'm sure. As I said, we are very organized here."

"I don't see how the landlord could have made such a mistake." Michael handed the list back. "I'm terribly sorry."

Monsignor Franchino smiled with forced affability. "No, please. Landlords are often negligent in their recording practices. The good Lord sorts these things out eventually."

"No doubt," agreed Michael. "Could I look at the priest's file for a moment?"

Franchino hesitated, then handed the manila folder to him. Michael sat back, read the file and then handed it back to the monsignor.

"You don't have any other information on the man?"

"No, but even if I did, I don't see the relevance."

"Just curiosity. I've been closely associated with the landlord and the building for many years and I still know nothing about one of our prize tenants."

Michael studied the room. Could some additional information be locked in the files? Something that might strip the mystery away from Father Halliran? But even if there was something, Franchino certainly wouldn't volunteer the information.

"No, there's nothing," concluded the monsignor.

Michael stood up. "I'll see that the rent records are corrected," he said apologetically.

"We will appreciate that," responded Franchino.

"Thank you," said Michael uncomfortably.

"It was my pleasure. Let me show you out." The

monsignor walked around the desk and across to the door.

"Oh, I almost forgot," said Michael. "Would you know a gentleman named Charles Chazen?"

The priest thought for a moment. "No, should I?"

"Perhaps."

"And who, may I ask, is he?"

"A neighbor of Father Halliran. He lives down the hall in apartment five A."

"As I said, it's been years since I've had any contact with the man, let alone his neighbors."

"You should advise the good father to contact Mr. Chazen, if he hasn't already. A perfectly charming old gentleman. Would make a wonderful companion."

"I appreciate your concern. I will note that for my staff. Good day now."

Michael hesitated. "There's one more thing, if I might ask your advice."

"Yes."

He searched his pocket. "There's this inscription I had translated from the Latin." He unfolded the paper. "I was wondering if it might be familiar to you, from some religious writing or something." He held it out.

Monsignor Franchino took the paper and held it in the light. He blanched, his lips tightening. Recognition! Without a doubt! The priest quickly assumed his earlier composure. But there *was* something. And perhaps the clues were in this room.

"No, it's not familiar."

"Are you sure?"

"Yes."

"It does seem religious in its language."

"Yes and no. It probably isn't. In any case, I've never seen it before."

"Never mind," said Michael as he left. "Thank you for your trouble."

The priest shut the door and stood frozen. Nervously, he rubbed the little tufts of white hair on the back of his freckled hands. Then he began to tremble. He crossed himself and stepped back.

His expression constricted; it was one of terror.

22

Monsignor Franchino and Father Halliran were the sole focus of Michael's thoughts as he raced down the hall toward his apartment and opened the door. "I just—" He stopped, hatred mirrored in his eyes. "What are you doing here?" he asked angrily.

"Lovely apartment," said Gatz. He was standing in front of Michael's desk. He lifted Michael's gold pen, held it in the light, read the inscription, then replaced it in the holder.

"That doesn't answer my question."

"I like the coloring. The style of furniture. I was telling Miss Parker that after living in a boardinghouse for so many years, I—you know, a cop, especially one who's been busted by a departmental commission, doesn't make much money and can't afford more—I come into a place like this and I can't help but be impressed."

"What do you want?"

Gatz picked his teeth with a plastic toothpick. "I'm glad you've returned. I've been here waiting patiently for"—he looked at his watch—"a half an hour on the city's money. I couldn't have waited much longer.

In fact I was about to leave." He placed the toothpick in his shirt pocket.

Allison writhed uncomfortably on the couch.

"Don't let me keep you," said Michael. He threw the door keys on the dining room table and walked into the living room.

"I wouldn't think of leaving now. That would show a lack of manners."

"Please. A show of manners would be unexpected. I'll even walk you to the elevator."

"You're so considerate you sometimes amaze me!" Gatz turned. "That's Detective Rizzo. I don't think you two have even met."

"Fortunately not!" said Michael, glaring at the impassive detective.

Rizzo shifted a packet of papers from his left hand to his right and extended them toward Gatz.

"Not yet," commanded Gatz.

"What do you want?" asked Michael impatiently.

"Want? Some friendship and conversation." He lifted a judge's gavel and rapped it against the desk. "Good wood," he remarked, then moved around, sat down in the chair, raised his legs and laid them on the finished walnut. "Me and Rizzo were down in the Tombs this morning, so I couldn't help but think of the courageous district attorney who once had so many friends down there behind the bars. Still smells pretty bad. Remember that stink? Sure you do."

Michael interrupted. "Take your feet off my desk."

Gatz waited, took out a cigar, then removed his feet. "Rizzo, I never told you about Mr. Farmer. A very famous D.A. but he didn't like the way the police handled the animals in the cages. In fact, I don't think he liked the police at all. He was very tough in court after someone else did the dirty work. Very thorough. And apparently honest, if you disregard the fact that he was accepting bribes from some nasty people in plea bargaining sessions." Gatz smiled thoughtfully. "Never could prove the bribe angle." He turned to Michael. "But that was a long time ago. Mr. Farmer's come a long way!" Gatz rose, walked around the desk and stood in the middle of the room. "This chair is uncomfortable. I hope you don't mind if I stand?"

"I don't mind if you die."

"You have a one-track mind. Death and more death. That's very unhealthy!" He waved his finger at Michael. "You've got to think about less violent subjects. Then you might stay out of trouble."

"Cut the humor! Say what you have to, then get out or don't say anything and get out now!"

Gatz backed off and lifted his hands, palms outward, as if to ward Michael off. "I just want some conversation, like I said." He turned to Rizzo. "Isn't that right?"

"Yes, sir."

"Then talk!" demanded Michael.

"Perhaps some subjects of current interest. Like the new city taxes. A paycheck ain't worth nothing no more! Or the hospital strike. Interested?"

"No."

"Perhaps"—Gatz tapped his lower lip with his index finger—"a body that was found in a vacant lot on the upper West Side, though he wasn't killed there. Interested?"

"No."

"Come now. This is a very intriguing subject. What's more interesting than a stiff?"

Michael silently stared.

Gatz continued. "A detective. William Brenner. Mutilated. Seventeen stab wounds. Quite dead!"

"So?"

"That's what I said," added Allison. "I don't see what that has to do with us."

Gatz smiled. He walked to the bar and poured himself a drink. Scotch. With a little soda. Two ice cubes. He raised the glass, toasted, "To your health," then sipped the whiskey and watched them. He laughed to himself. He knew what Farmer was thinking. The nerve of that cop bastard. To walk to my bar and grab a drink without an invitation. The thought of an angered Michael Farmer was pleasing. He would remember to refill the glass.

"It seems," said Gatz, "this Mr. Brenner specialized in some strange activities. Drug smuggling. Arson. Murder. Rather unique vocations, don't you think?" He snapped his fingers. Rizzo sifted through a packet of photos, pulled an eight-by-ten and handed it to Gatz, who walked to Michael and shoved it in his face. "Notice the wounds. Single-edged knife. The killer was right-handed. Look at his face. He didn't die of pleasure. You wouldn't have known him, would you?"

"No," said Michael.

"Of course not. What would an ex-assistant district attorney be doing with a guy that the police have been trying to bust for the last five years?"

"Frustrating, isn't it?" said Michael.

"Yes, it is." Gatz scowled. "Sooner or later he would have been caught. Too bad someone killed him first." He turned to Allison. "Did you ever hear Brenner's name before?"

"No."

"You're sure now?"

"I'm sure."

Gatz stepped to the couch and handed her the picture. She studied it briefly and looked away in disgust.

"Rizzo," Gatz said, as he handed the picture back, "take good care of this."

"Yes, sir."

Gatz took a deep swig of whiskey and began to pace again.

"Mr. Brenner's blood type was AB, Rh negative. Interesting, isn't it?"

"You missed your profession. You should have been a vampire."

Ignoring Michael, Gatz added, "And it should prove even more interesting after they break down the other components and match them against the blood that was found on Miss Parker."

"I can't wait," observed Michael.

Gatz readied himself for a few conclusions. "Let us look over a few of the facts." He drew a mousetrap from his jacket and cocked the spring. "Miss Parker has her story, which we're all familiar with, and she still clings to it right?"

"Yes," said Allison.

"Now we mix it together with the background of some of the individuals involved and add the major ingredient which up to now has been missing—a body—and what do you think we might have?"

"I couldn't guess in a thousand years."

"Murder."

"Nonsense."

"Murder. Or something like it."

"Something like it? Like what? Passing a red light or parking in a school zone?" Michael was livid.

Gatz looked at his empty glass, walked to the bar once again and refilled it, this time adding a little more Scotch, a little less soda and a ready-sliced thin lime rind. "I approve your choice of liquor," he said as he continued. "Now let us take the case of a renting agent named Joan Logan. Nice looking. Even sexy in a funny way, or so I've been told."

"A very funny way," added Allison.

"She was the renting agent for Miss Parker's building."

"Was?" asked Allison.

"Was," replied Gatz.

"Say what you mean!" demanded Michael.

Massaging his chin, Gatz announced, "It seems Miss Logan has disappeared off the face of the earth. There are no records of her existence, other than her agency registration and the ownership papers 'o the building where she had her business. Apparently she lived in a vacuum and one day decided to disappear—or perhaps was removed forcibly."

"What day?" Allison asked, knowing the answer.

"As near as we can tell, the same day our friend Brenner was ventilated," answered Gatz.

Michael sat down on the couch next to Allison, put his arm around her shoulder and tried to steady her trembling body. She looked straight at Gatz, shocked and confused.

Gatz released the spring on the mousetrap and placed it back in his pocket. He grabbed a match from the bar, struck it against the heel of his shoe and relit the cigar stub, which had long since burned out. He puffed hard; billows of strong-smelling smoke curled into the air and settled along the ceiling. "Coincidence?" he asked.

"Coincidence!" Michael replied. "People disappear all the time. As for the detective, people also frequently pop up in this city full of holes."

"The facts say 'no coincidence' and the facts are never wrong. They're like brilliant suns in the night."

"You're making me sick." said Michael disgustedly.

"How unfortunate," stated Gatz. His expression hardened. "Why did Miss Logan disappear and how? Why is it that the detective's wounds are so easily explained in Miss Parker's story and why is a fine gentleman like yourself seemingly involved in yet another mysterious death and an apparent disappearance."

Michael jumped from the sofa. "Your reference to our friendship was presumptuous and the conversation you so desired has proven to be a big down. If you have nothing else to say, put your drink back on the bar and get out. You've got proof of nothing and I don't want to see your face in my apartment again."

Gatz smiled. He drained the last drop of Scotch, replaced the glass, grabbed his hat from the armchair and walked over to Michael. Pointing his finger at

Michael's face, he said, "You're right. I've got no proof, yet. And I'm not sure how these pieces fit, but my nose tells me that they do, and like I've said a thousand times, my nose has never been wrong."

"It was wrong once."

"As far as I'm concerned, never!"

"Get out!"

Gatz saluted Allison and walked to the door. Rizzo followed him out.

Michael slammed the door. "That monster is getting on my nerves."

Allison sat motionless on the sofa. That one bit of information. Joan Logan definitely missing. Why? And then the detective. Could he have been the person she had stabbed? The man Michael had said had come in the door? But if he was, how did he get to the lot? Transported by her "father" and two naked women? And what was he doing in the building at that time of night? Every question offered no answer, just many more questions. "Where could Miss Logan have gone and why are there no records of her existence?" she asked meekly.

"I don't know," answered Michael, his temper worn short.

She trembled, not out of remorse for the agent, but from the overwhelming pressure of events. "And that detective, could he—"

Michael interrupted. "That detective had nothing to do with this." He sat down and gently stroked her hair.

She viewed him ambivalently, not sure whether he was involved in a terrifying scheme to drive her mad or legitimately concerned for her welfare. She lifted her hands and laid her head into the cup formed by the meeting of her two palms.

"I didn't get the material translated," he said to distract her, "but I'm going to hear from someone by Monday who will have the answer." He knew that was a lie, but he still didn't know what the inscription meant, and for some irrational reason thought it best to conceal the little he had learned.

He kissed her on the forehead.

She wept.

23

Michael looked in both directions—toward Fiftieth Street and toward Fifty-first—satisfied himself that no one was approaching, circled the brown metal gate and disappeared around the side. It was late, approximately four; the moon was in its first quarter; the shadow was short, thin and almost imperceptible. As he crept quietly next to the building, he examined the first row of windows, barely two feet above the ground. They were barred, heavily plated and fused shut with gray mortar.

He stopped and looked back over his shoulder at the spires of St. Patrick's Cathedral, which rose into the sky and formed a proscenium for the stars and hovering moon, then he continued forward, musing that he now was doing the precise thing for which he had sent countless felons to jail. Imagine if he, Michael Farmer, were caught burglarizing, of all places, the Archdiocese of New York.

He crawled to the fourth window, removed a chisel from his pocket and unsuccessfully attacked the shielded bases of the bars. They were buried too deep; he would have to get into the building another way. He looked at the second row of windows about eight feet above the ground. The one he wanted was directly over him. He stepped onto the lowest ledge and reached upward; his hands touched the edge of the sill. He stepped onto the next ledge and pulled himself up. The window was now accessible, the sill at chin level. Forcing the chisel into the mortar, he pushed under the bottom edge of the frame and jiggled violently. The heavily encased glass shuddered; the coating cracked like dry sand. He began to push upward. Slowly, the window started to move, until in one violent spasm it slid halfway up the frame. He leaned against the wall, replaced the chisel in his pocket and climbed into the building.

Standing in the darkness, he closed the window and lowered the shade. He waited until his eyes had adjusted to the darkness, then he reached into his pocket, drew out a flashlight and laid the beam on the wall. Part of the crucifix filled the circle; it seemed more prominent is the solitary light than it had that afternoon when the vastness of the room had mitigated its commanding effect. He hesitated. The figure of Christ was comforting and majestic, but at the same time it was a big brother watching his every action. He removed the beam, studied the pictures of the pope and cardinal and then tiptoed to the file cabinets from which Monsignor Franchino had removed the folder on Father Halliran that afternoon.

They were open. He searched until he located the G–J file; quickly he pulled it open, inspected the contents and removed the manila folder that contained the information on Father Halliran. Laying it across the open drawer, he examined the papers once again. There was nothing of additional interest; nothing had been added since that afternoon. He replaced the file and selected several more at random, finally concluding that if there was material of any relevance in Monsignor Franchino's office it would be in a more secure location—possibly the locked file cabinet behind the desk. He quietly closed the last drawer and tiptoed back across the room. He removed a cloth from his pocket, wrapped it around the handle of the chisel and inserted the point beneath the double-locked drawer. Then he grabbed a bulky stapler from the desk and slammed it against the tool. A sharp crack shot through the office. He listened; the risk of noise was unavoidable. He hit the chisel again, but the drawer wouldn't budge. The combination lock had to be broken first. He removed the chisel and placed it under the edge of the dial. Once again he rammed the chisel with the stapler. Then again, The dial snapped off, the mechanism broke and the combination lock was freed. He reinserted the chisel into the side space, smacked it authoritatively and wedged the drawer open.

With the flashlight he searched the file; the first folders were clearly labeled and obviously irrelevant. But in the rear was one that read "WILLIAM O'ROURKE/MATTHEW HALLIRAN."

He removed it, sat in Franchino's chair and opened it on the desk. It was divided into two sections. The first was on William O'Rourke, the second on Halliran. He decided to review the Father Halliran material first. It was identical to the other Halliran file, except that a picture of a shriveled old man—obviously the blind priest—was stapled to the upper right inside corner of the manila folder. He focused the light on the wrinkled face and noted the worn, tired features, the most striking of which were the eyes; they were wide and glassy and possessed a strange glow that gave Michael a chill. The focus and intensity were those of a lunatic, but there was something more, something he couldn't define. He turned the file over, hiding the picture, placed it to the side and picked up the written material once again. Yes, it was the same—from 1952 onward—and like the file in the other cabinet it contained no information for any period prior to that date.

He frowned and picked up the papers on O'Rourke. He started to read rapidly, then slowed. The information was startling. It gave the life history of William

O'Rourke, a teacher from Boston who was born in Brockton, Massachusetts, in 1891. And though the history contained nothing extraordinary other than an extended reference to an attempted suicide, the termination date was mind-boggling. It ended in 1952.

There was a police document dated July 12 of that year certifying the disappearance of a man named William O'Rourke on July 9. And there was a picture. Although the man was young, with a fine complexion, well-spaced eyes and a handsome shock of sand-colored hair, there was no mistaking the fact that this man was the same one who appeared in the snapshot of Father Halliran. They were the same person.

He analyzed the information, unsure of its meaning or significance. He flipped the résumé over and removed an additional piece of paper from the rear of the file. It was a deed to realty. The paper vested the ownership of the brownstone to a David Caruso. Obviously Franchino knew him or knew of him, and just as obviously the monsignor had been aware that Michael was not the attorney for the building and that the whole interview had been a charade.

He quickly flipped through the double folder once more, replaced the deed and put the file back in the drawer. He grabbed the remaining folders and took them to the desk. Carefully, he began to examine each one. The first was labeled "ANDREW CARTER/DAVID SPINETTI." The pattern of the file followed the other. It gave a history for Father Spinetti, a Jesuit priest, dating from June 1921 until July 9, 1952, the day on which Father Halliran's identity was assumed. In the second section of the file was a long résumé on a man named Andrew Carter. He was born in 1863, spent most of his life as a professional soldier, participating in the Spanish-American War as a member of Roosevelt's Rough Riders, the First World War as a French officer and prior to those two conflicts as a soldier of fortune for the Turks in the Russo-Turkish War. By the date of his disappearance on December 25, 1921, he had retired and was working as an instructor at a military academy. The only additional things in the file were the two pictures—one of Father Spinetti, the other of Carter, both the same—and a detailed description of Carter's two attempted suicides.

Michael laid the file aside, adjusted the position of the flashlight and opened the next file in the pile. This one was labeled "MARY THOREN/MARY ANGELICA." Again, the pattern was the same. An ecclesiastical identity—a nun evolving from a secular. And again an attempted suicide.

He reanalyzed the information and concluded that at given intervals certain laymen had vanished to reappear with complete manufactured clerical identities. The question was why? And why were the files so carefully secreted?

He riffled through the next. The most immediate was in French, unintelligible to him. So were the next three. Then there was a series in German, then French again. The only information he could glean from these files were the dates. They went back at least as far as A.D. 731.

Hastily, he gathered the folders and replaced them in the cabinet. He closed the drawer, pondered the missing knob and opened it again. It was ridiculous to replace the files; Franchino would certainly know someone had broken in. Michael took the most recent out again and laid them on the desk within easy reach, ready for his exit.

He moved the light around the room, looking for anything else of interest. Seeing nothing, he returned his attention to the desk and began to open the drawers. Again, nothing. But the middle drawer on the right side was locked. He took the chisel once more and jimmied the drawer open. It was empty, except for a manila folder similar to those in the locked cabinet. He held it up, his eyes widening in terror. The folder was labeled "ALLISON PARKER/THERESE." His hands trembling, he opened it. In the Allison Parker section was the résumé of her life up to December 19, 1973, including a detailed history of her attempted suicides, her defection from the church, the complete series of events surrounding Karen Farmer's death—all incredibly accurate—and a résumé of his own activities over the last three years. In the Therese file was a complete nun's history, beginning on December 19, 1973.

Today was December 18. Michael carefully examined both résumés and studied the picture of Allison that was attached. Then he closed the folder and placed it on top of the others he had removed. The room had suddenly become stifling. Sitting down in the desk chair, his eyes lifting to the ceiling, he thought about what he had uncovered—the magnitude, the horror. But he still couldn't understand what was happening. Or how they knew all those details.

The church was involved with Allison, she was involved with the old priest and something diabolical was planned for her. Why? He did not know. Where? He did, The brownstone. When? He knew that also. Tomorrow. Maybe she hadn't imagined the presence of Chazen and the others. Maybe they were part of what was now appearing to be some monstrous, inconceivable plot. The Catholic Church! Involved in something like this. As irreligious as he was, he still couldn't believe it. He looked up at the cross and restrained the impulse to rip it from the wall and smash it.

He lowered his head; whatever was going to happen he had to stop it. Both for Allison's preservation and in view of what he had read, his own.

He turned off the flashlight, lifted the files, gingerly made his way to the window, and jumped out into the darkness.

24

The sky was blue, a rare occurrence in New York. The sun, angled toward its winter solstice, shone brilliantly. As Michael hurried down the crowded street, he squinted against the blinding rays that reflected off the moving cars and massive glass and steel skyscrapers. He shivered, wearing only a light jacket. One hand continually rubbed his shoulders to maintain the circulation; the other remained at his side, wrapped tightly about the handle of an attaché case.

He walked east on Fifty-second Street across heavily traveled Third Avenue and into the residential neighborhood that bordered the business district. His thoughts in chaos, he stopped outside a garden apartment, squeezed his hand to verify that his case was still safe and protected, and opened the frost-covered door. His handprint remained for several seconds, gradually clouded and disappeared as the warm moisture left by his sweaty palm froze, coated the glass, then evaporated.

He consulted the list of tenants and pressed the button next to apartment 3 R. After a second ring, the speaker crackled. "Hello?" it said.

"It's Michael," he replied.

The speaker clicked off.

He grabbed the doorknob; the lock buzzed. He pushed through, walked around the bend in the lobby to the right and entered an open elevator which was filled with garbage bags collected on the superintendent's rounds. He scowled—the odor was dreadful—pushed the button marked "3" and, while counting the passing floors, reviewed the precise information he would reveal and the plan of action he would undertake. He needed help, but unfortunately the usual sources were foreclosed to him. Jennifer would have to do, and in all likelihood she would be perfect. With Allison's life at stake, he could count on her to do exactly what he would tell her and then keep her mouth shut. She was Allison's best friend, wasn't she?

He stepped off the elevator, quickly greeted Jennifer in the doorway of her apartment, entered, laid the contents of his case on the dining table, reviewed the events in the brownstone, then quickly explained the significance of the documents.

She listened incredulously.

He repeated everything to emphasize the seriousness of the problem and his absolute certainty as to the facts. Finally he sat back and waited to field what he hoped would be very few questions—and unprobing ones at that.

He was wrong.

"What about the person she supposedly stabbed?" asked Jennifer as she walked toward him from the far end of the brightly furnished living room. She stopped by a tall bookcase, removed a slow-burning cigarette from a shelf, puffed nervously, then continued to his side, cigarette in hand.

"I don't know," he replied, knowing full well that it was Brenner who had been cut to ribbons when he had stumbled into the apartment. "I still think she imagined the murder. Don't forget, she was still hysterical during the entire sequence from the moment she woke and heard the footsteps." The rationale appeared sound. In actuality, though, Brenner had failed to complete a relatively simple assignment. Anyone could have done it right, but Brenner couldn't keep himself out of trouble, so the idiot was dead for no reason whatsoever, and because of it he now had that little bastard Gatz on his back again. As if he didn't have enough problems. Yet he had only himself to blame; he never should have run the risk of using Brenner again for anything.

"Why don't we go to the police?" Jennifer was saying.

"No," he countered quickly.

"Why not? Nobody's done anything wrong. Even if Allison did stab someone, it certainly wasn't murder."

No, it wasn't, he thought to himself. There at least he was in agreement. If anything, it was an unfortunate accident. But he couldn't go to the police. He was concerned with the identity of the detective and the possibility that the police might establish a link between himself and the corpse. And God forbid they should discover or be told the information in Franchino's files.

"No police," he declared.

"You're not making any sense," said Jennifer.

"If the police get involved, they'll deal with this the way they would deal with a burglary and do it incompetently. Then nothing will save Allison. If we don't do things my way, she's finished." He stared at Jennifer intently.

"But—"

"No!"

"We're dealing with something we don't under-stand," said Jennifer.

"If we don't, the police certainly won't. No, I won't go to the police, and that's final." He began to shuffle the papers on the table. "Let's assume for one minute that we accept all this as the truth." He held several of the documents in the air and shook his head. "Allison is meant to lose her identity and reappear as someone else."

"Sister Therese?"

"Whatever that is."

"A nun," added Jennifer needlessly.

He nodded, the absurdity of the situation not mitigated by the evidence—at least as far as he was concerned. But since he was making assumptions, he had no alternative but to follow them to their conclusions, no matter how illogical.

"And Halliran?" questioned Jennifer once again.

"Judging from these histories, Halliran will also disappear, and Allison in the person of Sister Therese will take his place."

Jennifer dragged hard on the cigarette.

Michael lifted the translation and read, " 'To thee thy course by Lot hath given charge and strict watch that to this happy Place no evil thing approach or enter in.' It's obviously directed to Allison. Sets her up as a sentinel of some sort. Father Halliran, if we continue with our prior assumptions, is also a sentinel."

They stood silently reviewing the files.

"What about her father and the other people she saw in the brownstone."

"I thought they were illusions. It made sense. She had always despised her father."

"Yes."

"The scene she confronted in the brownstone was the recreation of an event earlier in her life. Could I have made any other logical conclusion? What was it? A hallucination? A nightmare? A breakdown? Take your pick. But now I'm not so sure. And that goes for Chazen and the others also. No, I think they were actually in the brownstone, supplied by the Archdiocese." He paused, drank from the glass of Coke which she had poured for him and continued. "They might have her under some kind of hypnosis. That would explain many things. How she saw that book passage. How she found the ad in the paper where there was no ad."

Jennifer removed the deed from the stack of papers and held it out.

"I went to the landlord's apartment to ask him

some questions. He wasn't there. Monsignor Franchino must have known I was lying when I said I was Caruso's lawyer. For all I know the inquisition could be meeting right now to determine what to do with me."

"Michael," said Jennifer, "this is all well and good, but how do you stop them?"

"I don't know, but I will. According to those files, whatever's going to happen will happen tomorrow. I intend to stand guard at the brownstone starting at twelve tonight."

"But—"

"I'll be damned if I'll let a bunch of religious fanatics destroy Allison." He spun from the table and paced nervously around the room. "And let's not get too carried away with this mumbo jumbo. We're dealing with some very real characters, not magic. The question is, what are they after?"

"I think we should call the police."

"No. For the last time, no!"

"Please?"

"I don't want to even discuss it. No police."

"Why? Because you're afraid of them? Because what I've found out about your past may be true?"

"I don't think—"

She interrupted. "What you did is unimportant right now. Allison is in trouble; if you really care for her you'll put her first, no matter what you're afraid might come out."

"I am putting her first!"

"No, you're not!"

"No? Do you think I'm involved in this for my health?"

"I really don't know why you're involved or how." Jennifer paused, then continued. "Maybe you made up all these files. Maybe you did take Allison into the museum intentionally to see the statue of the woman. Maybe you're involved with these priests of yours. Maybe there are no priests. And maybe you want to set me up as an alibi, so that you can

kill her like you did Karen and place the blame elsewhere."

Michael grabbed her by the hair and bent her over
the back of the chair. She shook him off, unafraid.

"Don't mention Karen again," he warned. "For
once and for all, Karen killed herself because I left
her."

Jennifer straightened her hair. "You know, Michael, I've always known that under that legal calm
was a vile temper."

"I still insist on handling this my way."

"And that is?" she asked skeptically.

"I'm going to bring her here tonight." He paused,
thinking, then continued. "I want you to have a dinner
party. Get on the phone and call everyone you know.
Have them here by ten, so that by the time I bring
Allison, there'll be enough people to keep her surrounded and occupied while I'm at the brownstone."

Jennifer stared, her expression implying agreement.

"And make sure she stays here! No matter what
happens, keep her here."

"What if she gets sick?"

"I'll leave you her doctor's number. He'll come
right over."

Jennifer nodded haltingly; she had no alternative.

He put his arm around her and placed his mouth
next to her ear. "No matter what you think, I love
that girl and no one's going to hurt her. No one!"
It was an admission—a significant gesture of emotion
for him. "I mean that."

She stood back. "I suppose you do," she said, still
regarding him suspiciously.

He gathered the papers and placed them back in
his briefcase.

"Shouldn't I keep them tonight?" asked Jennifer.

"Why?"

She lowered her eyes. "Just in case."

"No, I think I'd better keep the papers with me,"
he said. "I might need them."

He opened the door and walked out with the brief-case at his side. Had he told her too much? He wasn't sure. He wasn't even sure if she could be trusted. She could be on the phone with the police right at this very moment as he was on his way uptown toward home. Yet, he'd had no choice. Someone had to be with Allison this evening, someone who had some knowledge about what might occur.

He walked up Madison, ignoring the window displays, then he turned onto Seventy-first, stopped and stood on the corner looking toward the gray stone wall in the distance that bounded Central Park on Fifth. The long bench that lay shielded beneath the shoulder-high wall had only one occupant—an old hunched-over gentlemen in a top hat, with a long black cane. The street was quiet.

Michael kicked at the discolored leaves that had fallen from one of the trees. He was nervous. The role of the hero did not become him. He realized that more than ever as he said to himself, "Mr. Gatz, I wish you were dead." Then he turned and entered his building.

"Good evening," said the doorman.

"Hello, George." Michael started to hurry through the hall.

"Mr. Farmer?"

"Yes."

"A gentleman went up to your apartment a moment ago."

"Who?"

"I don't remember his name."

He thought for a moment, then asked abruptly, "What'd he look like?"

"Kinda short with a shriveled cigar in his mouth."

"Damn you. Why'd you let him up?"

"Miss Parker said to," he stammered.

Michael shook his head and turned to the elevator. Then he stopped and looked back over his shoulder. "His name is Gatz. Detective Gatz."

"Yes, sir."

"Don't forget it. And don't ever let him back in here again without my okay."

"Yes, sir. I understand."

Michael raced around the bend in the hall to the elevator and pressed the "up" button. He waited. The elevator doors opened and Detective Gatz started out. Seeing Michael, he jolted to a stop and stepped back into the empty elevator.

Michael hesitated. The other elevator arrived; the doors opened. He quickly squirmed in past a small boy. Gatz quickly jumped from his elevator and rammed his hands between the closing doors. The doors stopped and reversed.

"Bastard!" cried Michael, bracing himself.

"How crude," said Gatz, smiling.

Michael coiled and pushed himself off the wall toward the doorway. Gatz reacted quickly; he blocked the exit, jammed his hand into Michael's throat and hurled him back.

The elevator shook violently, as if the suspended cables were about to snap.

The detective jumped into the car. The doors closed behind him. "Now you keep your ass still."

"You've got a warrant?"

"No."

"Then up yours."

"We don't need a warrant to talk."

Michael tried to press the "open" button, but Gatz smashed his hand and pinned his shoulders against the panel.

"Cool it, my friend," the detective cautioned.

"You cool it and keep your hands off me." Michael pulled away. "What did you want with Allison?"

"Nothing."

"Then what are you doing here?"

"I wanted to see you."

"For another friendly chat?"

"How'd you guess?"

"I'm not interested."

"Yes, you are!" Gatz's voice was raised, his meaning

unmistakable. He and Michael were going to talk whether Michael liked it or not.

Michael stared angrily, then lowered his raised fists. "I can't resist your charms," he finally said.

"I've had a hunch about you ever since I first heard that big mouth of yours," Gatz began. "And I have a hunch about you now. Few facts, no real proof. Not much more than an idea as to what you're up to and why. But my nose told me—"

"And it ain't never been wrong. I've heard that a thousand times."

Gatz pointed his second finger at Michael, holding it an inch from his face. "I'm warning you."

The doors of the elevator opened. A middle-aged woman with a small white poodle in one hand and a gift-wrapped package in the other, stepped inside.

Gatz raised his hand. "Please use the other elevator."

"Excuse me," said the startled woman.

Gatz dug his hand into his pocket, removed his wallet and held it open in front of her, his badge showing. "Police business. Take the other elevator." He wasn't asking; he was commanding.

The woman ogled the little detective, then turned to Michael for some explanation. Michael looked away and the woman stepped back. The door closed.

Gatz bobbed his cigar and continued. "I got hold of Andrew Parker's will. A lot of money and almost all of it left to his beloved daughter. A most tempting sum of money. Like a big lump of cheese." He grabbed the trap from his pocket and rolled it in the fingers of his right hand. "Now this is interesting, but then again a lot of people get left big sums of money from their fathers."

"So what?"

"So what? That's a very interesting fact. Perhaps the reason why you might want to get rid of the girl or scare her to death or just plain scare her."

"That's the most ridiculous thing I've ever heard. If I ever tried something like that, I'd be sure to have married her first. Now, my friend, I'm getting off the elevator."

"No, you're not."

"You're going to force me to pull some strings again."

"Be my guest."

"I take it you've forgotten that—"

"No," said Gatz, his eyes glistening. "You can be sure of that. But you're going to listen to me and answer questions and then you can call anyone you want, even the President of the United States, but after I'm done."

Michael gritted his teeth as Gatz went on.

'I couldn't put this case together until I got a call from an informer we use. I had asked him to do some quiet investigating into Brenner's past. He went back into the muck and came out with exactly what I needed. Mr. Brenner, along about February 1969, accepted a contract to do in a broad. Was paid a lot of money. Wasn't that about the time Mrs. Farmer killed herself?"

"Fuck off, flatfoot. You know better than to get started on that. You'll wind up back in Brooklyn chasing bums off park benches."

Gatz smiled, undeterred. "It seems my party couldn't find out who was to be killed or who took out the contract. But I know!"

"You know nothing."

Gatz placed the trap back in his pocket. "Oh, but I do. My informer also learned that Brenner was hired recently by the same person who took out the original contract to do some additional 'detective work.' I asked him what kind and he said he didn't know but that he was trying to find out. You know guys like Brenner always leave some information about what they're working on in case there's a double-cross. It just takes time to find the right dupe to spill the beans."

"I'm not interested in a course in criminology."

"Very bright lawyer."

"And I don't know what you're talking about."

"I think I've made myself clear."

"I'm afraid your deductive reasoning so dazzled me that I failed to grasp the substantive accusations."

Gatz nearly blew through the roof of the elevator. He whipped the cigar stub from his mouth and threw it into the corner.

"I'm gonna lay it on you straight. You killed your wife. You hired Brenner to do it. Which accounts for those beautiful alibis that had you elsewhere. But I saw through your scheme then and I certainly see through it now, only a little clearer."

"I don't know what you're talking about. I don't know any Brenner and I never have known a Brenner."

"Shut up, I'm not finished. You got rid of your wife, because not only wouldn't she give you a divorce, but she promised to tell the police about the extensive bribes you were taking—if you left her. Then you found your girl friend Allison Parker's old man was rich. You also found out he was going to leave her almost every cent he had because he couldn't stand his old lady. And greedy men never change. You dreamed up a way to get at the money. You needed someone you could trust; you went back to Brenner."

"Are you through?" asked Michael.

"Not yet! Brenner appeared in the house looking like the dead father, and Miss Parker, who we know has a shaky mental history, stabbed him to death. Apparently she wasn't as defenseless as you thought. Then, when she ran off into the rain, you sneaked in, cleaned away all the blood, hid the body, and appeared the next day like a dutiful boy friend, hoping that the unexpected turn of events would not destroy you. And it probably wouldn't have, except for one thing."

"What?"

"Me. You never thought that I'd be involved."

"I think you're out of your mind," said Michael. "You've been watching too much television."

"Don't knock it. You can learn a great deal from television." Gatz smiled. He was satisfied that he had Farmer pinned against the wall.

"Let me ask you a question, Mr. Gatz," said Michael. "You know darn well that the information supplied by your informer couldn't be used in a court of law, so it comes down to the fact that you have no proof of anything. Just an overblown theory packed with nonsense. A fantasy dreamed up by that ridiculous ego of yours that can never admit to being wrong. You'd be out of your mind to make formal charges, and you know it."

"But I'm gonna find acceptable evidence and I'm gonna pin it around your neck until it chokes you. I want you to know that for the record."

"I assume that you're through now," said Michael.

"Yes."

Michael leaned toward the doors and pressed the "open" button. "Don't work too hard," he cautioned.

Gatz stepped from the elevator, leaving Michael to pace the rising cabin until it stopped on the tenth floor. He reached his apartment, threw open the door and shouted, "I told you not to let that cop in here! Don't you listen to a goddamn word I say?"

Allison jumped from the couch, trembled, and shook her head. Noticing how pale she was, he lowered his voice. Funny, she had seemed better the last few days. But now? A total relapse?

"How do you feel?" he asked as he placed his hand on her shoulder. The question was unnecessary; he knew the answer already.

"Terrible," she said. Her entire body registered visible evidence of the fact.

"What's the matter?"

"I don't know."

"The headache is back again?"

"Yes, and the dizziness and nausea. I feel like

I'm losing control of my reflexes." She shook her head. "I feel I'm losing control of everything."

He tensed. Was it starting already? "Did you feel this in the morning?"

"No."

"When?"

"This afternoon." She hesitated, as if she wanted to say something, couldn't, and was searching for the strength. "I fainted while you were gone."

"What?" he cried.

"I fainted," she repeated.

"How long were you out?"

"An hour."

"Did you call the doctor?"

"No."

"Why not?"

"I was scared." She sat down on the couch. "I'm too scared to do anything but die." She started to shake. "It's funny, but I'm not afraid of that."

He put his arms around her, hiding his anger. "Everything is going to be all right." He held her close for several minutes, then walked to the bar, poured a small jigger of Scotch and downed it.

She looked up beseechingly, half for pity, half for understanding. "While I was unconscious I dreamed of an old man sitting in a window."

"Father Halliran?"

She nodded. "Don't yell at me! I know you don't want me to think about the priest and the house, but—"

"I won't yell at you. If you saw the priest, you saw the priest and that's all there is to it." He poured a second jigger of Scotch. "I don't like the way you look." He walked to her again, kneeled down and kissed her gently on the forehead. He raised his hand and touched her lids and upper cheeks with his fingers. "Does that hurt?" he asked.

"Yes."

"And that?"

"Yes."

"Do your eyes still burn?"

"Yes."

He re-examined her face. The dry, lifeless texture that had gripped her eyes for the past two days had now spread to the bridge of her nose and her upper cheeks. The lines were very delicate—almost unnoticeable unless one looked very closely—but they seemed to be expanding over her face, eating away at the skin. It was terrible. He knew that the battle was on and that it would have to be joined by him. There was no one else.

She reached out and put her arms around him. "I love you," she whispered painfully.

Should he tell her? No! Let her be ignorant as long as possible. Keep her from looking closely in a mirror.

"Michael, help me!"

"That you can be sure of. I have no intention of letting this go on any longer."

She tightened her grasp.

"I'm taking you to Jennifer's tonight. You're going to stay there and sleep there also. She's having a party tonight. You'll enjoy it."

"Why can't I be with you?"

"Because I have to do something tonight."

"What?"

"Some investigative work."

She began to tremble more violently. "Michael," she said in a low, tremulous voice. "In the house?"

"No. I have to see some people."

"Michael, my head hurts."

"I'll get you some aspirin. That will help. But I want you to listen to me and do as I say. No questions."

She nodded.

"I'm going to give Jennifer the address and number of Dr. Steinberger, just in case. But while I'm gone I want you to see if you can mix in the party and keep your mind busy and clear of all your problems. Promise me you'll try. It's very important!"

"I promise." Once again she was like a helpless child, dependent on him for her strength and perhaps even for her life.

"Why don't you try and get some sleep for an hour or two. Then we can get dressed."

She silently got to her feet and walked unsurely out of the living room toward the bedroom.

He poured another glass of Scotch and held it to his lips. Then he squeezed the glass, harder and harder, until it shattered in his hand. He looked at the large sliver of glass that was buried in the skin below his thumb. He was so angry that he felt no pain. He grabbed the end of the sliver and pulled it out. Blood ran down his palm. He wrapped his handkerchief around the wound, poured another glass of Scotch, downed it in one gulp and followed Allison to the bedroom.

25

"Hello," Michael said.

"You're late."

"It was my fault," Allison said lifelessly. "I took a long time getting dressed."

"Don't worry. No one's started eating yet," said Jennifer.

Michael smiled wanly.

"Come in. The party's in here, not in the hall." Jennifer closed the door. "Let me take your coats."

"It's cold out there. It could snow." Michael waited

for Allison. "Here, let me help you." He pulled the jacket off her back. She had been floundering, unable to summon sufficient coordination to take it off herself.

Jennifer lowered her eyes. Michael winced.

"Do you really think it will snow?" asked Jennifer, searching for something to say.

"You can almost smell it in the air." Michael looked through the foyer toward the living room and the guests. When they had entered, the noise had been raucous and intense. But now the crowded room had grown strangely quiet; there was still a rustling of voices and laughter, but the sounds were strained.

"Give me. I'll put them away," said Jennifer. She grabbed the coats, hung them in the hall closet, turned and stared silently at them.

"Could you put my briefcase in the closet also?" Michael asked.

Jennifer glanced at the black case. "Oh, yes, of course."

He passed it over and she put it on the shelf, hesitated for a moment, then turned and stared at them again.

The noise from the living room remained muted.

Jennifer fidgeted. "Allison," she asked incredulously, "do you feel okay?" She had expected Allison to look weak and drawn. But like this? Drained! Colorless! Worse—infinitely worse—than when she had last seen her in Michael's apartment. Never!

"She feels all right," declared Michael. "A little headache and nausea, that's all."

"Yes," agreed Allison hollowly as her eyes wandered aimlessly.

"Michael, I . . ." murmured Jennifer, still shocked.

"Shut up!" he whispered hastily. He raised his voice. "The party looks fantastic."

"Yes," said Allison unsurely.

He frowned, touched her arm and led her out of the foyer into the living room. "Come, I'll get you a drink," he said as he pulled her through the crowd to the bar. He poured her a glass of ginger ale, dropped some ice into a glass of Scotch for himself, helped her to the sofa and left her with a group of friends. Dangerous, but he had to force her to try to act naturally. He mumbled angrily as he saw Jack Tucci cross the room and join her. The last person he wanted to see near her was that meddlesome fop. But there was nothing he could do.

He turned away, glass in hand, and walked unobtrusively to a corner where he could remain vigilant and undisturbed. He thought briefly about what lay ahead, then smiled as he watched Jennifer scurry about the room, bobbing from one guest to another.

He finished his drink, looked disgustedly at the empty glass and walked back past the buffet to the bar. "Could you pass me a Scotch?" he asked.

A partially filled bottle was pushed in his direction. He grabbed it, poured half a glass, added water, some ice, and placed the bottle back on the table.

"Excuse me," he said as he angled toward the window and opened it slightly. Then he turned his attention back to Allison. He couldn't hear what she was saying, but he could see that she was having difficulty moving her lips.

"Can I speak to you a moment?" asked Jack Tucci. He carried a glass in one hand and a hand-carved pipe that reeked of cherry-flavored tobacco in the other. His expression was very agitated.

"How've you been?" asked Michael coldly.

"Fine." He paused, then added, "And you?"

"Couldn't be better."

"Could you say the same for Allison?" Jack asked dryly.

"Why not?" Michael said with a pretense of ignorance that could have fooled no one.

"I called your office several times this week. Why didn't you return my calls?"

"I didn't get the messages. No, really," he added as Jack narrowed his eyes. "My secretary is very inadequate."

"This is me you're talking to, Michael, not some bloody moron. If you're avoiding me, which you are, please give me credit for sufficient intelligence to realize it. That way neither of us need blither on like the Mad Hatter." He took Michael's arm and pulled him into a corner. "What's the matter with Allison?"

"She's sick."

"With what?"

"A kidney ailment."

"What kind?"

"Jack, if you want a detailed medical analysis, call her doctor."

"I just talked to her and she looked right through me, almost as if she were in a trance. That's not the result of a kidney ailment."

"What do you want me to say?"

"The truth. Something's wrong with her, but it's not physical. It's mental, and I'd like to know so that I can help."

Michael eyed Tucci impassively. "Like I've told you, Jack, she has a kidney ailment."

"You must take me for a fool!"

"If you insist."

Jack grabbed Michael's arm. "I don't—"

Michael shook off the hand. "Let me be as blunt as I can. Whatever is wrong with her is none of your business. *Capisce?*"

"It's only yours?"

"Right."

"By what divine command? The marital vow?"

"No! By possession. And a firm resolution to break the neck of anyone who sticks his nose where it doesn't belong. I don't want to argue with you any more. She's sick. A kidney ailment. That's all." He walked away, angry at Jack, angry at himself for having lost his temper. He slowly moved to the wall and sat down on the floor. He surveyed the crowd, then checked on Allison once again. She was still speaking mechanically. He tried to put himself in her place. To feel the agony, the pain and fear she was suffering. Or the cumulative effect of the recent horrors that had robbed her of her former self. But he couldn't.

"Hello," said Jennifer as she sat down next to him. "Despise our world?"

"Yes," he responded coldly.

"It's eleven twenty."

He consulted his watch and nodded. "I'll leave in five minutes."

"Not a bad party," she said, knowing that neither cared.

"The usual. Keep Jack Tucci away from her after I leave."

"Why?"

"Gut reaction. He may ask too many questions, and she's so out of it that she might answer."

"Okay."

"Is there anyone else who might get overly snoopy?"

"I don't think so."

"Know so!"

"Yes," she answered, annoyed.

"Watch her carefully. And keep them away or at least talking about nonsense. I don't want anyone to talk to her about her condition."

"I'll watch her. Don't worry."

"I heard from Gatz this afternoon." He paused. "If he comes back to my apartment again and doesn't find us there, he may come here. Under no circumstances is he to get to her. Hide her, sneak her out the back or put her under the bed. But don't let him near her."

"I won't."

He palmed a slip of paper into her fingers. "Her doctor's number is on it. If she gets sick, call him. He's familiar with her condition and he'll come."

She nodded.

He hoisted himself to his feet, tidied his jacket, and walked across the room, head lowered to prevent any time-consuming conversation.

Allison looked up from her seat on the couch.

Michael took her hand. "Excuse me," he said as he pulled her up and across the room, where he leaned her against the wall. "How do you feel?" he asked.

"All right," she replied. Her lips barely moved, her voice was distant.

"No worse than before?"

"No."

"I'm leaving now," he said, trying to avoid her eyes. They disturbed him, ate at his conscience. "I'll try to get back before the party's over. If I can't, you'll sleep here and I'll be back as soon as I can."

"Where are you going?"

"I'm not sure yet."

"But if—"

"No more questions." He looked toward the crowd. "Jennifer!" he called.

"You're leaving?" she asked, coming over.

"Yes. Make sure Allison doesn't feel uncomfortable."

Michael opened the closet, removed his coat and threw it over his arm. Then he grasped the handle of the black briefcase and pulled it out.

"What's in that?" asked Allison, seemingly noticing it for the first time.

"Nothing." Michael turned to the door.

"Michael," said Jennifer, "be careful."

Allison glanced at her quickly, then threw her arms around Michael. He held her and stroked her hair, then he pulled her arms away and pushed her in Jennifer's direction.

"Let me go with you," Allison pleaded meekly.

He did not respond. Just opened the door and left.

26

Michael blew on his hands; the cold wind and temperature had frozen them white. Cursing, he replaced his gloves, turned the corner onto Eighty-ninth Street and walked slowly down the street.

There were no people, few sounds. It was as if all life had fled the area, perhaps in expectation of an unnatural event.

Two cars turned onto the block, passed him and rumbled into the distance. He stopped and stared. Across the street was the brownstone.

As he scanned the front entrance and the black windows, a violent gust of wind whipped across his back. By some quirk of the senses the wind magnified both his visual impression of darkness and the already terrifying knowledge that he would have to engage the brownstone alone.

He began to cross. In the center of the street he stopped. The angle was perfect, the light just sufficient. He had seen nothing in the fifth-floor windows from his prior position, but in this exposed setting, somewhat nearer than before, he could see a form, undefined but seated—apparently staring out the window—waiting. It was the priest. Father Matthew Halliran. Or William O'Rourke by birth. Was the man really blind? If there was a plot, he doubted it. No, it seemed logical that the blindness was a ploy, an assumption that,

if correct, allowed the old man to sit and stare with
impunity.

Aware suddenly of his own visibility, he quickly
jogged to the sidewalk. He removed a set of keys
from his pocket, cautiously walked up the stone staircase and ducked into the vestibule. No one could
see him now, but he was anything but secure. He
was expecting company, and unless he was overesti-
mating his opponents, they would be expecting him.

He placed the black briefcase on the ground, removed a flashlight from his jacket and tested the beam.
Nodding his satisfaction, he withdrew a revolver and
inspected the chambers. The gun was loaded, the
safety off, ready to use. He placed it in his belt.

He peeked from the vestibule and, seeing no one,
picked up his case, inserted Allison's key into the
front door and opened it. As the door closed behind
him, he looked up at the ceiling where the isolated
bulbs burned alone, producing a strange moonlike
effect. He turned on the flashlight and waved it about
the walls to observe the effect of the haze on the
beam. It was minimal. He turned off the light, placed
it back in his pocket, removed the revolver and began
to move forward.

Flinching violently, he whipped the gun around.
There was movement—but it was his own. He regarded
his reflection in a full-length mirror, emitted a silent
breathy laugh, and threw his gloves on the table. Looking up into the void that was the second floor, he
pulled himself up the stairs, one hand on the gun,
the other on the banister.

Allison clutched her head and screamed; she staggered. Jack grabbed her to prevent a fall.

"Somebody get some ice!"

Allison pitched and swayed. Heads turned.

"Quick!"

Allison waved her right arm and righted herself.
With her palms pressed against her forehead, she
murmured, "I'll be all right."

The party had stopped. Everyone stood motionless.

Jennifer rushed to her side. "What is it?" she asked, panicked.

"I'm all right," Allison answered unconvincingly.

"Come sit down." Without waiting for a reply, Jennifer pulled her to the sofa and forced her to sit. "I'll get some ice."

"I don't need it. I'll be all right. Just leave me for a few minutes."

"Allison."

"Please!"

Jennifer assented and stood up. Sixty eyes were glued on them, inquisitive, concerned, perplexed.

Michael reached the top of the stairs and leaned back against the paneled wall. The floor lights were out. He pulled the flashlight from his pocket and flicked it on. The beam highlighted an empty hall. Apartment 2 B lay directly to his right, apartment 2 A at the far end. He reached across to 2 B, turned the knob, but the door was locked. Disappointed, he raised his hand, grabbed the little bulb and turned it. It was dead. He shook his head, satisfied that the preparations had been made. Whoever was in control of the situation had seen that the proper atmosphere for a night of horror had been arranged. The doors were locked; the lights were out. He focused the beam on the walls, seeing the new paneling that had been laid over the old, something he had never noticed before. It looked strange, almost beckoning to be inspected. But that could come later. First he was going to search each apartment and tear them apart hoping to find a clue—any clue.

He started with Allison's. Apartment 3 A. When he finally left it, the living room was wrecked. He had torn out every piece of upholstery, emptied the closets and dumped the drawers, looking for hidden microphones, speakers or any other gadget that might have been used to frighten her. He had performed the same surgery in the bedroom, but since that was the site of most of the noises, his operation had been far more extensive. Where would I hide a microphone? he had asked himself as a point of departure; then he had searched. He had found nothing; his only reward was a veil of dust and plaster that covered his entire body, giving him an appropriate ghostlike appearance.

Standing in the hall he looked at his watch; it was twelve forty-five. He considered the available alternatives. He could go up to the priest's apartment or stop at one intermediate. The former seemed more expedient but in effect might not be. The old man had never opened the door before and he was sure that he was not about to now—at least not for him. The two apartments that remained of interest were 4 A and 5 B. First would be 4 A.

Allison held the ice bag to her head. Most of the guests had returned to their food and drink.

"Feeling better?" asked Jennifer.

"Yes, much," replied Allison softly. She certainly didn't look it.

"Keep the bag there a while longer. In a little while you can lie down in the bedroom and close your eyes."

Jack approached. He stood over Allison momentarily, then sat down and placed his hand on her thigh. "Shouldn't we call a doctor?" he asked, turning to Jennifer.

"I . . ."

Allison interrupted by shaking her head fiercely.

"Allison . . ."

"No, please. No doctor," she struggled to say. The words were muffled, as she had difficulty coordinating her lips and tongue.

Jack looked at her uncomfortably, Allison tried to smile. Then suddenly she screamed. "My head!" The blood-curdling cry pierced the room. "I . . . can't stand it. I . . ." The ice bag fell to the floor, she grabbed her scalp frantically, continuing to scream as Jennifer and Jack tried to hold her spastic body still. Her mouth opened and shut in a convulsive spasm, foam rose along the corners of her lips as her tongue coiled to snap back into her throat and choke her.

"Pry her teeth open and get her tongue," screamed Jennifer amid the commotion.

Jack rammed his hand into Allison's mouth; her teeth ripped his fingers. "Get me a spoon, quickly!"

"There are some on the table."

Two men ran for a spoon as Jack locked his fingers over Allison's lower teeth and, placing his palm under her chin, pried them downward. With his other hand he grabbed her tongue.

"Here!" he shouted as he shoved the spoon into her mouth and pulled out his bleeding hand.

Suddenly she stiffened, then rocked forward and pitched off the couch onto her face, unconscious.

The precinct corridor was empty. An occasional sound of laughter drifted through closed doors, filtered down the hall and echoed from the cinder blocks.

Gatz and Rizzo exited an office and ambled down the hall to the end. Gatz opened a door to his left, entered his office, walked to his desk and threw his hat on the blotter. He sat down in the swaybacked chair and leaned back, placing his heels on the desk. Then he ripped a match along the underside of the chair and lit the remainder of his cigar. The end flared, heated and burned. He inhaled deeply, enjoying the taste of the tobacco. He scratched the stubble on his chin; he hadn't shaved since early morning—almost nineteen hours before. He yawned, then yawned again.

"Rizzo, go down to McGuire's office and get me a cup of coffee."

Rizzo nodded and hurried out.

Gatz rubbed his eyes, closed them and leaned back in the chair.

"Sir?" asked Detective Richardson who stood at the door.

Gatz sat up. "What is it?"

Richardson approached the desk and dropped a typed note on the blotter.

Gatz cleared his throat and moved the paper under the desk lamp. He stood excitedly. "Where'd you get this?" he asked.

"In a hidden compartment in the rear of one of Brenner's desk drawers."

Gatz slammed his fist on the blotter. "I've got him!" he cried. He turned to Richardson. "Thank you," he said.

The detective wheeled away from the desk and out the door as Gatz flicked the intercom.

"McGuire, is Rizzo still there?"

"Yes," bellowed a deep voice over the static.

"Can you hear me, Rizzo?"

"Yes."

"Bring in Farmer."

"To question?"

"No. To book."

He released the knob on the intercom and once again reclined in his seat. He smiled broadly, his grin reflecting hatred more than anything else. The moment had arrived for the thrust, right to the jugular.

He picked up the desk phone and dialed. The phone at the other end rang several times.

"Inspector Garcia," he asked, and then finally said, "we've cracked the nut. Richardson just brought a detailed note on Allison Parker, establishing the connection we need. They found it in Brenner's office. No. No. I've already sent him, and we should have Farmer here in less than half an hour."

Gatz lowered the receiver, reached across the desk and grabbed the mousetrap. He pulled it in front of him, picked up a wire and inched it slowly forward.

The trap snapped and cracked down on the hook. He had made no effort to remove his weapon.

"Caught like a rat," he announced.

The room was filled with whispers.

Allison lay in bed with an ice pack on her forehead. Her condition had not improved. She seemed nearly comatose, at times moaning unintelligibly, at times completely insensate.

Jennifer sat next to her, speaking quietly into the white phone. Jack lifted the ice bag, felt Allison's head, then squeezed the sack. "Get some more ice," he asked someone as he leaned protectively over the bed.

A young woman pushed through the crowd, removed the flattened bag and replaced it with a new one. Jennifer set the phone down and said, "The doctor's on his way." She pulled a cigarette from a crushed pack and lit it nervously. "He suggests we keep everyone out of the room except someone to watch her. He's afraid a crowd may upset her more." Watching Jack's positive response, she stood up and extended her arms, motioning as if she were herding sheep. "I'd appreciate it," she announced, "if everyone would go back to the living room."

The onlookers turned and walked out.

Jennifer closed the door and dragged deeply on the cigarette. "Did you notice the texture of the skin on her cheeks and eyelids?" she asked as Jack looked up.

"Yes," he replied.

"Like sandpaper or dried-out wood. As if something had sucked out all the life. I've never seen anything like it."

Jack gently touched Allison's skin, then sat up and opened the collar of his shirt. "Where's Michael?" he asked.

"I don't know."

"You don't?" His tone indicated skepticism. "He's a jackass! Kidney disease? I don't know what she has, but I'll be damned if it has anything to do with her kidneys." He stiffened. "He should have his bleeding teeth rammed down his throat."

"Now is not the time for that. Will you watch her while I go back outside?"

"Yes."

She smiled, touched his arm affectionately and walked out of the room, concerned for Allison but at the same time concerned for Michael, who she knew would be up to his neck in trouble if Allison's condition was any indication!

Preceded by the beam of light, he walked down the corridor, past the kitchen and bathroom and out into the living room. Behind him he had left another room in shambles. The bedroom of 4 A. The nexus of the confrontation. In his belt he carried a screwdriver and a chisel, which he had taken from Allison's kitchen. Both had been useful. But again the results were disappointing.

He walked to the sofa and sat down. He was tired and frustrated—mostly frustrated. He pulled the screwdriver from his belt, buried it into the couch, ripped out a wad of stuffing and threw it to the dust-strewn rug. He had an uncontrollable urge to lash out and destroy, but he was restraining himself, waiting for the right target.

He flashed the light around the room. "Damn!" he whispered. "A rotting mess." The same living room where the mistake had been made, the mistake that had cost Brenner his life. There was really no reason to examine the area again. He was sure he would find nothing. But then again he had nothing better to do—yet.

He pulled himself off the sofa and began to dismantle every drawer, closet and floor piece.

The search was unproductive.

He walked into the hall and looked at his watch—one forty-one—and listened to the rhythmic ticking. He had been in the house almost two hours. Maybe he was wrong. Maybe nothing was going to happen. Could they have called it off? Afraid that he had found out too much. Afraid that he had come to the house with help.

He started up the staircase to the fifth floor. Halfway there he stopped. Should he break open the priest's door and declare his presence even though the old man could not help but know that he was there already? He had few options and few ideas. Yet, his gut reaction was to delay his confrontation with Halliran, at least until he had no alternative. So he reversed himself and started down the staircase.

He heard a sound, the creaking of a door.

He felt a cold shiver and then an intense sensation of fear. There was something evil behind him. He wasn't sure, but he sensed it and he had to get away.

He descended like a heavy weight falling to earth, gathering speed and momentum with each step, pulled by the force of darkness below, repelled by the uninviting unknown above. Every sense in his body was intensified, the slightest groan in the building was like a screech of a hideous gorgon. Down and down he went, his feet sliding from one step to the next, one hand holding the flashlight, the other wrapped around the gun with the index finger on the trigger. The darkness. The rapid footsteps echoing. Past 3 A and 3 B. His pulse began to race and pound. He lost his perception of time, descending through a cyclone that was the brownstone. Away from the unknown. Faster. Faster.

Then he stopped.

He whirled abruptly and threw the beam of light down the hall. There was nothing. He sighed, restraining his panting. He was scared, so terrified that he questioned himself. Had he been the one to conjure a fantastic plot from the antics of a few old fools and some crazy clerics?

He flashed the light toward 2 A. He listened. Nothing. And the chill was gone. He turned and swung the light around the corridor, near the staircase and up on the wall. The beam hit the dead bulb and then danced onto the new paneling.

The new paneling! He moved toward it. Yes, it looked strange and certainly worthy of a quick inspection. He looked up, removed the chisel from his pocket and rapped it against the wood.

The initial sound was puzzling. He examined the edges of the slab and then knocked his fists on the wood to test its density. A hollow echo returned. The overlay seemed thin and was not laid flush against the material underneath. He knocked again. There was no mistaking it. Perhaps he had found the spot for the speakers, or whatever. He did not even know what he was looking for, just that he was looking.

He jammed the chisel under the side edge of the paneling, levered it and began to pull the wood out.

He tore through the boards at the center and along two planes of parallel lines, one horizontal, the other vertical. Large chips of wood hung from the wall. He surveyed his work in the light of the flashlight, which he had placed on the floor on top of the gun so that the beam landed directly in the center of the slab. Frantically, he began to tear at the exposed boards until, under a hail of dust and wood slivers, all the strips had fallen away and the area underneath lay exposed.

Jennifer opened the door quietly and tiptoed into the room. She screamed.

Jack lay on the floor, his skull split, a trickle of blood running from above his right ear, down his neck and onto the floor. The lamp, which had stood on the night table to the right of the bed, lay on the rug, a collection of fragments, large and small—all covered with blood.

The bed was empty; the window, which led to an emergency fire escape, was open.

As she stepped into the room the other guests piled up behind her.

"What happened?" someone asked. No one answered.

She walked to Jack's body and kneeled down. His hand moved; he was alive—if barely. She sobbed, overcome by the horror, a horror to which she had a special insight. She had seen too much. She had heard too much. Enough was enough. The time had come to stop playing Sherlock Holmes. Jack lay on the floor, bleeding and unconscious. Who was next? And where had Allison gone?

She grabbed the phone off the night table and dialed once. She waited, tears streaming down her face.

"Operator, give me the police. This is an emergency."

He laughed hysterically. There was something disturbingly horrible about the sound, hollow, trebled and distant. And as it echoed throughout the seemingly empty building—from the fifth floor, where the blind old priest sat watch, to the first-floor hallway with its misty fog—it carried with it a message of frustration, then disbelief, then anger, one replacing the other until the echo of the bellowing sound receded into the most uninviting reaches of the brownstone and dissipated into toneless vibrations.

Michael brushed off the long-accumulated dust that adhered to the uncovered surface and flicked away the lacing of spider webbings and insect matting. He stood back, lifted the flashlight and trained the beam on the letters that were carved in the wood. He reviewed his initial reactions. He reappraised their propriety. And as he began to read the inscription once again, he broke into that same uncontrolled laughter.

He read:

Through me you go into the city of grief.
Through me you go into the pain that is eternal.
Through me you go among people lost.

Justice moved by exalted creator,
The divine power made me
The Supreme wisdom and the primal love.

Before me all created things were eternal,
And eternal I will last.
Abandon all hope, ye who enter here.

His laughter continued unabated until all the air
had dissipated from his lungs. He whispered to himself,
"Thank you, Dante," raised his hand and simulated
a tip-of-the-hat gesture. Once again he rocked with
laughter—a convulsive laughter which both appreci-
ated the humor of his discovery and its preposter-
ousness. The thought that a brownstone on West
Eighty-ninth Street in the heart of the city of New York
could be the entrance to the underworld, the portal before the River Styx, was ludicrous.

He quieted. Although the words seemed ridiculous,
they were part of something sinister and real, something which he still did not understand. Involving Allison. Involving the church and the forced disappearance of numerous people over the years.

He kneeled down. Suddenly he felt his blood rush
from his body. There was someone behind him.
Breathing on his neck. Short choking breaths like
the efforts of a victim in the final stages of pneumonia.
He reached down and felt along the floor for the
gun, aware that the figure behind him was waiting.
The snub-nosed barrel slipped into his fingers.
Carefully, he drew the gun into his palm and slid
his index finger around the trigger. His breathing
stopped. He whirled around, flashlight pointed ahead,
gun drawn and finger ready on the trigger.

Father Halliran was standing directly over him.
His face matched the picture in the Halliran file. The
deep undulating wrinkles circled his skull as if the
skin had been strip-mined, and his cheeks and forehead
were blotched with black and blue specks, the result
of bursting corpuscles. The eyebrows were gone. So

too were most of the lashes. The veins and arteries that carried the blood supply under the decayed skin stretched perilously close to the surface—distended, swollen and discolored from the advanced decomposition of tissue. Topping this vision of horror was a matted web of hair, choked with dirt as if the old priest had risen from a grave beneath six feet of soaked earth.

Michael emitted a gasp and focused on the priest's eyes. There were no pupils. Neither eye had a distinguishable iris. Encased in cataracts, both were white like eggshells.

The old man was wearing a long black robe which cuffed just below the Adam's apple, supporting the layers of dried flesh that hung from his neck; the robe covered his entire frame, including his feet. His two spindly hands, tipped by clawlike nails, were joined chest high; they held a gold crucifix which reflected the hard light of the flashlight back into Michael's eyes.

Michael squinted and moved the beam off the metal.

The priest stood still. Michael kneeled, motionless. Their eyes were locked on each other—his perceiving the challenge, the priest's blinded to what lay before him. Yet he continued to look down as if he were cognizant of every move Michael made, as if Michael's thoughts lay open before him and his future was in his power.

The priest parted his lips. His fragile diaphragm contracted. He let the air slowly out of his lungs, producing a low moan. He seemed incapable of forming words with the deadened muscles that supported his jaw. Slowly, his head began to swing back and forth. The gesture was communicative. It implied trespass and transmitted pity and remorse. With the slightest twitch of his withered head the priest conveyed many thoughts, all of which carried the impression that horror had not yet begun and that once commenced could not be stopped.

The old man moaned once more, turned and walked, holding his cross before him, back to the staircase from which he had descended.

Michael steadied himself. The sight of the priest had nearly stopped his heart. Now, moments after the initial shock, it was beating wildly. Yet underneath his panic the same resolve with which he had entered the brownstone remained. It was just a matter of subordinating primitive reactions to his inherent disciplines: the ability to reason, to apply logic to given stimuli, and to respond with calculated decision and uncommon self-control. But in the end it was more self-deceit than anything else that caused him to follow the priest down the hall. Although his very fiber doubted it, he told himself that the old priest was just a man and that though the events of past days whispered that he was challenging the unnatural, the very essence of evil, there still was a logical explanation for everything, and that by retaining his composure and challenging directly he could confront, intersect and prevail.

He caught Father Halliran at the base of the staircase. He grabbed him by the arm, flashed the light in his face and unsuccessfully tried to spin him around. The old priest, possessed of unexpected strength, continued slowly upward, one step at a time, the cross extended in front of him, his eyes glassily staring straight ahead.

"All right, my friend," said Michael. "It's about time you let us in on the game."

The old priest turned his head slightly in Michael's direction, pulled his arm free and turned away again, dismissing Michael's presence like one would shoo a bothersome gnat. He began to chant softly in Latin.

"I want to know why these things have been happening! I want to know who's behind it. I want to know the object of the game. What are you after? And I swear to you, if I don't find out, I'm going to break that cross over your head. Christ and all."

The priest stepped off the stairs onto the third floor.

He was oblivious to the cries, the clutching arms and hands that pummeled him as he continued to climb, and the angered, distorted face that followed immediately to the right of his shoulder.

Michael screamed. "'Talk, you bastard! Talk or I'll crush your skull!" He was quickly approaching an unrestrained fury. "Why were all those people playing charades? Chazen, Mrs. Clark, the others. How did you know so much about Allison? About her father? About me? The psychiatrist's reports? Did you see them?"

He shook the priest again. The old man stopped and slowly turned his head. His eyes were glowing, more opened and piercing than they had been before. If they reflected real emotion, he was mad.

Michael backed off; the glow hurt him.

The priest nodded—as before—pityingly, then climbed to the fourth-floor landing and disappeared around the banister. Michael hesitated, then with the beam of light the only path through the darkness, tore up the stairs, ran down the hall, climbed up the last staircase and caught Halliran as the priest began to cross the hall to his apartment.

"Do you want me to play games with you?" Michael cried angrily. "Then let me assume from recent reading that this place is the entrance to the underworld and that you're the resident bogeyman. Congratulations. I just hope your union has a good pension. If not, I'll renegotiate the deal." Michael realized his words sounded ridiculous, but he had run out of intelligent things to say. And even so, saying anything was useless.

Halliran continued to chant.

"Say something, for God's sake!" screamed Michael at the top of his lungs.

Gatz charged through the front door of the precinct house and hurried down the stairs. His expression was serious. His movements deliberate. Beside him was a patrolman.

The patrolman opened the rear of the squad car and got in as Gatz slid into the front seat next to Rizzo.

"No idea where they might have gone besides Learson's?" asked Gatz.

"No."

"Did you have the line checked?"

"Yes. Off the hook."

Gatz nodded, his concentration intense. The car sputtered, whined and sped down the block.

"Where's the apartment?"

"In the Fifties."

"Go through the park," ordered Gatz.

"Yes, sir," replied Rizzo.

"Rizzo," Gatz announced, "I got a feeling that tonight something is going to happen."

Chanting continuously, Halliran opened the door that had been so frustratingly closed.

He walked toward the window before which he had invariably been seen sitting still and quiet. Before it stood an antique wooden chair. As Michael followed the man, he noticed the severe angles and inflexibility of the seat. It looked uncomfortable. It must have been torture for the old arthritic cleric to sit hour after hour in the same position against its hardwood frame. But as Michael flashed the light about, he realized that the old priest had no choice. There was no other furniture in the apartment.

In the center of the room he turned the beam toward the bedroom. The door was open; there was no furniture in there either. Could it have been possible that the entire world of the priest, his entire existence, was tied to that baroque piece of furniture? That he sat there and slept there and ate there. He shivered. There was no sign of any food or kitchen utensils.

The old man sat down, held the cross in his lap and looked out the window. "Bastard," yelled

Michael. "Bastard. I'm going to tear you apart with my bare hands. I'm going to choke what I want out of you."

He moved around the side of the chair and wound his cold, bloodless fingers about the old priest's neck. He began to squeeze. The old man continued to chant in unintelligible Latin.

"Bastard! Talk, you bastard!" Michael raged. Halliran continued to chant, but now the rhythm was hyphenated by choking. His windpipe was being depressed; breathing was becoming difficult. But no matter how hard Michael squeezed, the priest did not defend himself. Instead, he just continued to hold his shaking hands about the cross.

The chair toppled over; Michael and the priest sprawled across the floor. "I'll kill you," Michael cried, struggling. "Bastard! Bastard!"

A heavy object swept out of the darkness through the soft light that trickled in through the gray-tinted window. It landed heavily against the skull. Again and again! Blood splattered onto the barren floor. The sound of flesh being pulled across the wood. More groans. More blood. And then silence.

Allison opened her eyes.

She shook her head. She was groggy. Where had she been? Where was she? And wherever she was, how had she gotten there?

The air was still cold and dry; the wind continued to blow fiercely. And she wasn't wearing a coat. She was freezing.

She raised her eyes from the sidewalk, looked around and then straight ahead. She gasped. Across the street was the brownstone. Dark, quiet and uninviting.

One thought took precedence; Michael was in the house. She stepped off the curb and paused, sensing the weakness in her limbs as they shook from the effect of the feezing air and wind. Her teeth chattered mercilessly; she rubbed her hands together. Then, summoning her strength, she ran across the street and into the house.

The light above was still shining; the air possessed the same foggy density.

She walked to the mirror, lifted the pair of gloves off the table and examined the leather closely. They were Michael's. He was possibly within reach, certainly within the sound of her voice. She turned from the mirror which held her sallow reflection and screamed, "Michael!" The sound echoed overhead and died. "Michael, are you here?" she repeated in a loud, quivering voice. There was no answer. "Why did you come here?" she said more softly. "Why?" And then she cried again. "Michael!"

She fidgeted with the thin leather gloves. She would have to climb the stairs into the darkness and inspect each apartment. Perhaps he was in one of the bedrooms, shielded from the sound of her voice by the thick plaster walls. Or maybe he just wasn't able to answer for some terrible reason.

She pulled at the fingers, turned them inside out and threw them back on the table.

"Michael, please answer me," she screamed again.

She waited momentarily; there was no response. She grabbed the rail and began to climb. The yellow fog sped away as she ascended the old wooden steps. She stopped halfway up and shook the banister. It was still as sturdy as ever. At least there was something in the brownstone on which she could rely. She shook the banister again and step by step climbed the rest of the way to the second floor.

She turned sharply at the top of the staircase, bypassing the barely visible inscription, and walked down the hall. "Michael!" she cried again.

She looked up the staircase to the third floor and sighed deeply, relieved to see that the small yellow light that jutted from the wall at the top of the landing was working, illuminating the stairs. She went on slowly, remembering once again the night she had stepped on the cat.

She reached the third floor, walked toward the far end of the hall and stopped abruptly. There was something on the tile: a large round stain with smaller streaks and stains reaching down the corridor. She puzzled, then kneeled down and touched the substance. It was liquid, viscous and warm. She lifted her hand, smelled the ends of her fingers and rubbed them together, each one tinted with the fluid. And then she knew. It was blood.

She gasped and looked along the floor at the smaller pools and scratch lines which suggested that a body had been dragged along the floor. She looked in the other direction. The trail seemed to end in the middle of the hall, as if the body had been picked up and hurled out of the brownstone. She trembled. "Michael, please help me! Please, wherever you are." Then she fell to her knees and began to crawl, exhausted, incapable of standing, heading for the door to her apartment and the only safety she knew in the entire building.

As she was about to pull herself up and insert her key into the lock, her hand touched something hard and cold. She lifted the dull piece of gold-colored metal and examined it closely. It was a cufflink. Fourteen carats. With the initials MSF: Michael Spencer Farmer. Covered with blood.

She screamed and clutched it in her fist while the other hand reached for the immediate security of her crucifix. Frantically, she inserted her key into the keyhole that seemed to be dancing all over the metal plate, unfastened the lock, pushed in the door and fled from the hall. Leaning back against the wall, she closed her eyes and gasped, "Michael! No!" She rubbed her forehead, then grabbed strands of her hair, pulling them out at the roots. "Help me! Help me!" But there was no one there. Only darkness. "I confess! I have sinned," she cried. "Sinned. But leave me alone. Whoever you are, leave me alone!"

Her hysteria increased in its violence. Her nails dug into her skin, leaving long scratches.

Suddenly she whirled around, snapped the lock shut, rammed the bolt across the door and closed the guard chain. She turned again, studied the dark apartment, ran across the room to the granny lamp and pulled the switch. Nothing. She tried the main light, but it too was out. She sped across the room to the coffee table and pushed the button on the small lamp. It went on and illuminated the room. She was alone.

Shuddering, she returned to the door to check the locks once more. Then she rushed to the bed-room hallway, poked her head into the kitchen and the bathroom. They were both empty. The kitchen light was out; the bathroom light was working. What was going on with the lights? she wondered as she carefully traced her steps to the bedroom, tried the main switch and then, it being out, flicked on the wall lights. The bedroom was empty also. She was safe; at least while she was in the apartment. But was it really safety? She had no phone. No means of communication. Sooner or later she would have to leave the apartment and enter the halls. And no matter what time of day, it would be like night in the corridors. What could she do? She looked around the room, then suddenly bolted from the bedroom and tore down the hall into the living room. The front windows! She could open them and scream. No matter that it was late. Someone would hear her, go for help and bring the police.

She raced around the couch, past the lamps, the guardian grandfather clocks and the fireplace, finally stopping in front of the draperies. Furiously pulling them apart, she gasped! The windows were gone; in their place was a solid wall. "No!" she screamed as she rammed her fists against the wood. Again and again she pounded, her knuckles swelling, her dry eyes aching. She shuddered. The back window faced a solid wall. From there no one could hear her cries. She was trapped!

She turned nervously away. "Oh, Mother," she whimpered as she thought of home. She needed her mother now. More than anything in the world. Her mind was wandering, and as she began to pace, her brain slowly welcomed the return of the dizziness and nausea to compound the fierce headache that had been building since she had awakened in the street. She was alone. Shut off from the world. By whom? For what purpose? And Michael. Poor Michael. Her pace quickened. She needed someone to protect her. She stopped and looked at the television. Yes, she could count on it. She turned it on. The tube buzzed and sputtered. A test pattern! She changed the station. Music. "The Star-Spangled Banner." Again. Nothing. Again. Finally! The late show. She stared at the screen. It was alive, filled with movement and noise. The myriad of colored dots swallowed her consciousness. She continued to walk about the furniture, but now her eyes remained fixed on the screen. And they remained so until her feet and body could no longer bear the stress. Painfully, she wrenched her focus from the set and moved down the hallway to the bedroom, where she fell to her knees next to the fourposter and laid her head in her trembling hands. The fingers touched skin that at any other time would have scourged her senses, but she perceived nothing. "Angel of God, my Guardian dear" she prayed hypnotically. The television buzzed in the background. She continued her prayer, but the rest of the words were garbled and lost in the palms of her hands. If only she could get back to that church and sit in the confessional again. It had been her only moment of peace. She rolled her forehead on the bedding, lay inert for a few moments, then looked around wildly. Footsteps. Again? Back and forth they went just like on those other nights. Thumping. Then she realized the sounds were not coming from above.

The television snapped off. She jumped. There were footsteps in the living room. Then silence. Someone was in the apartment! She gagged her mouth with her hands. How? She had checked the apartment. And she had bolted the door, and the windows were now a wall. Then she remembered the living room closet which she hadn't checked. Whoever was in the other room had been in there, probably behind the clothes, waiting.

Two more footsteps. The sound of heavy breathing.

She looked wildly about for anything that might protect her. In desperation she ducked into the bedroom closet and shut the door. Holding the knob in her right hand, she leaned back into the hanging clothes. Her muscles were frozen in place, her body motionless.

Heavy footsteps resounded in the hallway. They were moving slowly but deliberately toward her, and as the magnitude of the echo increased, so did the feelings of hopelessness—for the closet held no protection for her. Whoever was in the apartment knew she was there and would find her.

The footsteps stopped at the entrance to the bedroom.

She pulled harder on the knob, as if she were trying to permanently fuse the door closed and isolate the terror outside.

She inhaled, the acerb odors of the naphthalene that protected the clothes from moths scorching her lungs and eyes. She lifted her hand and held her chest. Her already overworked heart was beating with frantic irregularity, exerting so much stress that at any moment she expected it to blow her organs through the door into the bedroom.

The footsteps resumed; they seemed to course over the far side of the room, stop near the window for several seconds, then move back to the dresser.

She pulled the knob harder.

The footsteps started again and moved to the bed.

She held her breath, afraid to make any sound,

risking suffocation rather than discovery. She took her hand off the knob, dried it and returned it to its place. Her other hand was wrapped around the crucifix. She was soaking wet.

As the footsteps circled the bed and moved in the direction of the closet, she felt her entire body constrict. A warm flow of fluid ran down her leg and onto her feet. She had urinated. She looked down at the soft light that crept in under the door and saw the wretched liquid slowly filtering under the crack and into the bedroom. She cringed and tightened her muscles, hoping to cut off the flow. But it was impossible. She squeezed her eyelids shut as she thought of the pool that was oozing into the bedroom and betraying her presence.

The footsteps moved by the dresser and stopped in front of the door. She could see the shadow of the two feet in the light. This was it! Again came the surge of horror, nausea and dizziness. The doorknob began to turn; she receded.

The door opened an inch and stopped. The intruder breathed deeply, then pulled back the door with a violent thrust. She opened her mouth in terror.

27

"Michael!" she cried.

"What are you doing in the closet?" he asked in a perplexed tone of voice as she fell forward and dropped her powerless arms over his shoulders.

"Michael, Michael, Michael," she moaned, burying her head in his neck.

"Everything's going to be all right. I'm here now."

"I can't—"

"Just relax. I'm holding you." He squeezed her tightly, trying to reassure her of her safety.

"I saw the blood, the cufflinks."

"Everything's going to be all right," he said. "Everything!"

"The headache," she cried, clutching at her throbbing forehead. "I feel so sick."

"I know, and I now know why, and soon the sickness will be all gone and you'll be fine."

He pulled her to the bed and sat down with her. "Take it easy, no one's going to hurt you," he said softly, as if there had never been any danger.

"Michael, why?"

"Soon, soon," he said.

"You're here."

"Yes, and there's so much to explain."

"Explain?"

"Yes. In the last few hours I've found out the secret of this building. And the role of Father Halliran." She squinted at the mention of the mysterious priest. "Believe me it's almost beyond the comprehension of the human mind."

She looked at him quizzically.

"I'll tell you everything, but I want you to compose yourself first and relax. You're still too shaky."

"I'm fine," she said. "And I want to know. Tell me!"

He looked at her, gauging her preparedness for what he was about to say, and then began. "It's unbelievable!"

"What?"

"This!" He dug his hand into his pocket and pulled out the slip of paper on which the translation had been written by Ruzinsky. "Have you ever seen this before?"

She grabbed the paper, held it close and read the inscription. "No!" she declared pointedly.

"You have, but in Latin, in the book. You see, I had it translated. But it wasn't in the book, although for some reason you perceived it through the book."

"Where was it?"

He pointed to her head.

"The Latin version of that transcription was imprinted on your mind so that by the time your mind had been stripped of all other faculties, that would be the only thing to remain. A command!"

"Michael, I—"

"And because your mind and body were being stripped you were sick, dizzy and had a constant headache."

"But—"

"I'll explain everything. Just be patient." He lifted himself off the bed, walked to the dresser and lifted a book off the top; he returned to her side. "Do you know this book?"

"Yes, vaguely."

He laid Milton's *Paradise Lost* on his lap and thumbed through the pages. He stopped, marked a page and held it up. "What do you think?"

She gasped. Printed on the page was the inscription "Part of Book Four."

"Michael, this doesn't make any sense. I never read *Paradise Lost*, in English or in Latin."

"Ah, but it does. Remarkably so!" He stood up and moved to the middle of the room, book in hand, like a lecturing professor. "The quotation in question was a warning from the Angel Uriel to the Angel Gabriel, who had been stationed at the entrance of Eden to guard and protect it against any incursion from purgatory. Uriel had perceived a sinister form flying toward Eden and with his warning caused Gabriel to dispatch two angels to guard Adam and Eve's bower. They found Satan at Eve's ear and threw him out of Eden, but Satan guilefully returned as a mist by night and breached the bounds of Paradise, entering into a sleeping serpent. Then came man's transgression! Interesting?"

"Yes," replied Allison, astonished by his display of erudition.

Michael consulted the book. "The Guardian Angels returned to Heaven," he said, and he read:

Up into Heaven from Paradise in haste
The Angelic Guards ascended, mute and sad
For Man, for of his state by this they knew,
Much wondering how the suttle Fiend had stolen
Entrance unseen.

"God absolved them and sent his son to judge the transgressors. But Satan bade Sin⁻ and Death to proceed to Paradise."

"Michael, this is ridiculous!"

"Shh," he admonished, holding his second finger before his lips. "Just listen!"

She nodded, winced in pain and nodded again. He smiled, held the book in front of him, walked to the back window and continued, "Satan turned to his legions and told them of his conquest, told them of the new world and bade them follow him once again to their new kingdom. But God, hearing these vilifications, turned them all into foul creatures, set them upon each other with awful hissing, and sentenced them to yearly humbling in order to dash their pride and joy over man's seduction."

He closed the book and laid it on the dresser.

"I feel so sick. I want to leave here, please."

"I haven't finished."

"Later."

"No, now!"

"But Michael, this gibberish—"

He looked at her angrily. "This is not gibberish. I'm trying to explain to you what has happened here and who you are!"

She cocked her head and looked at him inquisitively. "Who am I?"

"The Sentinel," he said coldly. "The successor to Father Halliran, the Sentinel before you, who was the successor to a long line of guardians leading all the way back to the Angel Gabriel."

"What?"

"You heard me!"

"No," she said, shaking her head. "I didn't."

"When mankind was thrown out of Eden and set upon the world, Satan swore that he would return with his legions. God thus had to maintain his guardians about the new world. But he chose not to use his angels for this task, for they had failed through no fault of their own. Rather, the perversion of Eden had been caused by man's transgression, so man was charged with the task of guarding the world—just like Gabriel had been charged—Father Halliran and now you. And all Sentinels were chosen because of their iniquity—attempted suicides—chosen not only to guard the Kingdom of the Lord, but for their own preservation, to sit in penance for their sins against themselves and thus save themselves from damnation."

"This is ridiculous!"

"Is it?"

She laughed through her agony. "If God was going to choose a guardian, he certainly wouldn't have chosen me!" She laughed again. "After all I've done—and been—."

He smiled wryly. "The Lord works in mysterious ways."

She had heard that before, most recently at the church.

"You know how you found this brownstone?"

"The notice in the paper that you couldn't find."

"You were lured. There never was a notice in the paper. It was imprinted on your mind as was the book passage. You were literally commanded to come here and wait for the moment when Father Halliran would pass the crucifix to you and you would take his seat to watch. Your entire existence has been orchestrated and your safety insured by a vigilant priest. Miss Logan's associate. A Monsignor Franchino. He removed the body after you stabbed the detective to death. The detective I hired to check out the building and verify or contradict what you had told me. It was Franchino who gave orders to Miss Logan, also an agent of the church. He arranged her disappearance when things got too hot."

"Michael—"

"This brownstone is the bridge over Chaos. It is the connection between the Gates of Hell and the boundaries of the earth. It is the place where the Sentinel, God's angel on earth, is charged to sit and watch for the legions of hell." Michael's voice had risen and was now tinged with revelatory strength. "It is where you are to sit when the transfer has been completed—tonight—unless it is stopped. If it isn't, you will be stripped of your remaining faculties, physically deteriorated to hide your identity and confined to the chair to watch and wait."

"What do you mean stopped?"

"Stopped. They are trying to destroy you by forcing you to renounce yourself. Take your own life. The ultimate sin. It is a difficult task. That is why the chain has never been broken. Mrs. Clark, the lesbians, the others you saw—your father—all soldiers in the legions. They tried once before—the night you met your father—and they will try again tonight. And if they succeed, they will unleash their hordes on the earth."

"Stop it! Stop! What are you trying to do to me? Drive me crazy? This is all insanity."

He rushed to her side, sat down and threw his arms around her. "Calm down. I'm here and I said everything is going to be all right. I'll stop them, but you must believe that what I'm telling you is the truth."

"Michael . . . I . . ." she stammered as she held her hands to her head. "How can I believe this?"

"It's true, that's how! Now come with me. I want to show you something."

She placed her hands on the bed, began to push herself up, then stopped and looked strangely at him. She raised her hand to her lips, thought for a moment, then asked, "Why didn't you answer me when I was calling to you?"

"I didn't hear you."

"I was screaming."

"The doors to the apartments are thick."

"Yes, but not when I was in the living room."

"Excuse me," he said, not quite understanding her point.

"When you were in the closet in the living room, you had to have heard me."

"No," he said innocently.

"You had to," she screamed.

He frowned. "I wasn't in the closet."

She gasped. "The door was bolted. How did you get in? And how do you know all this?"

He breathed deeply, then opened his mouth to answer. Suddenly she screamed. In the darkness by the bedroom entrance stood the cat—Jezebel—eyes opened wide and back arched.

"The cat!" she screamed, scrambling back on the bed to the headboard, the farthest point in the room from the dreaded animal.

The cat spit and hissed and started to inch forward.

"Kill it!" she cried.

"No, let's see what it wants," Michael said.

"Kill it!" she screamed again.

Tracking its prey, the cat slithered to the edge of the bed, hissed, spat into the air and jumped up.

Allison pushed herself against the headboard, then froze with terror. Michael grabbed her hand reassuringly.

"Kill it."

The cat slowly crawled along the bed until it stood directly in front of them, coiled to leap and attack. It spat viciously at her and then sprang—into Michael's lap, where it cuddled under his arm, then turned toward her and spat again.

She gasped and looked at him queerly. "Michael . . . I don't . . ." she said, repulsed by this excrescence of horror.

"You don't understand?" he asked calmly as he petted the animal.

"No!" she screamed. She shot off the bed and began to move to the window. "I don't understand—but you're evil."

"I'm good." He began to laugh with an intensity that seemed to build with each intake and expulsion of air. Louder and louder it became, and slowly the hint of the unnatural crept in and her skin began to shrivel on her body. It was horrible.

He screamed, *"I was killed by the priest Franchino when I tried to strangle Father Halliran, and I've been damned to eternal hell for my sins! For having arranged Karen's murder by Brenner."* He continued to laugh as his body began to vibrate. *"I am one of the legion!"*

Before her very eyes his soul, which caressed the cat, assumed a posture of eternal vexation. The body possessed little substance, only a sallow coloring and a skin that seemingly would have blown away in the wind. And the laughter; the sound of his voice seemed to emanate from someplace distant, a place of evil and detestation. No, he was evil. She was good!

She bolted from the room down the hallway and to the door. As she fought with the locks and listened to his slowly moving footsteps, she knew that she could not win. He wins, she is destroyed. She wins, she is also destroyed, sentenced to sit forever in penance for her sins. But as the lock snapped open and the bolt drew back and she attacked the chain, she knew that if she had to lose she would rather lose to God, sit and watch and be his sentinel, and by doing so save herself from damnation.

She threw open the door, ran down the staircase to the second floor, hesitated momentarily in front of apartment 2 A, continued to the end of the hallway, stopped with her back to the still unnoticed inscription and peered down to the first-floor hallway. She wavered, then grabbed the banister to steady herself, heard the sound of footsteps behind her—Michael—and surged down the staircase, stumbling, falling, forgetting to test the railing. She ran past the mirror and came to a dead halt.

"Welcome home," said Charles Chazen benignly. He was standing in front of the door, dressed as he had been the night she had first met him. "Don't be afraid," he said. "I've been waiting for you. I so want you to help me redecorate my apartment. You have such flair for that, you know. And you're such a sweet child that I just love having you around."

She began to step back. "Jezebel was so happy that you were able to make her birthday party, even though you didn't have time to buy her a gift. Next year I'll let you know a little earlier. Definitely so!"

"No!" she screamed.

"Tut, tut, so much noise; it hurts my ears. Why should such a delicate child make such a racket!" He started to walk toward her.

She gasped! Her reflection in the mirror! What had happened to her? She looked like an old woman, a hundred times worse than when she had entered the house. She screamed and tore at her face.

And Chazen kept coming, slowly, his paces marked and steady.

"Yes," he said. "Welcome home." Suddenly the somber look evaporated from his face, his eyes grew stern and cold and his mouth clenched in fury. He stiffened his body, raised his hands like a prophet calling to his people and hurled from his mouth a thunderbolt of entreaties. The entire foundation of the building shook. "I call ye and declare ye now returned," he cried like a madman. "Successful beyond hope, to lead ye forth. Triumphant out of this infernal pit. Abominable, accurst, the house of woe, and Dungeon of our Tyrant!"

Her vision clouded as she could feel the rumblings in the air and hear the clamor building.

"Now possess, As Lords, a spacious Wold, to our native heaven little inferior, by my adventure hard with peril great achieved."

She continued to move backwards as he slowly approached, flaying his arms in expectation.

"Long were to tell what I have done, what suffered with pain voyaged the unreal, vast and unbounded deep of horrible confusion, over which a broad way now is paved to expedite your glorious march."

As she became enveloped she began to move backward up the stairs. A path was cleared behind her so that her retreat would be unimpeded. Back she went, oblivious to her enslavement.

"What remains but up and enter now into full bliss!"

He stood, hands raised.

She felt the tremor under her feet. She turned. The stairwell and the hallways were jammed with colorless, emotionless forms.

She was going to come apart. Every part of her body burned in agony as if the fires were already upon her. And she did not know where to go. Back? Into those hordes! Or forward? Back she went, involuntarily. Back! Along the second-floor corridor, up the next staircase to the third floor. Completely surrounded. There was Michael's blood. And there were the lesbians, Sandra and Gerde, staring at her, their hands fondling each other, their bodies naked. Malcolm and his wife. There was nowhere to go. Behind her Chazen was ascending the staircase.

She looked around, hurled herself through the door to apartment 3 B and screamed. On the floor was Michael's blood-soaked body, his lips purple and discolored.

She ran to the wall and turned. Mrs. Clark entered from the bedroom. Behind her came the Klotkin sisters, still enormous, but now repulsively horrible. Then

Detective Brenner. They all stopped several yards away and remained motionless—waiting.

"Leave me alone," she screamed. "Let me die in peace!" She screamed again. Standing motionless across the room was her father. She whimpered. Her father did not move. He waited.

The door swung open and Michael entered. He stood still a moment, then stepped to the side, near his mortal body, and waited for the entrance of Chazen, who was several steps behind. The old man came in the door—Mortimer hopping about on his shoulder—walked to the center of the room and raised his hands as the cries of his children rose to an incredible head-splitting crescendo. Amid the clamor, Jezebel entered and ran to his side, spitting at Allison.

Chazen lowered his arms and the clamor instantly ceased.

"You are the chosen of the Lord God, the Tyrant and our enemy," he said to Allison. "You are she who is to guard and protect the entrance to the earth. You are she who must take up the scepter of the Lord from the present sentinel and take his place. You are the appointed one who must be destroyed if we are to be successful. Now is the hour of decision and action." He turned around to his army. "The work will be done, she shall become one with us and then we shall up and enter into full bliss to join Sin and Death!" He turned back to Allison and extended a scepter. "You shall damn yourself with your own hand—for you must!"

Chazen raised his arms again and the clamor rose anew. Singing voices, clanging armor, and hell's own echo filled the room, the halls and building. And she began to crumple to the ground—shaking, bleeding from the mouth, vomiting, losing self-control, wanting death.

The door to apartment 5 A sprang open, held by Monsignor Franchino. Father Halliran stood next to him in the doorway. His cross was extended in front of him with one hand. The other was held on his pained chest. He started forward, gasping for breath—forward to find and transfer the crucifix to Allison, lest the chain be broken and the path cleared for iniquity.

The armies of the night rebelled, rattling their spears and armor. They hurled themselves against the cross but fell in the wake of the superior force. Thousands challenged and hurled themselves against the ancient priest. But on he went amid the outcry. On and on. Searching for his successor. The chosen of God. The Sentinel!

28

"Everyone back!" The policeman turned. "Put the other one over there."

Eyes peered in the darkness.

"I want everyone behind the barricades or on the sidewalk."

Leather and rubber heels scratched the macadam; a consumptive cough split the frigid air.

"That means you too."

"Press."

"Which?"

"*Daily News.*"

"Your pass?"

"Yes." The man dug his hand into his overcoat and removed a card which he handed to the officer.

The policeman studied the identification. "You can come around," he said.

"Thank you," the reporter said as he stepped between the two barricades that blocked the street and headed toward the center of activity about a hundred feet down the block.

The cop surveyed the scores of people that huddled behind the police lines. He listened to the charged voices, spat on the ground and watched the spotlights that were fixed on the front of the building.

The police had arrived some forty minutes before. Two cars. The first with Detective Gatz, Rizzo and two other detectives. The second with several other policemen, a doctor and Jennifer Learson. Gatz, Rizzo and three others had immediately entered the building, leaving the girl outside in the company of the remaining officers. They had stayed inside, without word, for ten minutes before one of the uniformed police and Detective Rizzo left the building, spoke with their associates and placed a call over a car radio. Within minutes scores of police cars descended on the area. Spotlights were brought in and barricades were set up to hold back the gathering mob.

There had been no word as to what had happened inside. Except for the two who had made the call earlier, none of the policemen who had entered the building had reappeared. The tension was extreme. And it had begun to snow.

The front door to the brownstone opened slowly and Gatz walked out with Rizzo at his side. At the base of the stone staircase were the reporters. Gatz stopped in the vestibule, looked down at them, then turned to Rizzo. "Call the lab and get a man down here." Rizzo nodded and ran through the reporters and to the police cars. Gatz stared down at the expectant newspapermen. "There is no statement as of yet. It is a homicide. More than that I can't say. As soon as Inspector Garcia gives the okay, we'll call you all together and go over the whole incident. Now I would appreciate it if you all would step aside. There's going to be a lot of traffic in and out of here."

"Who was killed?"

"Later, I said. Now let's go." He motioned to Richardson who stood behind the reporters. "Put up a blockade over there and put the reporters behind it." He turned to the other officer. "What time is it?"

"Three forty-five."

Gatz extended his hand outside the vestibule and grabbed several snowflakes. They were large and presaged the onslaught of a heavy fall. He squeezed them together, fused them into a tiny ball and tossed it to the ground.

"It's a cold night, sir."

"Yes, more than you think."

"Why?"

"Why?" He smiled. "It would take a long time to explain." He walked outside, felt the snow hit his face and turned to the policeman. "Stay in the doorway. Don't let anyone in except for the normal crew."

"Yes, sir."

He walked briskly down the stairs, surveyed the crowded street, and walked to an empty patrol car. He leaned against the front fender, adjusted his scarf and looked at the building from top to bottom.

"They're sending a blood man and a crew to take prints," said Rizzo as he joined his superior.

"Good."

Rizzo unfolded a scrap of paper and handed it to Gatz. "Here's the woman's name who called the police."

"Which building?"

"That," he said, pointing to the yellow apartment across the street.

"Where's she now?"

"At the station house. They won't question her until you get there."

"Did you speak to her?"

"No."

"Who did?"

"Jake."

"And?"

"It was Parker. The description fits. The woman said she was looking out the window—she couldn't sleep—saw the girl go in."

"Where do you think she went?" asked Rizzo.

"I don't know, but we'll find her. Does Learson know?"

"I just told her."

"She take it hard?"

"Yes. The doctor had to give her a sedative."

Gatz spit into the thin layer of snow that had accumulated on the cold cement and stared at the entrance to the brownstone. "Did you ever have a real disappointment—one that ripped you apart?"

"Yes."

Gatz glanced back to Rizzo and squeezed his fists.

"Why do you ask?"

"Because I wouldn't want to have been the only one."

"I don't understand."

"I think I was wrong, Rizzo. Dead wrong. After being so positive!"

"You can't be sure."

"No, I can't. But then again, I have this feeling in my gut." Gatz was uncharacteristically reflective and somber. The events of the night and their apparent implication had destroyed countless hours of effort and analysis.

Jake Burstein came toward them. "The doctor examined the old priest," he said. "Apparent cardiac arrest."

"What about the marks on his neck?"

"They were made by hands and nails."

"Strangulation?"

"Maybe. But it didn't kill him."

"He's sure?"

"No. It'll have to wait for autopsy. But he's confident it was a heart attack."

Gatz nodded. "Anything on Farmer besides the wounds?"

"No."

Gatz shook his head.

"I showed the black attaché case to the girl," said Jake.

"She recognized it?"

"Yes, but she wanted to know where the papers were."

"What papers?"

"I don't know. She seemed frantic, but when I asked her about them, all she would say was that Farmer had some papers in the case."

"No papers were found?"

Jake shook his head.

"Have them search the whole building for them. I'll have to talk to her."

Jake started to leave, then turned back to Gatz. "Tom, cheer up."

"Rizzo!" said Gatz suddenly.

"Yes?"

"Get a warrant out for Allison Parker."

"Charge?"

"Attempted murder of the photographer. Suspicion of the murder of Michael Farmer. Suspicion of conspiracy in the murder of Karen Farmer."

"Yes, sir," he said obediently. He stared at Gatz for a moment and then turned away.

Gatz leaned back against the police car once again and rubbed his gloved hands together. It was over. God, he was tired. He thought about Allison Parker, the girl he had absolved of all complicity in the "suicide of Karen Farmer." Could he have been so wrong? Could she have been involved and now have destroyed her co-conspirators to cover her past? He slammed his fist against the car door, sniffed at the cold night air and turned his attention to the front of the brownstone.

The heavy door opened. A uniformed police officer stepped through and held it back. There was no movement for several seconds, then a figure clad in white appeared, followed by a stretcher and several more attendants. The body that lay on the stretcher was covered. The stretcher was carried to a waiting ambulance and placed inside. The rear door was closed. The driver gunned the engine and the ambulance steered around the barricade and into the night.

Gatz threw his cigar into the snow.

The front door opened again and another group of attendants exited with another stretcher and another covered body. The white sheet was stained red.

Gatz turned away to find the girl and question her about the contents of the briefcase.

Gatz had finished detailing the evidence accumulated in the four days since the murder, most of which consisted of Jennifer Learson's statements. Although little made sense, he finally was paying a visit to the Archdiocese.

The cardinal stared at him. "With all due respect to the authorities and your investigation," he began, "I can only say that what you have told me is an impossibility. It is beyond the realm of reason, though no doubt the forces of God and Satan are continually locked in confrontation."

Gatz nodded respectfully.

"There is little more that I can say," continued the cardinal, "other than to assure you that the truth lies elsewhere."

Gatz stood. "I certainly do not question Your Eminence, but if I might ask one more thing."

The cardinal nodded.

"The priest involved was a Monsignor Franchino. I have tried to locate such a man in the archdiocese, but have been unsuccessful."

The cardinal stood and smiled softly. "That is easily understood. There is no one with that name under my authority." He turned to an aide, who nodded agreement, and then turned back to Gatz. "Nor has there ever been."

"I see," said Gatz, standing. He flushed, somewhat embarrassed. "Thank you for your time," he added politely as he turned to leave.

Moments later he climbed into a patrol car next to Rizzo and proceeded uptown to his final appointment of the day, with David Caruso.

Caruso met them at the door in his wheelchair. He and Gatz exchanged some pleasantries, after which he repeated that he had told Gatz everything and could conceive of no other information to add.

"Only a few questions," Gatz responded.

Caruso gestured Gatz to a chair.

"Have you heard from Miss Logan?" asked the detective.

Caruso shook his head.

"Were you able to locate her home address?"

"I told you before, I never had it."

Gatz glanced at Rizzo. "Have you ever heard of a priest named Monsignor Franchino?"

Caruso reflected briefly, then said, "No."

"Did you have any dealings with anyone from the Archdiocese concerning Father Halliran?"

"You've already asked me that five times."

"Tell me again," said Gatz.

"No. The old owner made the arrangements with the church. I merely bought the building from him before he died. Miss Logan had no contact with anyone that I know of. We just received the rent checks signed by M. Lefler, the comptroller."

Gatz shook his head, then thanked Mr. Caruso for his time and patience. "Let's go," he ordered Rizzo, and after they had left the apartment he added, "take the Jennifer Learson statement and file it away."

Behind the door, David Caruso positioned himself at the window. He watched as Gatz and Rizzo climbed into their car and sped away. Then he shook his head and calmly rubbed the little tufts of white hair on the back of his freckled hand, convinced that the open chain had been permanently closed and the truth buried.

He pulled the shade, stepped out of the wheelchair and walked away from the window.

Epilogue

The number 5 lit up on the board.

"Music is piped into the elevators. Unfortunately, the system is out right now, but it should be back in working order within two or three days."

The man smiled at the young couple. Newlyweds, fresh out of college. Ideal tenants.

"You've just come to New York?"

"Yes. My company transferred me here from Chicago."

"Which one is that?"

"United Airlines."

"You're a pilot?"

"Not quite. I'm in the advertising and promotion department."

The man smiled. Good company. Good position. He liked them. "When is the little one due?"

"I have a long time to go. Five months." The girl patted her bulging abdomen and smiled.

The number 20 lit up on the board. The elevator stopped and the door slid open. The agent straightened his inexpensive brown suit and motioned them out.

The walls were papered richly. The floor was covered by a thick carpet.

"There are fifteen apartments on each floor," he said as he turned the corner. "The incinerator is next to the elevators." He removed a key from his pocket. "Here it is, apartment twenty L." He inserted the key and opened the gray-painted door.

They stepped into a small foyer, turned to the right and walked into a very large living room. There was

275

no furniture but the entire apartment had been recently painted. The room was rectangular with an L-shaped dining area which opened into the kitchen.

"It's a very large living room."

"Almost too large," replied the young woman. She walked across the floor to the window and turned back. "We might not have enough furniture to fill it."

"We'll buy more if we have to," answered her husband. He glanced at the renting agent. "I'm primarily concerned about the closet space and that there's enough room for us and the baby."

"Understandable. Here, look at this." The agent opened a closet in the foyer area. "It's a step-in." He flicked on the light. "There's enough room in here for many things. You could even keep the baby carriage inside."

The young woman nodded approvingly, then ducked into the kitchen, which was equipped with the most modern of appliances, including a dishwasher and a garbage disposal unit. The agent and her husband followed.

"Do we pay gas and electric?"

"No. Just electric. You'll notice the washing machine."

She nodded and walked to the refrigerator. She opened it, peered inside briefly and closed the door. "It's fine, plenty of room. Can I see the bedroom?"

"Of course. This way."

The agent led them through the other door, down a short hallway into the bedroom.

"I like it," said the girl. "I had my heart set on a brownstone, but I guess this will be better for us. It's safer and more convenient."

"There's no doubt about that. Far safer. Though I must agree with you, some brownstones are quite attractive. There used to be some beautiful ones on this block. But they were ripped down about five years ago when this building went up. I'm sure that within a few years there won't be any brownstones—except for those that are used as town-houses—in the entire city."

"If we decide to take the apartment, when can we move in?" asked the husband.

"Tomorrow if you like."

He turned to his wife. "What do you think?"

"I think we should take it."

"Good. Let's go downstairs and fill out the necessary forms. The application must be approved by the building management, but I'm sure there'll be no problems. I'll make sure it's put through today."

At the elevator the agent pressed the button; they waited.

"The building seems very quiet," said the young woman.

"Yes, it is. We insist on it. If you tolerate too much noise, no one can live in peace. This floor is especially quiet."

"Why?"

He shrugged his shoulders. "The luck of the draw."

The elevator arrived. The young woman stepped in first, then her husband.

"What about our neighbors?" she asked.

The agent thought for a moment. "Your neighbors? Yes, let me see. There's a Mr. Jenkins in apartment M. A nice man. He plays the violin in the New York Symphony Orchestra."

"Does he practice in the apartment?"

"No, you won't hear a thing." The elevator started down. There was silence.

"And the K apartment? Is it empty?"

"No." He stopped and thought. "I suppose I should tell you, since you'll be living here. The woman who lives in twenty K is a recluse. She's a nun and I've been told she's blind. You can see her sitting in the window if you look carefully from the outside. She's been here since the building was put up. But she's no trouble at all. She never makes any noise and she never leaves the apartment."

"Sounds ominous," said the woman.

The husband smiled. "I guess it will be good for our souls to be living next to a nun."

They laughed.

It was late afternoon when the couple walked out of the building, having completed the necessary forms. They crossed the street and began to walk toward Central Park West in order to catch the bus.

The young woman stopped. "Look," she said, pointing.

Her husband turned, followed the direction of her finger and stared at the top floor of the ultramodern building.

"At what?"

"The window. Next to the end. Can you see anything?"

He stared intently. "Yes, I think I can."

"The blind nun?"

"I can't be sure. But according to the agent it is."

"What do you think?"

He looked her in the eyes and smiled. "Something to write home about." He kissed her on the cheek and they both walked down the block, satisfied with their new-found home.

The apartment was dark. There was no furniture except for a high-backed wooden chair that stood before a closed window, in front of which hung a semi-transparent drapery. In the seat was a form —human—aged beyond recognition. The eyes, bulging and swollen, were covered with hideous white cataracts. The skin was wrinkled and cracked like dried clay. The lips were thin and blue. The hair along the eyebrows and on the head was dead, stringy and broken; the complexion was waxen.

The breathing was protracted. There was no movement other than the minute lifting of the chest.

In its lap, the hands were folded, still and lifeless.

They held a gold crucifix.

We know you don't read just one kind of book.

That's why we've got all kinds of bestsellers.